P

"Dimon turns genre expectati⋯ ⋯⋯ ⋯⋯⋯⋯⋯⋯ ⋯⋯⋯ ⋯⋯⋯ ⋯⋯⋯⋯⋯⋯⋯ly hot erotic suspense sequel . . . Dimon's ability to weave together such strong, engaging plots is commendable, and her characters are surprising, complex and sensual. With a subplot as addictive as the main arc, this is a sequel—and a series—that simply should not be missed."

—*RT Book Reviews*

"This entertaining cast of whip-smart, sardonic former felons will keep readers turning the pages for the sex and the snark alike."

—*Library Journal*, starred review

PRAISE FOR

MERCY

"Everything I want in a book by HelenKay Dimon—emotional, sexy and smart." —*New York Times* bestselling author Jill Shalvis

"From the first page I was hooked. Captivating, steamy, with an intriguing hero and heroine, *Mercy* is one of the best books I've read this year." —*New York Times* bestselling author Vivian Arend

"Masterful. Edgy. Hot, hot, hot. Read this now."

—Alison Kent, bestselling author

"Dimon turns up the heat in this sizzling romantic thriller . . . Perfect for readers who appreciate intense intrigue and very erotic romance with overtones of questionable consent." —*Publishers Weekly*

continued . . .

"Romantic suspense fans should give this one a try. I think you won't be disappointed." —Fiction Vixen

"Dimon writes an engaging story . . . Enough tension and hot sex to keep readers who like it that way happily turning pages . . . Hot and bold in a hard-shell-over-a-soft-center kind of way that romance fans will find sexy, fun and satisfying." —*Kirkus Reviews*

"Dimon pulls off a rare balancing act, successfully blending a taut, intriguing caper with a searing, unsettling and profoundly compelling romance." —*RT Book Reviews*

PRAISE FOR HELENKAY DIMON

"She's a delight." —*New York Times* bestselling author Christina Dodd

"Sharp writing and plenty of sexy romantic sizzle." —*Chicago Tribune*

"HelenKay Dimon is a genius." —Joyfully Reviewed

"So smart, sexy and fast-paced, I devour her stories." —*New York Times* bestselling author Lori Foster

"Sexy, emotional, funny . . . Dimon gives it all to her readers . . . [This] shouldn't be missed." —*New York Times* bestselling author Jill Shalvis

"The sex is steamy. The repartee is witty. There are some things in life you can just depend on, thank goodness." —Dear Author

"I didn't want to stop reading." —Smart Bitches, Trashy Books

"Dimon's fresh new series is enjoyable, and the plot will appeal to many different readers. By turns funny and romantic, the sexual tension between the main characters is portrayed perfectly." —*RT Book Reviews*

Titles by HelenKay Dimon

MERCY
ONLY
MINE

MINE

HelenKay Dimon

HEAT | NEW YORK

HEAT

An imprint of Penguin Random House LLC
375 Hudson Street, New York, New York 10014

This book is an original publication of Penguin Random House LLC.

Library of Congress Cataloging-in-Publication Data

Dimon, HelenKay.
Mine / HelenKay Dimon. — Heat trade paperback edition.
p. cm.
ISBN 978-0-425-28209-0 (softcover)
1. Man-woman relationships—Fiction. 2. Sexual dominance and submission—Fiction. I. Title.
PS3604.I467M56 2015
813'.6—dc23
2015016678

PUBLISHING HISTORY
Heat trade paperback edition / October 2015

PRINTED IN THE UNITED STATES OF AMERICA

10 9 8 7 6 5 4 3 2 1

Cover photo of sexy man © Tankist 276 / Shutterstock.
Cover design by Diana Kolsky.
Text design by Kristin del Rosario.

Penguin
Random
House

ONE

Tuesday at six fifteen. That's when Gabe MacIntosh's patience officially expired.

He'd been listening to Natalie Udall argue her case for over an hour. The woman sure could talk. She sat in the office chair and swiveled the seat back and forth. Tapped her fingernails against the conference room table. Ignored the water bottle he put in front of her more than thirty minutes ago while she battled every point he made. Treated him to her whole I'm-a-pissed-off-woman routine while repeatedly making it clear she thought she was in charge.

Smart and sexy but so wrong.

"Are you almost done?" he asked, hoping to wrap up the discussion and move on to the protection part of the program. He had to get to work. Much more non-bodyguard time alone with her and it would be a race to see which one exploded first, his brain or his dick.

The whole mind-wandering thing was new to him. He'd never had trouble concentrating or staying focused during an operation. He'd been trained by the best. An untold amount of government money had been spent, years consumed, honing his skills and turning

him into an ace sniper. He could hunker down in a field for hours
with hostiles lurking nearby, almost stepping on him, and never make
a sound. Not until he was ready. Not until *he* decided to unleash a
rash of fury and fire.

With her, something shifted. He noticed too much. Thought
about her when he should have been concentrating only on her safety.
Everything about her reeled him in. The straight long blond hair he
dreamed about wrapping around his hand while he entered her. The
way her slight southern accent slipped in when she rushed her words
or got really pissed off.

The first time they met she wore a suit. The skirt had hit just
above her knees and had his brain misfiring as he dreamed about
running his palms up those pale thighs. Wrapping those lean legs
around his waist. Today, weeks later, she wore pants, but the impact
on him didn't lessen one bit.

No question the strong female type appealed to him. So did
that body, fit yet curvy. Hips that would fit his hands. Every other
part of her perfect for licking and tasting. He never fucked on a
job. He viewed an assignment as just that, a file he memorized
and a body he watched over. Emotionless and straightforward.
But with her he saw a woman, smart-mouthed, determined not
to be a victim, competent and hard to scare.

So fucking hot.

But he'd been hired to protect her and that put her on the off-
limits list . . . no matter what his dick thought.

She'd left her black-ops position with the CIA after a lengthy
negotiation through her attorney, and an extraction agreement
stored in a vault somewhere proved it. The pages of legalese spelled
out her rights and responsibilities, and acted as a supposed guarantee that she would not be harmed. They both knew better. A pile
of papers wouldn't stop some ticked-off asshole in power from

taking her out. From deciding she knew too much or made a wrong move.

Back when she had a job she'd been brave and determined. Refused to take a seat when the idiot men in her office had insisted she be quiet and blend in. That kind of shit made enemies. Which was why she needed him right now. Just for a short time. His presence as bodyguard added some assurance no one could get to her. That was the theory anyway.

Now he just had to convince her of his value.

He would watch her while his brother Andy and the rest of his team looked for signs of an impending attack against her. Once they were convinced the extraction agreement would hold and she'd remain safe, she could go lead whatever life she wanted and he'd go back to the office and his next assignment. Simple and efficient. He'd played this game many times. Unfortunately, Natalie didn't appear all that excited about her role as potential target.

As if she read his mind, she started talking again. "I don't need your protection."

She'd been saying the same thing for what felt like hours. So many times that the refrain ran through his brain even when she wasn't talking. "I heard you."

"Then unlock the door, let me out and point me in the direction of my house."

Thanks to all her time at The Farm, the CIA's top secret training facility in Virginia, and who knew where else, Gabe guessed she'd get along just fine with so little direction. She'd somehow find her way back from their undisclosed location to wherever she intended to hide. Then she'd probably get shot in the head.

Yeah, not on his watch. "You're staying with me."

"You don't get to decide."

"I actually do." He had a work contract in his office back at his company, Tosh Industries, that trumped her denials. She might not like the protection but her friends, concerned friends who were players among the Washington, D.C., power elite, had arranged it for her, paid for it, and she agreed in front of them. Now she was stuck. Gabe intended to see the operation through even if he had to lock her in a closet and sit in front of the door to keep her there and safe.

She continued to tap those fingers against the tabletop. "I'm a grown woman."

"Believe me, I know." He'd eyed every inch of her. Watched her walk and studied her file. He hadn't seen her naked, but he could guess. That confidence, the swish of those hips. It all played in his mind on an endless loop until he ached with the need to strip that proper navy suit off her.

She froze in her chair. "I make my own decisions."

"Not right now." He did. He was in charge. He meant for work, but the idea of taking control in every other way appealed to him, too. Way more than it should.

"What is that supposed to mean?"

He suddenly needed to say the words, to clue her in that she had him on edge. "Your body belongs to me."

Tension flooded the room. Quick and without warning. Heat surged through him. Her big blue eyes blinked. She didn't say anything, which should have been a relief, but Gabe felt anything but calm. His skin drew tight, felt stretched, his stomach hollow. The need to fuck her gripped him.

She leaned forward, not a big change in position. No, very subtle, almost imperceptible. "Excuse me?"

He cleared his throat. "For now. Until we know you're out of danger. I decide what happens with you."

Adding the context didn't help to settle the energy pinging around the room. He shifted in his seat across from her and tried to rein in the thoughts bombarding him. She was a job, and an annoying one. When the first mental reminder failed, he tried again.

Most people appreciated his protection once they got over the shock of the cost. He didn't do everyday shit. His business focused on covert, need-to-know cases. He didn't advertise or go looking for work. Jobs came to him by reputation and through people who knew all the dirty little secrets. And the never-ending flood of those in Washington, D.C., kept him very busy.

He eyed the water bottle in front of her, thinking she'd have to take a breath or a drink soon. "I can name three members of your old team at the agency—the team you ran for the CIA—who are now dead."

She shrugged. "Things happen."

Like a fireball written off as a gas explosion. A murder-by-vehicle explained away as a fluke car accident. Accidental shootings, random robberies gone wrong. Gabe had seen it all, and so had she, which was why she needed to stop fighting and let him help.

"I'm not in the mood for games." He needed to stand up, pace around. He forced his body to stay still.

"Which means what?"

"Give me some credit and don't pretend I don't know how your business works."

She finally grabbed the water bottle. Held it. Tapped the bottom against the desk. "My old business. I'm unemployed. I followed my instincts, protected my team, and my boss pulled my security clearance. I couldn't even get the okay to take a public tour of the building these days."

He'd picked this office building as a neutral stop before they took off because it sat miles away from her condo in Washington, D.C., and her office at Langley. Outside the metro area. He'd hustled her out and kept her under wraps. But they needed to keep moving. They actually had a plane to catch. Not that she knew that, but it meant they were on a timetable and if she didn't work with him soon he'd have to take drastic steps.

Just thinking about what that meant started a countdown ticking in his head. "You have five minutes."

"Then what?" She rolled the water bottle between her palms. "You shoot me?"

This woman never stopped. He pushed, she pushed back. He just wished he knew why he found the back and forth so fucking hot. "Tempting."

"Keep in mind I'm an expert with weapons."

If he were the eye roll type, now would be the time. Since he wasn't, he stood up instead. If he needed to implement Plan B he wanted to be on his feet. "I'm better."

Her gaze followed him around the small conference room. "Are you trying to intimidate me?"

"Do I?"

"I'll ignore that." She stopped playing with the bottle and unscrewed the cap. A ripping sound cut through the room as she broke the seal.

Thanks to that death grip he half expected the plastic bottle to explode in her hand. "You now have four minutes."

"It doesn't matter, because in three minutes I'm going to get up and walk out of here." She took a long drink then refastened the lid. "Without you following at my heels."

She managed to make something so mundane look sexy but at least she finally drank from the damn bottle. Gabe mentally switched back to Plan A. "If you look around you'll see a lack of windows and one door."

"So?"

"You have to get through me before you can get out, and I think you're too smart to pick that option." But suddenly he wanted like hell for her to try.

She stood up and her balance faltered. Slightly and just for a second. With a hand against the table, she righted her body again. Then she came straight at him. Stopped right in front of him and in her high spiky heels almost met him eye to eye. Their bodies didn't touch but the thin layer of air between them didn't act as much of a deterrent.

She leaned in until her mouth hovered next to his. "You think I'm that easy to take?"

Son of a bitch. "I don't know, Natalie. Do you want me to take you?"

She pulled back. "You assume because I'm a woman I'd be submissive during sex."

Jesus, she went there. "Who said anything about sex?"

She snorted. "Oh, please."

Just as he thought. They were finally on the same page, and it was the wrong damn page. Sure as hell the wrong time. "I know what I like."

"I can guess." She tipped a bit to the side and grabbed on to his shirt in a rough hold to stand upright again. "You demand complete dominance."

"Mutual pleasure."

Her body began to list to the side and she blinked a few times. "What did you . . ." She visibly swallowed as she shook her head. "What's happening to me?"

"I think you know." He slipped his hands around her elbows in a gentle touch. The room was going to sway for her and he needed to be ready.

"I don't . . ." Her knees buckled as her grip on his shirt tightened. A second later her gaze flew to his. "You—"

"Drugged you." He nodded as his gaze searched hers, trying to figure out how far gone she was at this point. "Yes."

Before she could answer, her head tipped back and her body went limp. That hand dropped from his shirt and her body fell as if her bones had disintegrated.

He caught her before she hit the floor. Scooped her right up in his arms and stared down at her. Enjoyed the feel of her in his arms far too much. But he didn't mind the sudden quiet. "Now you'll follow my directions."

The lock clicked and the door opened. In walked Gabe's younger brother, Andy.

"Talking to unconscious women." Andy shook his head. "Is that your thing now?"

Gabe refused to get diverted by bullshit talk. "Our scheduled transport should be here. We need to get moving."

Andy glanced at Natalie then back to his brother. "I thought she'd never drink the water."

That made two of them. The rush of relief stole some of the stiffness from Gabe's shoulders. Since the alternate plan involved knocking her out, he'd been pretty damn grateful she got thirsty or nervous or whatever caused her to reach for that bottle.

"She's careful." He admired that. Admired so much about her.

"Really worried there for a few minutes that I'd have to listen to a lengthy discussion of the type of sex you preferred." Andy shivered. "Not interested in that, by the way."

At thirty-six, Gabe was six years older than Andy but sometimes felt like the grandfather of the company. He kept them on task. So, treating his brother to a front-row seat of the attraction kicking his ass was not Gabe's idea of a good time. "She was testing boundaries. A smart strategy, actually."

Andy smiled. "Boundaries?"

Enough standing around and talking nonsense. That wasn't Gabe's style anyway. "Do you want to die today?"

"Are you tough all of a sudden?" Andy pressed in the code and unlocked the door again. Opened it to the private area leading to the emergency stairs and the helicopter waiting on the roof. "To be honest, I was more concerned she'd get the drop on you, then I'd get stuck trying to get her out of town."

"You're hysterical." Gabe followed his brother out the door and down the long hall.

"I'm not sure why you think I'm kidding."

He held her close with her head tucked under his chin. The smell of her shampoo, something floral, filled his senses. "I can handle her."

"Uh-huh."

Unable to reach out and punch in the code, Gabe stopped at the door to the exit. Looked down at her face and that mouth. "Meaning?"

Silence pounded around them. Andy didn't make a move for the door or say anything. The quiet had Gabe's head snapping up. He looked at Andy, shorter with more of a runner's build. He worked with a quiet confidence, but this time something else moved in his eyes. Concern, maybe?

They didn't have time for this. The helicopter would take them to a private airstrip, then they needed to get on a jet and disappear.

Gabe was about to bark out orders when Andy piped up. "You're looking at weeks alone with her in a snowed-in cabin."

A fact that gnawed at Gabe. The close proximity would test

the limits of his control, but he could not admit that. "I'll refrain from strangling her."

Andy's eyes narrowed. "Maybe, but will you be able to keep your other body parts away from her?"

Good fucking question. "She's a job."

Andy typed in the code and the emergency door opened. "You keep telling yourself that."

That was the plan. Gabe just hoped he could stick to it.

TWO

Natalie stood at the window and watched the snow come down. More snow. Buckets of it fell every minute, or so it seemed. She knew because she'd been watching since she woke up fifteen minutes ago.

Exhaustion still pulled at her muscles and clouded her head. She didn't panic or wonder what happened. She knew the answer— Gabe.

He'd drugged her to get his way. Not that she blamed him for using whatever means necessary to get a job done. She'd been in his position in the past and used the same knockout tactic. Back then if she couldn't extract someone from the field with permission, she did it the hard way. Well, the hard way for them, not her.

Still, being on the receiving end ticked her off. Being dragged to *who the hell knew where* didn't sit well either. From the topography and weather, she knew she'd been asleep for some time. She now saw towering trees and snowcapped mountains in the distance. No other houses were visible for miles. She had the eerie sense he'd stolen her away to the wilderness, leaving her dehydrated and woozy. And that meant being out of it and unable to fight back for a long time.

Yeah, he'd given her something that jacked up her system. It could take her some time—she had no idea how much—to regain her equilibrium. Until then she'd be vulnerable to all sorts of dangers. The type she normally handled with ease, from assassin attack to the simple task of regulating her own body temperature.

That's what she got for leaving the CIA on bad terms. A farewell gift that included having her life flipped inside out while she waited for the fallout in the middle of nowhere.

First step: find her so-called bodyguard and set down some ground rules that included no drugs unless she was the one administering them. And if she found the opportunity to punch him, she just might grab it. Paybacks were a bitch and he should know that.

Nothing moved in the towering trees weighed down with thick white powder. Every now and then she'd hear a whoosh and snow would tumble, adding to the piles already covering the ground. The place didn't work for her. It was too quiet, too isolated. Someone could approach through the makeshift forest around the small cabin. That meant she needed to move. Make a plan, probably find viable transportation.

Not that she was dressed for tracking and running. She stood in jeans and hiking boots. Gabe would have to explain that part since the last time she remembered she'd been wearing a suit. Blue, most likely. Probably had her hair pinned up, which she did for work. Now it rested on her shoulders and spread down her back.

Forget about the rest of it. The man was going to get his ass kicked for stripping her. She glanced down at the gun in her hand. Maybe more than an ass-kicking, but at least he left her a weapon. She'd just need to be clear that didn't exactly make up for the rest.

She looked out over the bright white landscape and squinted, searching the ground for footprints. The gray sky, so thick with clouds and cutting off any natural light, made it hard to judge the actual time of day. But she could guess, because over the years and through numerous assignments she'd developed an innate sense about this sort of thing.

She'd spent months at The Farm and later been dropped in the middle of Germany for survivalist training. Spent time in the desert and Arctic. She'd seen it all, which made the idea that she needed a bodyguard to watch over her so strange. Early in her career *she* had played that role. Once she came out of the field and took an administrative job at the CIA, she watched over her team. From a distance, but she still thought of them as her responsibility and did anything to keep them safe, which was how she ended up getting fired. With all that time acting as the protector it was difficult to switch roles and accept being the protected.

Not that she could see her supposed bodyguard right now. His ability to blend in surprised and impressed her. He wasn't exactly small. He had the big, burly, bearded thing down. Not her usual type. Not even a little, which made her wonder why the look worked for her now. Or did before he drugged her . . . the jackass.

Blocking out the mental image she'd stored of Gabe and the fogginess in her brain, she wrapped the oversized flannel shirt around her and reached for the doorknob. It turned in her hand, which both stunned her and didn't. Leave it to Gabe to keep her guessing. To act as if she were free to go but trap her in a place that made leaving nearly impossible . . . or so he thought. Looked like he underestimated her. Good. She hoped he kept doing that.

The snow now bordered on sleet and made a clicking sound as it fell to the ground. Ice crackled in the trees. People who loved winter would appreciate this scene. She didn't. She grew up in the south and craved heat. After years in D.C.'s humidity, venturing out in several feet of snow just added to how much she hated what her life had become.

She stepped out on the small porch. The frigid air blew around her, whipping through her clothes and chilling her skin. It took only seconds for her to know that the drugs really had dropped her body's defenses, ratcheting up the shock against her skin. A thought tugged at her, that she should stay inside, but she blocked the tiny voice in her head. She'd been in deep-freeze shooting situations. Owned special gloves. She didn't have them on her now, but she had skills.

The bitter cold cut through her as she moved around, going down one step then the next, from the porch to what probably constituted a lawn in non-snow season. Her boots crunched against the layer of ice covering mounds of white. Snow pelted her face. She glanced around, checking for any sign of her protector, the former sniper turned bodyguard she didn't want. Only the quiet sounds of the forest echoed back to her.

She took a few more careful steps and rounded the cabin to peer into the wall of trees crowding around the side of the building and stretching out as far as she could see. Her hand tightened around the Glock. Numbness settled in her fingers. She flexed them to keep the blood running, careful not to touch the trigger. She'd seen more than one blood-soaked accident caused by fingers contracting, poor gloves or a bad grip. The cold brought death.

The eerie quiet had her on edge, waiting. A wave of tension crashed over her. She'd insisted the CIA wouldn't come after her now that she retired, but she never believed it. She only shared those denials to keep from getting stuck with a bodyguard. That didn't work out so well. But on her own she'd be faster. In charge. Not beholden to a six-foot-two mountain man.

She ignored the biting cold and took a few more steps. Then froze. The slide of footsteps echoed back to her. She heard . . .

something. Faint. Almost like a scratching. Her body snapped to attention and her brain switched to analysis mode. If they were coming, if people wanted to take her out, they'd go down with her.

A heavy thump sounded behind her and she spun around. She tried to lift the gun but her muscles suddenly weighed too much. A hit knocked her wrist and the weapon flew. Her instincts kicked in and she switched to autopilot. The world blurred around her. She concentrated on the figure moving into her view, not focusing on a face but, instead, seeing a target.

Adrenaline pumped through her, making her forget about the chill and the drugs still slowing her mind and her movements. She landed a roundhouse kick then pulled back and slammed her foot into a hard stomach. A heavy grunt registered but she didn't let up. Fighting off the lethargy weighing her down, she struck out with the heel of her hand, aiming for a chin. Knowing she suffered from a height and weight disadvantage, she readied to launch a quick third attack.

Before she could raise her head and size up her attacker, he crashed into her. Strong arms wrapped around her in a crushing hold. The band tightened across her chest as her body took flight. A blanket of white whizzed by her and she saw the ground coming. Knowing didn't lessen the hit. Her body slammed into the packed snow. Actually bounced.

The air left her lungs as hundreds of pounds of furious male pressed her deeper into the cold snow. Determination fueled her muscles. She thrashed and hit and kicked.

Hands tightened around her wrists and trapped them against the ground. "Natalie, enough."

The rough voice stopped her, and the haze cleared. She looked up into the dark eyes of Gabe MacIntosh, the man charged with protecting her. His broad shoulders blocked the view of the world around her.

Black hair, slightly too long with a bit of curl at the edges. The brooding expression and quiet dignity that matched the mystery winding around him. Retired military, current owner of a security company. Right now with the rich scruff around his mouth he looked more lumberjack than professional rescuer.

And she hated that she noticed any of it.

"What's wrong with you?" She spit out the question over the rage building inside her.

His intense glare didn't let up. "You pointed the gun at me."

He had to be kidding. She tried to lift her hand and punch him, but he had her arms pinned to the ground on either side of her head. The landscape came into focus as the killing frenzy pulsing through her eased. But the anger still simmered. "Because you snuck up on *me*."

Those dark eyes narrowed. "Are we really doing this?"

Sometimes he used too few words and she had no idea what he was saying. "What?"

"Fighting about nothing."

The minutes ticked by and she became aware of the hard body balancing against her and the scent of the outdoors on his skin. She stood five eight in bare feet and up until recently held a position that required her to stay fit and battle-ready at all times. Not exactly petite and certainly not weak. Still, he overwhelmed her. Being this close to him set off a battle between her brain and her body. He was a distraction. He tried to be helpful, but deep down she still believed heading out on her own and going into hiding without any contact with her old life was the only way to survive.

She struggled to remember what she was saying. "You are the one who—"

"You wouldn't have heard me if I wanted to sneak up on you." His frown eased. "I let you know I was coming."

"A normal person would have called out my name in warning."

"Never said I was normal."

"No argument there." She'd known him for about five weeks, and he'd been anything but.

At first, he followed her around as her lawyer, Sebastian Jameson, negotiated her extraction agreement with the CIA. Gabe never said a word back then. He slid into the background and watched until she could sense him. Until his presence made her jumpy. But Bast had insisted on the extra layer of protection.

Those days passed with each one stretching longer than the one before. The more Gabe hovered, the more she'd fought her awareness of him. The towering frame. The rough exterior. That face and those eyes that followed her everywhere.

She'd pretended she wasn't aware of him. All through the negotiations as he stood by the door, she'd tried to mentally block him. When Bast finished the deal, Gabe took over and started planning. He switched from quiet but determined watchdog to drill sergeant, issuing orders and making decisions as if she didn't get a vote. She'd been planning to put an end to his dictatorial reign when he drugged her water bottle, scooped her up and brought her here . . . wherever "here" was.

He shook his head. "You even wake up arguing and difficult."

Not the first time she'd been called either. Still . . . "Excuse me?"

"Makes me sorry the drugs wore off so soon."

The idea of nailing him in the gut tempted her. Lower would work even better. "Since you knocked me out against my will, changed my clothes and dragged me out here, you shouldn't try taking the high road."

"Had to be done."

Typical. He thought he knew what she needed. She decided to remind him of a very basic fact: "I am trained."

"True, but I'm better."

When it came to stalking his prey, he likely was. Snipers excelled at shooting, but the real skill came with the ability to move in and around without anyone knowing where they were. Not that she was ready to concede anything to this guy. "Get off me."

"No."

The bruising cold of the ground contrasted with the warmth of his body. He wore an outfit similar to hers, jeans and a flannel shirt, but heat poured off him. Forget the dropping temperatures and never-ending fall of snow. None of it appeared to affect him.

She shifted her hips and felt the bulge in his pants and the way it pressed against her. Not erect, but the man was not small and seemed to have an issue with personal boundaries. That only made her more determined to impose a few. "Are you so hard up for sex that you tackle random women?"

"No."

"I can feel you."

He didn't bother to lift up or move. Didn't spend one second hesitating or looking guilty. "I would think so, since I'm basically on top of you."

It was hard to argue that point. She started to buck her hips with the idea of knocking him off balance but changed her mind. The friction could take them in the wrong direction, and she needed every ounce of concentration right now.

The icy cold of the ground seeped into her bones. The combination of the drugs and the dropping temperature had her body in freefall. She'd start losing feeling soon, much faster than she normally would, and if she didn't get inside and dry, she could be in huge trouble. The weather appeared to have no impact on him. He stayed warm, got hard. Never even shivered. Of course, no one had messed with his body or brain to get him out here.

She decided to go with the obvious problem. "Your dick is against my thigh." She could feel all of him everywhere. The muscles across his chest and his flat stomach. For a big guy he didn't have an ounce of fat on him.

"Where should it be?"

The way he acted, like it was no big deal and not a threat in any way, had her thinking he might have even fewer people skills than she did. "Not on me."

"Sorry about that." Nothing more. Not even a shift to the side.

"That's your response?"

"Yes."

The whole he-man thing should have pissed her off. Instead, confusion had her brain cells sputtering. He didn't take any crap but didn't flinch when she fought back. She couldn't intimidate him. He didn't resort to stupid insults like the ones she used to hear whispered behind her back at the office.

She couldn't put the pieces together in her head, but she could fall back on the denial that served her so well in the past. "I don't want your protection."

"So you keep saying."

His exasperated exhale blew over her, but she ignored his frustration. "You should listen then. I'm not great with repetition."

"Fine, I heard what you want."

"And?"

"Tough." He sat up and moved back. Still straddling her thighs, he pulled her up and got her back off the ground.

Her instincts told her to take a shot. Knock him back and run. But she didn't. She sat there and waited to see his next move. Might have had something to do with the very real sense that Gabe was not a guy many people got away from easily.

Her gaze wandered down his chest to the bulge at the front of his jeans. "You think we're going to sit up here, have sex and wait for bad guys to come snooping around?"

The corner of his mouth kicked up, not in a full smile but close. "You seem obsessed with sex."

"I wonder why." She rubbed her hands over her arms as her teeth started to tap together.

His gaze fell to her lips then traveled back to her eyes. "Let's make a deal."

"No." The knee-jerk response came out before she could stop it.

"So prickly."

"Do you blame me?" She'd been run out of her job and made the fall guy for a rogue CIA operation that eventually uncovered a spy within the agency. Never mind that she resolved everything or that her team pushed through, with some of them losing their lives, and found the mole despite claims from agency higher-ups that none existed.

He nodded. "You've had more than a fair share of bullshit thrown your way."

"Understatement." Her crime had been simple in the eyes of her superiors. She'd exposed blind spots in the agency. She'd refused to take no for an answer when she knew she was right. She'd stuck up for the sole surviving members of her team and made a deal to spare their lives in exchange for her leaving her job and not exposing systematic flaws within the agency. In return, she got manhandled, drugged, and now had to hide just in case someone at the CIA decided she might not keep her mouth shut and needed to be eliminated.

Gabe exhaled. "I can't fix what you've been through, but I can give you some peace of mind."

For some reason that made her more skeptical, not less. "If you say so."

"I won't touch you without your permission." He lowered his head until he leveled that intense stare right at her eyes. "Ever."

"You're touching me now."

He held up his hands. "My job is to protect you. Nothing else will happen."

"Damn right."

"Kick me in the balls if I try." He stood up, pretty much jumped to his feet without making a sound, and held out a hand, letting it hover in front of her face. "You hold the power over what happens between us."

"I agree."

"*Us*, not how I protect you."

He still didn't get the churning inside her, that drive to run and not depend on someone else. She'd been trained for this, damn it. The idea of having a full-time bodyguard made her twitchy. Made it more likely that she'd end up looking to protect him than to keep herself safe. "I need to leave."

He exhaled as he shot her one of those you're-working-on-my-nerves frowns he excelled at throwing her way. "And go where?"

Seeing no reason to play the martyr, she grabbed his hand and struggled to her feet as numbness threatened to overtake her. "Hell if I know."

This time he did smile. Shot her a wide and sexy grin. "That's what I like about you, Natalie."

That look had her spinning. Whatever was dancing around in her stomach better be the flu. "What?"

"You're not stupid."

Smart of him to notice. "I guess that's a good thing."

"And sexy as hell."

Now that was a problem. If she let her mind wander for one

second she thought about climbing all over him. The need pounding through her could not be mutual. She could fight off her own attraction, but not his as well. Sex on the run, in the midst of gunfire and danger, sounded dumb. Like a one-way ticket to checking out of this world for good.

"Imagine me shooting you. That should kill the mood." She glanced around, trying to believe she lost touch with her weapon for even a second, or that she only had one.

He slipped the gun out of where he had it tucked into his belt and handed it to her. "You'd think, but no."

"You're a sick man." And by that she meant hot enough to have her common sense blinking out.

"Probably." He nodded toward the cabin. "Let's go."

Her defenses rose. "That sounds like an order."

He shifted his weight and leaned in closer. "You can either get in there, strip off your wet clothes and shower, or I'll do it for you."

Something hard clunked to a halt inside her. Her heart . . . lungs. Likely something she needed to keep moving. But she couldn't deny the shocking cold or how her mind moved a click or two slower than usual. How instead of talking and standing around, she should be running, but her muscles betrayed her.

"And now threats." She forced the words out over the rush of blood whooshing in her ears and the sudden shaking in her knees.

Those dark eyes gleamed. "Consider it a promise of things to come."

For a second she thought about taking her chances in the cold and snow. Seemed safer. "Be careful what you wish for."

That smile of his came whipping back. "Challenge accepted."

THREE

Gabe got her back inside without strangling her. He had to win some sort of prize for that restraint. That and for not kissing her, because he sure as hell wanted to, almost did. Now came the ultimate test . . . keeping his mind on the job and off her.

He reset the trap that guaranteed he'd know if someone ventured past his outer line of defense to the porch. Then he locked the door. Spinning around, he came face-to-face with Natalie. This close, he could see shivers race through her and hear her teeth click together.

Her eyes clouded with a telltale haze and she headed for the wood-burning stove along the far wall. All that did was give him a front row seat to that ass. Not that he could take any time to enjoy the view. Not with her in this condition. She looked ten seconds away from a hypothermic coma. Which was weird since his skin was on fire. Just trying to breathe made the walls of the tiny cabin close in.

Other than a threadbare love seat to his right and a small kitchenette running along the wall to his left, there wasn't much else in the cabin. Except her. She was right there in the middle of the room, which put her about six feet away from him. Six short fucking feet.

He drew in a deep breath and fought for the well of control he normally took for granted. "Take your clothes off."

She turned around nice and slow. The move had her flannel shirt gaping open to show off a peek of skin and the thin white T-shirt underneath. "If that's your line, it needs work."

"The order has more to do with not wanting you to freeze to death." The way her nipples pressed against the tee had his gaze bouncing up and down her impressive body, but he forced his expression to stay blank.

She scoffed. "Nice of you to care."

"I doubt I'd get paid if you died because you got cold." And she was not dying on his watch. He forbid it. To help make that happen, he scooped a blanket off the love seat, thinking to wrap her in it after.

"Aren't you practical?"

"To the bone."

She glanced at the doorway to the bathroom. Doorway, no door. Not enough room for those in the small space. The person who built the place had the good sense to tuck the toilet around the corner for at least a shred of privacy, but the shower was *right there*. Right in the line of sight from the doorway. No curtain. No wall. Nothing.

She looked back at him. "You can wait outside."

Tempting. If he didn't worry she'd pass out and drown herself, he would. Maybe the fresh air would kick-start his common sense, but that would have to wait. "I'll stay here."

She crossed her arms in front of her. "I'm not going to run."

"You're right." He doubted she'd take that risk. They shared some skills, and she had to know running meant jumping into one of the traps he'd set for the people who might come after her. "I wouldn't let you."

Her eyes narrowed. "Is this some sort of play for control? Like you're trying to break me or something? Because you can't. Others have tried and failed."

Interesting. The assessing gaze. The stiff body stance, which said she'd closed the door on listening to reason. He suddenly knew what it must have felt like to work for her. She didn't take any shit. A good philosophy and one he shared, but now he needed her to just obey and make his life easier. "Stop with the modesty. This is about getting you into a shower and warm again."

She glanced over her shoulder at the open doorway then back again. "You think I'm embarrassed to get naked in front of you?"

"I don't know why you would be." He assumed she'd had sex before. A woman didn't look like that, go through life with that confidence, without enjoying some pretty hot and heavy hours in the sack. At least he hoped so for her sake. She deserved good sex. Hell, everyone did as far as he was concerned.

He didn't buy into the whole idea of a strong woman automatically being cold in bed. That struck him as television bullshit nonsense. Weak didn't interest him. She did, and he hoped like hell she liked it dirty because he did, and they would get there . . . eventually.

Before he could say anything else, she dropped her arms. Those long fingers went to the remaining buttons on the flannel shirt. In less than a second, she had the shirt open and off her shoulders. Dropping it on the floor, she reached for the hem of the tee and that slipped over her head next.

"There." She stood with her arms out, wearing only a bra.

Full, high breasts. A collarbone he ached to kiss. He blocked it all even as his insides started to tighten in anticipation. "Your skin is red."

"What?" She glanced down as a shiver overtook her.

The longer she stood there, the more her words slurred. What started as a slight hesitation in her voice outside and a haze over her eyes turned scary as she grew more disoriented now. The unusually brutal temperatures for this early in the winter, dipping well below freezing, the harsh wind and the thin layer of wet clothes combined to steal her body heat.

Normally, she'd be fine. She had the training and her time in the elements had been limited. But the drugs he'd used on her turned everything upside down. Robbed her of the ability to adjust. She'd been on a downhill slide from the second she stepped outside.

He should have hustled her back inside sooner. That was on him. His fuck-up.

Enough talking. "Damn it, get in there before you pass out on me."

Giving her a choice hadn't worked so far, so he didn't try now. With a hand under her elbow, he half guided and half pushed her toward the bathroom. Thanks to the homemade off-the-grid water heater in there, she had a chance. He turned the handle so the shower came on and the water started to warm.

"Everything off." When she just stood there with a dazed look on her face, he dropped the blanket on the corner of the makeshift sink and took over. "Lean on me."

Dropping to a knee on the floor, he got her boots untied and off. Her hand landed on his shoulder as she struggled for balance. When he felt the chill pouring off her and seeping into him, he moved even faster. His hands brushed over her and his fingers flew. Tugged on the button at the top of her jeans and skimmed the material and her practical cotton briefs down her legs, revealing inch after inch of pinkish-red flesh.

He tested the water one more time before slipping the straps of her bra off her shoulders. The fact that she didn't fight or insist she could handle it told him how bad off she was.

She glanced up at him with eyes clouded with a deadly haze. "That won't—"

"In." One hand at the base of her back, he shoved, not even trying to be gentle. He needed her under the water.

"Argh—" Her shout cut off and her mouth dropped open as the spray hit her skin.

She tried to turn away, to shift back, but he held her there. "Yeah, it's going to sting."

"This isn't frostbite."

"No." Probably not even frostnip, but now wasn't the time to talk technical terms.

She started shaking hard enough for her heels to thump against the floor of the old tub. "I'm still freezing."

He could barely hear her as her jaw rattled and knew he'd fucked up this timing. Ignoring the cold and her body and every other signal that this had been a piss-poor idea, he stepped in next to her. The second his shoe hit the tub bottom, she turned. Her fingers curled into his wet shirt as she buried her face in his neck.

"There you go." The position let him maneuver her closer to the spray. With his arms wrapped around her, he pushed her back, submerging them both in the spray. He rubbed his palms over her. Whispered into her hair. He didn't even know what he said, but the mumbling had her clenched muscles relaxing and her body falling deeper against his.

Another few seconds and her body warmed. Then he hit the tipping point. When the touching went from saving to savoring. When he stopped worrying about her breathing and struggled to control his own. Her body, all lean muscles and sexy curves, fit against him as he knew it would. The slow, sensual torture as she blew soft puffs of air against his throat confirmed one thing he knew before the private plane had taken off to bring them here—he was fucked. That was the only explanation for breaking into a sweat in these temperatures.

He cleared his throat and inched back so he could look into her eyes. "Better?"

"Yeah."

The haze had gone, and something else replaced it. Something he couldn't think about for more than two seconds or he'd be rationalizing how fucking her could warm her right up.

He waited until she nodded to drop his hands and reached around her to shut off the water. The brush of his arm across her ass was pure accident but pretty damn great. "Good to hear it."

Her fingers relaxed against his shirt, but she didn't let go as she glanced down between their bodies. Focused on the bulge in his wet and confining jeans. "Is that still nothing but harmless reaction?"

"Depends on how you define 'harmless,' but yeah." The bigger worry was that he'd be in this state until he delivered her back to civilization.

What qualified as worse than being fucked? He was that.

She tried to swallow as he moved away from her. She'd been cold, too cold, and every action he took made sense. Brought her back to sanity faster. Even now her mind clicked into gear. Reality crashed into her right after.

Big, sturdy, commanding and so rough around the edges—she wanted it all. They'd met back before she left the CIA. Him hovering at the fringes of her life. The limited space between them had taken a toll.

Blame the adrenaline rush or the blanket of danger she'd been under for so long, but she wanted this—him. For her. Not pretty, not a commitment, not even a date. Just hot, out-of-control sex. Abandon her hang-ups and forget everything sex. Get-lost-in-him sex.

But it couldn't happen, or so she kept repeating in her head, hoping her body would catch up to her brain. Not if they were stuck out here, always on watch. Not if he saw her as a job. She had to rein in the need pumping through her and find a kick of self-preservation or she'd be crawling all over him.

She was about to point out that the whole cold, wet clothes thing had been his fault when he started to strip. Stood right in front of the sink and peeled the wet shirt off. Dropped it to the floor and let it slap against the hardwood. Then he reached for the Henley underneath and pulled it up, revealing miles of broad back with muscles carved into every inch.

Like everything else about him, his back, all that skin, wasn't perfect and pretty. Faint white scars marked his upper back as if he'd been lashed. A jagged line stretched along the right side of his back and disappeared around to his front. Likely from a knife. The wounds of a warrior. Of the man who went in first, took on the most dangerous jobs.

The ripping sound of a zipper cut through the room and her mental inventory. He shifted his hips, then the wet jeans dropped, taking a tight pair of gray boxer briefs with them. Her gaze slipped from the dip in the small of his back, down his ass cheeks, so round and firm. No fat, just perfectly formed and muscled.

His shoulders stiffened for a second then fell again. "I don't care if you look."

That comment had her fumbling as she reached for the closest towels, and not from the cold this time. She wrapped one around her chest and folded the end against her skin for a snug fit. Tucked her wet hair up in the other.

Somewhat dressed and feeling a bit more sturdy on her feet, she tackled the bigger issue. "This isn't going to work."

The door to the cabinet under the sink slammed as he reached for a towel. They'd somehow managed to use three of the total four available in a five-minute span. Still, him with a towel balanced on those hips, turned away from her, showing off that broad back and the outline of every muscle, proved potent enough. Naked and facing her might cause her to make a humiliating scene.

Which brought her right back to the topic he seemed to be ignoring. "We are never going to last a week."

He rubbed a hand through his hair, smoothing down the stray strands. "We get along fine."

She meant without having sex, but she took the easy out. "You know I'm trained. We both know sitting here waiting to get shot at or blown up is stupid."

"Neither of those things is going to happen."

She had no intention of letting either of them get injured, but that wasn't really the point. It was one of tactics and strategy. "I should be moving every day or two as I zigzag my way from here to nowhere in particular."

Still he didn't face her. "We're done with this argument."

"So if someone fires a grenade launcher—"

He spun around, those dark eyes snapping with fury. "I'll know before they try. If for some reason I don't, I will push you to safety."

Anger zipped through him. She could see it in every stiff line of his body. In the tiny lines at the corners of his mouth where his lips had thinned into a grim slash. No question about it. He would sacrifice his life for hers without even blinking. She got that but she didn't like it.

Ever since the whole CIA mess with her backing her team against her CIA superiors and landing on their target list, she'd been shoved into a position of accepting gratitude and help from other people. Bast acted as her lawyer, even when she didn't want one. Hired Gabe when she'd said no. "I don't remember agreeing that you're the boss on this gig."

"Humor me."

She picked up the blanket sitting on the edge of the sink, unsure how it even got there, and slipped it around her shoulders. "Fine. Since my plan was to go on the run by myself, not drag anyone else into potential danger, why don't you tell me your plan."

"We stick together. You follow my directions until we have confirmation that the CIA believes you intend to keep quiet about the secrets you know and plans to uphold their end of the agreement."

It sounded simple, but she knew from experience that little about the CIA operated that smoothly. "I'm unclear on how exactly we get that confirmation."

"The most obvious?" He shrugged. "No one tries to kill you. No one comes here and we don't pick up word about you being hunted."

That sounded a bit loose for her comfort. "'Pick up word'?"

"Andy handles that part. He tracks chatter and contacts and looks for signs that someone is trying to find you."

One man versus the CIA. The idea made her head pound. "That's not very comforting."

"If someone comes for you, if they find us and I get taken out, you run to one of the two sites where I've stashed supplies and weapons. Each has a satphone. There's a pack at each with directions, but you call Andy and follow his instructions about reinforcements and extraction."

She didn't bother to ask about the two drop points. "Okay."

Gabe's eyes narrowed. "Do you actually plan on doing any of what I just said?"

"I'll stop and grab the food and weapons—" His frown deepened and the rest of her answer cut off. "What? You would do the same thing."

"True."

The defensive words died in her throat. "Wow."

One of his eyebrows lifted. "What?"

"I didn't expect the honesty." With some of the fury gone, she let her gaze wander. Not far and trying not to be obvious about it, she glanced at his tight abs and the deep vee running from his shoulders to his trim waist. For a big guy, he was all muscle, no fat.

His chest bore more scars. Because she'd done her homework the minute Bast introduced them, she knew the wounds spoke to Gabe's time in battle. He wasn't the guy to rip his skin open as he tried to climb a fence in some immature drunken stupor. He'd earned every scar through fighting and bleeding and sometimes withstanding days of torture. Knowing that made it harder to hold on to the last of her anger over being manhandled and hustled away. Made it even harder to ignore the attraction kicking her ass.

The harsh lines of his face softened. "The one thing you can count on from me is honesty."

"Then you know that the two of us, locked up here . . . alone . . ." The need spun around inside her, threatening to knock her over. She knew if she even mentioned the word "sex" she'd be all over him, desperate to release some of the adrenaline pumping through her.

He glared at her. "Since I'm trying not to crawl all over you, I'm specifically not thinking about that scenario."

She let out the breath she'd been holding in. At least they were in this together. That knowledge provided some relief. It also made it clear that they were just running out the clock on the inevitable.

"We're grown-ups." Maybe a round or two between the sheets

would burn off all this energy and they could go back to mutually glaring as they sized each other up from opposite corners.

His hands balled into fists at his sides. "I don't fuck on the job."

She tightened the blanket around her, hugging it closer to her body. "You mean you haven't."

"Right."

Now that reaction proved interesting. She couldn't help but poke around. "You ever been tempted?"

"Not before you."

The words washed over her, leaving her insides jumping. Not a sensation she particularly needed or wanted right now. "I don't believe that."

"I don't lie."

"Maybe you just haven't had the chance yet." She stepped out of the shower stall, because standing in there felt like hiding from a conversation that had the power to strip her raw inside. "None of the women you worked with did anything for you."

"Now you're pissing me off." He made a sound that came close to a groan. "Women are more than interchangeable body parts for me."

For some reason she believed him. It didn't sound like a line coming from him. Not with that rough edge to his voice. "Most guys would play games and lie."

"Then most guys are idiots. It's pretty clear I want you. Or I do on those rare occasions when you stop talking for two seconds."

He could ruin a mood faster than any man she'd ever met. "Charming."

"I'm accustomed to quiet."

"Well, I'm used to sitting at a desk, setting up operations and guiding my team." In her early CIA days, she'd walk into danger prepared never to walk out again. Looked like her life had circled back around to that position.

His gaze roamed over her face, as if he was studying her. "Those days are over."

"Yeah, they are." She accepted that. Pissed her off, but she'd known that protecting her team would seal her fate. That was the bargain she'd made. The CIA left her team alone—Elijah and Becca got to live their lives in peace—and in return she stayed quiet and walked away from all she'd worked for in her career. Everyone's ass would be covered except hers.

Gabe took a step closer. "If you stop fighting me, I'll do everything I can to make sure you stay alive long enough to build a new life."

He didn't touch her, but he didn't really have to. Having all that intensity aimed right at her as a wall of shoulders blocked out the world in front of her held her attention. He'd enveloped her without ever lifting his arms.

"What does that look like?" she asked, because she really wanted to know. He'd navigated these waters and moved from government-paid sniper to businessman. He might be able to provide some perspective to a life that looked pretty bleak and spare right now. "The CIA is pretty much all I know."

He nodded as he shifted again, bringing them closer and shutting out the steady dripping from the faucet and the strange look of the coffeepot sitting on top of the homemade water heater. "I thought the same thing when I left the Army."

"With your firearms skills and contacts." That was just it. She had *nothing* else. "My extraction agreement doesn't really let me go into some random country and take down a dictator."

The corners of his mouth kicked up in a smile. "That's a shame, because I bet you could take a guy like that out without backup."

His confidence in her abilities left her more than a little breath-less. "I do have skills."

"So you've said." He lifted his hand and his thumb brushed back and forth over her bottom lip. "Damn, woman. You make me want to break every promise I've ever made to myself about mixing business with pleasure."

She fought off a shiver, because she refused to be the man-touches-me-and-I-go-tingly type. "You did say you were in charge. That you decided every move we made."

"Proves I'm a dumbass." He continued to swear under his breath as he adjusted his towel.

She got it then. He really wouldn't make a move until she gave him the green light. Even then, he'd need to be convinced they were safe. If she wanted a few hours of mindless sex—and she still wasn't sure that was a great idea—she'd have to push. To test the limits of his control. "You seem to think your work will be done at some point."

"Of course. You'll be safe and able to move on at some point, hopefully soon."

"And I won't be a job to you." Her fingers slipped over the edges of the blanket before balling her hands in the cloth. "Not then."

He shook his head. "Don't tempt me."

She felt the pull. Something in the air wrapped around her and tugged her closer. She wanted it, wanted him . . . wanted to forget.

The reality of that last one broke the spell. She stepped back. "I better get dressed."

"Good call." But the grumble in his voice said he thought otherwise.

That made two of them.

FOUR

Andy MacIntosh sat at his brother Gabe's desk, double-checking work emails and generally keeping Tosh running as promised while Gabe was away. Not that those were easy shoes to fill. Gabe might only be six years older, but he'd been an adult and responsible, stepping into family roles since Andy hit puberty.

That bone-deep dependability and solid work ethic only increased when Gabe opened Tosh four years ago. Instead of the usual floundering small company routine, Gabe's contacts and reputation launched them into a stream of steady work. Most days, too much work.

They had three on-the-ground assignments rolling at the same time right now, all high priority and all involving life-or-death scenarios. Safe houses with complex security measures and big gun protection. Usually Andy headed up a team, but Gabe's sudden willingness to hit the field one-on-one with Natalie grounded Andy this time. He got stuck behind with the paperwork, file preparing and directing the rest of the group as they guided operations from a distance. Andy knew the men depended on him for intel and surveillance, but that didn't make the big desk job any more interesting.

With few employees left in the office and those all focused on specific tasks, things had been quiet. They didn't get many guests. Few people knew the two-story nondescript warehouse in southwest Washington, D.C., housed an upscale, high-tech multimillion-dollar security company. No flash on the outside. No expensive cars in the parking lot.

The only hint something more than packing and unpacking of crates happened inside the beige building came from the state-of-the-art security system. The same one that flashed a visitor's face a few minutes ago. Even now Andy waited in the chair for the unwanted showdown to start.

He heard a beep, and the screen of one of the many monitors outlining the desk snapped to life. One of his mapping experts— a guy with years of technical experience and a brain that left them all breathless—played escort in the hall. Andy hit the buzzer before anyone could knock. He had enough of a headache without adding to it, and this scene would likely do just that.

The door opened, and Andy waved away his employee while Rick stepped inside. Rather than wait for the boring hellos to begin, Andy jumped right in. "Since you're here, I assume you know Gabe is out of town."

"Good to see you, too. Interesting you still choose to have your security act as a lockdown to keep you trapped inside." Rick walked straight in and took the chair on the other side of the desk. "I warned Gabe about that flaw when he set up this place."

They had contingency plans to escape if that became an issue, but Andy doubted Rick came in and agreed to hand over his weapons at the front desk just so they could talk about the building's blueprints. "Speaking of Gabe . . ."

"Fine, yes. I'm here about him."

The day officially turned to shit. They had been at it for a year, Rick and Gabe, locked in a family disagreement ever since Rick dropped his emotional bombshell. Andy dreaded taking a wrong step.

"I'm not getting in the middle of the game of mutually assured destruction you two are playing," Andy said, even though he had long ago sided with Gabe.

Rick waved off the concern. "That's not what this is about."

Andy didn't *want* to know what accusations Gabe and Rick were currently lobbing back and forth. But as soon as he thought it, he realized that wasn't quite true. The unrelenting tension outside the office grew more, not less annoying and Andy wished it would end. "Have you talked to him?"

"Last time I tried he threatened to blow my balls off if I didn't leave his property."

Andy laughed. Couldn't help it. He could almost see Rick standing outside the big gate while Gabe welcomed him with a gun. "You gotta admire the simplicity of his threats."

Rick leaned forward with his elbows balanced on his knees. "I need you to get in touch with him."

Just as suspected, Rick wanted to suck him into the middle of this. Andy had no trouble taking a pass on that. His personal life was enough of a shitshow without inviting these two to dump their garbage at his feet. "He's out of contact."

"This is about work. He's guarding Natalie Udall, and you know where he is."

Well, shit. So much for hoping Rick didn't know what happened inside Tosh's walls. Andy always assumed that Rick sat in his top secret, no-one-knows-he's-out-there-watching office and kept tabs on them, but now he had confirmation.

"I actually don't." Andy held up a hand before Rick could call bullshit. "Deniability."

So much of what they did at Tosh depended on secrecy. Rick might not work for Tosh, but he understood black-ops. Had spent most of his adult life heading up a group innocently enough called The Defense Initiative. He ran assets in the United States and overseas, providing backup on intelligence operations where the government needed a wall between what it could do by statute and what it needed to do to get the job done, legal or not.

Rick's work helped people sleep better at night, even though they never knew he existed or that he even did the work. Tosh got off the ground as quickly and as successfully as it did because Rick had thrown work their way. Back then Rick and Gabe got along. Now Andy doubted Gabe would accept a ride across town from Rick.

"But you're in contact." Rick blew out a long breath. "Look, Andy, this is serious. Gabe's job and my job just collided."

Which in Rick-speak meant not "personal" but "work related," and that got Andy's attention. "Tell me."

"Some people are concerned about Natalie's loyalty. That she was privy to some secrets that she now might be tempted to tell."

Andy had known Gabe was walking into a fucking mess. Forget the crap about this being a routine extract and hold. All those horror stories Gabe had told Natalie to get her on the helicopter, about the CIA potentially sending assassins to quiet her and eliminate all risk regardless of what her extraction agreement said. None of them had convinced Natalie or warned her about anything she didn't already know, but it now looked like they could be true. Someone was talking to Rick about Natalie, which meant someone was too nervous about her knowledge of internal CIA workings and the mole and the failures that allowed the mole to work his way onto a black-ops team. Gabe could have more than a lone shooter or group on recon knocking on his door.

The trick was to draw the information out of Rick, something that never came easily. "What people?"

Rick tapped his fingertips together. "People who control drones and have assassins on speed dial."

"You mean people in the CIA who won't make it look like she died in a freak accident." And took Gabe with her. Andy knew how this worked. Most of the team Natalie worked with lost their lives in just that way as the mole had panicked and tried to wipe out all of the evidence against him.

Rick nodded. "Her being out there, not communicating, not where they can see her and watch her, makes some people with a lot of power and even more to lose very nervous."

Fucking Gabe and this fucking assignment. They dealt with life-or-death situations every day. Gabe never flinched, but in those cases he had a team with him, resources. Open communication. None of that was in play here. "That's bullshit. She's not a threat to national security."

As usual, Rick didn't show any emotion. His expression remained blank, and the tapping of his fingertips continued a steady beat. "I agree, but I didn't give any orders here."

"But there *is* an operation to locate her and bring her in?" That Gabe could handle on his own. A full-scale attack designed to wipe her out of existence might be a different thing. "This *someone* in the CIA, or group of someones, hired you to track Natalie, correct?"

"We're speaking hypothetically, of course." Rick sat back with his perfect posture honed by years in the military.

Andy's patience expired. "Rick."

"It's a watch-only mission. I send my people in to make sure she isn't making contact with . . . undesirables." Rick almost smiled as he said it. "That she isn't selling information about holes in CIA security that would allow for a foreign government to infiltrate the organization and plant someone inside. That she isn't talking with the wrong people. Maybe other people who are disgruntled with the CIA."

"In other words, one of her old bosses fears she's turned." The idea was so ludicrous it made Andy want to shoot someone. "Natalie Udall, a woman who's dedicated her entire adult life to the CIA and the protection of this country."

"Basically, the job is to make sure she's out there holding up her end of the agreement as promised."

Relief flooded through Andy, but skepticism rushed in behind. "Do you believe that? We both know you could find her and then the next order you get will be for you to send someone in to take her out, all in the name of God and country."

Under that scenario Andy could have one brother out there trying to protect her and the other trying to kill her. The idea made him hate the division between Gabe and Rick even more.

"Some powerful people have a lot to lose if she talks about what she knows. Operational details." Rick kept tapping those fingers.

Rick danced around the topic in general terms, but Andy knew they were really talking about the problem with the mole. The job that cost Natalie her job and almost cost his ex, Elijah Sterling, his life. "I read Natalie's file. She had intel on everything from black bag jobs to abductions and rendition."

"It's more than that. From what I've been able to learn, she wasn't the type to just hang out in the room. She pushed operations in the directions she thought they should go, including the mole hunt everyone else but her saw as a waste of time."

"You mean, the point where she was right and everyone else was wrong." Andy agreed with Gabe on this point. Natalie's smarts and instincts had trumped those of most of the men around her. Could be one or two of those disgruntled lifetime desk jockeys didn't like her skills or her agreement to leave the agency without trouble. "She should have run that damn place."

"I agree, but there's a faction that doesn't. Others are smart enough to know harming her, going after her, means blowing her extraction agreement and setting in motion whatever contingency plan she and her lawyer—"

"Bast."

"—worked out."

"The latter group seems too smart to be working for the agency." All the pieces came together in Andy's head. The brewing internal war threatened to spill out and blow back on Natalie and, by extension, Gabe.

"The intelligent group has convinced the more vocal minority to hold off on taking any action for now and send in someone to watch her," Rick said in a flat voice.

Andy did not like where this was headed. "Which is where you come in, I assume."

"Gabe can't kill the guy who is about to start watching him because that person the CIA is sending to check on Natalie works for me."

It sounded so innocent, but the history between Rick and Gabe came with a load of baggage. If Gabe tipped from frustrated to furious while he was out there with Natalie, he could lose his edge. Gabe had never wavered in his dedication to the job before, but the issues with Rick were personal. They went right to the very heart of who Gabe was and what he believed.

"Goddamn it, Rick." Andy tried to push down the anger simmering inside him, but it spilled out. Rick's bombshell would fuck up all of their lives, not just Gabe's. "Are you looking for a new reason to piss Gabe off?"

"I'm trying to resolve our personal issues separate from this, but I can't even get there if he kills one of my men. He will touch off a landslide of shit from the CIA."

As if those two needed one more wall erected between them. That meant Andy had to step in, like it or not. "How close is your person to finding Gabe's location?"

Rick switched from tapping his fingertips together to drumming them on the armrest. "That depends on how long it takes for you to give it up."

"Wouldn't even if I could." That's how this worked. They had emergency protocols and ways to track each other down if communication cut out, but the specific details of where a team, or in this case Gabe, took an asset stayed with the team leader. The fewer who knew the safe location, the better.

"You can point me in the right direction and I'll ferret the rest out." Typical Rick. He didn't dig for details because he had to know there were none to give. So, he circled back and ran at the problem another way. "Look, the CIA wants a check-in with Natalie now. That means surveillance and proof she is upholding her end of the deal. I get why she ran, and it was smart, but her being in hiding isn't helping to smooth over the concerns."

On one level Andy appreciated what Rick was trying to do— handle the matter on his terms, which made it less likely Gabe would need to take action. But this still amounted to an assignment implosion. Rick might act as though officials only contacted him, but there could be others. Rick could accidentally be leading the real killers right to Natalie.

"Your job sucks." In that moment, Andy thought they all needed to rethink their chosen career paths. Forget his war hero father. Forget the mother he lost too young. Doing this shit day after day took a toll.

"If my men do the check, we don't need to worry about the safety of Gabe and Natalie. I can make this happen. Bring Gabe home faster and safe."

"You owe him," Andy said, adding the unspoken words he wanted out in the open.

"Like I don't know that."

That was something. Andy chalked it up to personal growth or some such shit, but still. "He's going to fucking hate the idea of you stepping into the middle of his assignment."

"I'll send a man. Gabe won't kill him. We can work together on this without the CIA really knowing."

Andy almost hated to ask the question. "Then what?"

A shrug. An exhale. Rick worked his way through all the gestures before finally spitting out a sentence. "After the job is done I'll work on repairing the personal damage."

That struck Andy as a "too late" issue, but he didn't say it. "Remind me to take a vacation during those days. Preferably one out of the country."

"I'll get him to listen to me."

"It's like you don't know our brother at all." After all these years, after all the fighting, Andy didn't understand how that level of ignorance was possible.

But Rick would learn that the hard way, just like he did with everything else. For being the oldest Rick sure did screw up the concept of family loyalty pretty often. Between Rick's stubbornness and Gabe's refusal to even listen, Andy had just about had it with being the youngest MacIntosh brother.

"He'll forgive me." Rick said the words, but the rock-hard certainty of his voice stumbled on the delivery.

Andy could not imagine a world where that could happen, and

he really couldn't blame Gabe for making any truce difficult. "You know something I don't?"

Rick shook his head. "He can't stay mad forever."

That sick feeling of rawness crept back into Andy's gut. Yeah, Rick didn't get Gabe at all.

FIVE

Gabe lifted the handle and swung the maul. The tool looked like a cross between an axe and a sledgehammer. He'd found it in the supply shed along with large pieces of wood, clearly cut by a chainsaw earlier in the season, before the snow started to fall. Cutting them even smaller seemed like the best way to burn off energy without doing it the way he wanted to do it.

He set the head of the maul in the log and lifted. It glided through the air, straight down in a vertical line through a mix of gravity, momentum and strength. He enjoyed the rhythmic thumping as he whacked into the middle of each block. The repetitive motion started a welcome burning in his shoulders.

The snow had stopped falling and the wind died down. The exercise kept him warm in his quilted flannel jacket and thick boots as he worked. So did her stare. He could feel it as the sweat rolled down his back. Natalie, on the porch, watching.

"How do you entertain the other women you bring up here?" she asked, the amusement obvious in her tone.

Just the sound of her voice sent a flush of warmth racing through him. "This is a safe house, not the back of a Chevy."

He lifted the maul again and brought it down with a heavy *thwack*. Sending the quarters flying brought a kick of satisfaction. Gave him something to focus on besides her, and God knew he wanted to look at her.

"It was an innocent question," she said with that soft southern lilt.

Sexy-sounding or not, he somehow doubted that. "Uh-huh."

This woman thrived on intel gathering. She knew how to drill down, ask the right question. Set someone off and test his patience. He didn't think she'd turn those skills off in her private life, which totally sucked for him. He'd been interrogated, soft and hard, and didn't need a repeat of either.

Thwack.

"Are you immune to the cold or something?" she asked.

He stopped before he could lift the maul for another swing. "No."

"Ah, we're back to curt responses."

"Never left them." He made the mistake of looking at her then. Forget yelling at her to get back inside. She stood there, leaning against a post, wearing his thick down jacket and wrapped in two blankets with an oversized hat plopped on her head. Only pink cheeks and those big eyes peeked out. "I'm not a big talker."

But he was a fucking goner. One quick glance in her direction and his common sense fizzled. He couldn't even see skin, and what few brain cells he had left blinked out as images of her, under him, over him, filled his head.

"You must be a joy on a stakeout."

She seemed a little confused about the difference between an

Army sniper and a detective. No way she made that mistake except on purpose, which meant she'd carefully crafted the questions to get at something else.

He balanced the head against the chopping block and leaned against the handle. "I don't really do those."

Her head fell to the side and that soft blond hair, now dry, slipped over her shoulder. "What do you do?"

"Now?" He followed the direction of the question but couldn't figure out where it led.

"Other than swing that axe, I mean." She pointed at the handle as her gaze wandered across his shoulders and down to his stomach.

"Maul. And I think you know the general gist of my job." Not that he could or would explain more. His clients deserved confidentiality. He extended it to her just as he did all the others.

She made an exaggerated show of dropping her head forward and sighing. "Honestly, this is going to be the longest few days of—"

"Weeks."

"I'm ignoring that." She pinned him with a serious glare. "Can't really imagine not killing you if we stay up here for weeks and don't say or do anything."

She'd basically summed up the reason he stood outside in the frigid weather chopping wood when they already had piles of it stacked up under tarps in the dry shed. Not that they had a lot of choices for activities that didn't include the bed or the outdoors. Other than a pile of mysteries with torn covers, a deck of cards and an old laptop loaded with a few movies and nothing more, they were on their own for entertainment. Next time he picked a safe house, he'd pick one with Internet service. "You want to go to a movie?"

"What?"

She clearly missed the sarcasm. "This is about keeping you safe." When she continued with the narrow-eyed frown, he skipped right to the point. The one he thought he'd made when he dragged her under that shower spray. "Hell, I don't even want you outside."

Instead of getting the hint and heading back in, she pushed away from the post. Took a few steps then started down the stairs. "I'm assuming you set up a perimeter."

Now that was insulting. As if this was his first damn day on the job. "Of course."

"Don't you think you should tell me where in case I accidentally walk into it? While you're at it, I need the locations of those two emergency drop sites. Just in case."

A trained operative turned handler turned administrator. While he intended to fill her in and would, he couldn't quite see her racing around without a care. "There's less chance of any trouble if you stay inside."

She stopped on the bottom step. Didn't venture into the snow this time. "I'm not someone who just sits around."

"I can appreciate that." Neither was he. He worked hard and played even harder. He didn't hover or sit around watching one game after another in a recliner until his ass fell asleep. He got up and did things.

She shrugged. "Then entertain me."

His mind went blank. Totally fucking blank.

"Oh my God." She burst out laughing. "You should see your face."

The sound echoed around him, wiping out every dark thought and the last of his frustration over her refusal to just follow his directions without question. "Do you know your accent comes out when you do that?"

"What?"

"Smile." There, in the background. The southern melody. The way she hit certain words. The light that brightened inside her, if only for a second, while she sparred with him and let the rest fall away.

She held his gaze for an extra beat before glancing away. All of a sudden, something in the sway of the towering trees held her attention. "Back to my point."

"You want me to keep you busy." A list of possibilities filled his head, each one dirtier than the one before. "Right."

"Then entertain me."

The handle dug into his palm as he tightened his grip. "You're playing a dangerous game here, Natalie."

A whooshing sound had them both turning to the side. Snow dropped off high branches in large clumps and crashed into a pile at the edge of the small open area around the cabin.

Nature provided the diversion. Gabe jumped on it. Whatever coursed through his veins likely hit her as well. He didn't buy into the idea of men being more sexual than women. The one looking at him right now, picking each word for maximum impact on his senses and taking his nerves to the snapping point, was no shrinking violet. But he had his limits, so he went with safe.

"I was talking about a game of Twenty Questions." Not that they hadn't studied each other's files . . . or at least the information that other people, even people with clearances and access, could unbury. The stuff she kept hidden, the information locked inside her and in unmarked files somewhere, did interest him.

"You won't know if I'm telling the truth."

The woman had a good point. Not that he'd conceded that just yet. "I will."

"You're some kind of human lie detector?"

He fought to keep his mind on the mundane conversation and off the hours that lay ahead. The night he had to get through. "Possibly."

She rubbed her boot over the salt he'd thrown on the step after clearing it off. "Indulge me."

The scraping sound screeched across his brain. "I thought I was doing that when I agreed not to tie you to the bed."

Her foot slid to a stop. "Is that your thing?"

"Actually, yes." She just stood there. Not quite what he expected. Hell, he deserved for her to tell him to fuck off, but she didn't. "No comeback to that?"

"You don't scare me." She tightened her grip on the edges of the blanket. "Having sex with you doesn't scare me."

It scared the piss out of him for some reason. "So that we're clear, what I'd do to you in bed would be about pleasure, not pain."

Silence roared between them. The creaks of the cabin and regular thuds of the snow dropping off trees blended into nothingness as they stood there, a few feet apart, with the words hovering between them.

She broke the spell with the muffled clap of her gloved hands. "Back to the game."

Damn but he liked her style. She didn't back down from a challenge. "You have to earn it."

She snorted. "I almost hate to ask what that means."

He held up a finger and waited until her eyebrow lifted in response. He'd piqued her curiosity. Good. A quick jog to the shed and he was back with a hatchet in one hand and a roll of red tape in the other. Using the chopping block, he balanced an extra piece of wood against another.

"I give up. What are we doing?" She came the rest of the way down the steps to stand beside him.

Before answering, he used the tape to create a makeshift circle on the log balanced and facing them. More of a hexagon, but close enough. He tapped the center. "If you hit the target, you get to ask a question."

Her gaze bounced from the red tape to the weapon in his hand. "Hatchet throwing?"

"You told me you have a lot of skills." He'd bet this woman could adjust to most situations, including this one. And if not, fine. He wasn't really in the mood to unload about his life anyway.

She shot him a sexy smile. "I meant the indoor kind."

The ground crumbled beneath him. He was amazed his knees didn't buckle from the force of the need driving through him. But he somehow forced his arm to lift and held the hatchet out to her, handle first. "Unless you want me to take you inside and test both of our control, you should think about throwing."

She took the hatchet and spun it around in her hand by the handle, looking far too comfortable with the lethal instrument as they moved back. "One of these times I'm going to accept your not-so-subtle offer before you rescind it again and hide behind your moral code."

The back-and-forth, the flirting . . . so dangerous. Every time he let his mind wander and slipped in a bit of innuendo, she rose to the challenge. One of these times he'd lose the will to walk a line back, then the real fun, and all the trouble he feared, would start.

He kept guiding her back until they reached a distance that guaranteed this wouldn't be an easy task for either of them. Unless she had experience with this. He didn't. Other targets, others games—yes. Not this particular one, but he guessed the skills would transfer. "I'll look forward to that."

"Not very professional of you." While walking, she turned and dropped the blanket on the steps before looking at him again. "I thought you said you didn't fuck on the job."

Hearing the harsh word in her soft voice shoved him right to the edge. She was playing with him now. Playing and winning. "One hit and you get a question."

"I think I'm familiar with the rules." She let out a low whistle. "You are a man who likes his rules."

When she finally reached the start line he drew with the toe of his boot, he moved around her. Let his lips travel over her soft hair as their arms touched and he shifted to stand behind her. His mouth lingered by her ear. "Oh, and when I hit the target I get to ask one of you."

She kept her focus on the target a rough twelve feet away. "Most of what I know is classified."

"Spare me the theatrics." He hated to pull back. Had to mentally order his muscles to obey and put some room between them. "You get three chances. Yes or no?"

She spared him a quick glance that let him know she'd accepted the challenge before stripping her gloves off and dropping them by her feet. "What you mean to say is I'll get three questions. Because I will not miss."

"I like the confidence." Hell, he was starting to like everything about her. Even those times when she got all haughty and demanding. He definitely liked her now, when her playful competitive side came through. "Hot."

She aimed. Really aimed. Lined up her feet then shifted her weight right before taking a step forward. Her arm rose over her shoulder and ended empty as if she'd just shaken someone's hand.

Gabe's gaze went from her wrist to the target. The blade wedged into the log, cutting right through the tape. Of course she could throw a hatchet. Why didn't that surprise him? "Even hotter."

"That will teach you to underestimate me."

"Yes, it will." He walked over and jimmied the blade out of the log.

She waited until he stood beside her again to say anything. "Where are we?"

He didn't pretend to misunderstand. "Montana, east of the Continental Divide."

"Huh." Her gaze traveled over the horizon. "Not what I expected."

"I'm an enigma."

"Not quite the word I'd use."

He'd debated going somewhere closer to D.C. but decided they needed unpopulated and away. "But it's colder than usual for this time of year, and there's much more snow than I anticipated."

"You couldn't check the weather report before the plane took off?" Her eyes narrowed. "And you're still not forgiven for drugging me, by the way. That one is going to haunt you. It will circle back around and bite you in the ass. Be forewarned."

He had a feeling her real level of anger didn't match her threats. She could have woken up in a rush and come after him. She hadn't. Not really. It was as if, on some level, she understood how the operation spun out.

"I wanted snow. The easier to hide you in, my dear." And that was true, so he stopped there and held out his palm to prove he held the hatchet. "My turn."

He skipped the big show and the perfect form. He'd been throwing things at targets since he could walk. His father, the perfect military man who vowed to raise the perfect future soldiers, would drag all three boys outside and teach them how to shoot at cans and throw knives. The hatchet weighed more, but the technique should be about the same. He squinted, lining up the target as he concentrated, then let go.

As the blade hit, she swore under her breath. "Figures."

She wasn't a great loser, but that didn't exactly surprise him either. He guessed she didn't get all that much practice. "Why join the CIA?"

"To serve my country." She didn't miss a beat. Threw out the answer then reached for the hatchet.

No way was he accepting that answer. "Bullshit responses not allowed."

She glared. He glared back.

She finally broke the stare-off with an eye roll. "There are men who need to be tracked down and killed. Forget the excuses about hard childhoods and not having enough milk when they were babies or being told the truth about Santa too early or whatever ridiculous excuse passes for a reason not to take personal responsibility these days. Some view human destruction as a game, and those men need killing. They have to be stopped."

The way she said it mirrored how he would have said it. On this, they were on the same page. "And you joined to stop them?"

"Yes." She held up two fingers and wiggled them in front of his face. "That was two questions, by the way."

Before she could say anything, she grabbed the hatchet. Performed the same drawn-out routine. Ended with her arm out and in perfect alignment with the target. With the blade embedded in the pseudo-circle she matched her first near-perfect throw with a second one.

She spun around on the heel of her boot and smiled at him. "Why did you leave the Army?"

"I was done being the government's bitch."

Her smile fell. "*Now* who's giving a bullshit response?"

He held up his hands in fake surrender. "Totally true. I had been trained to track, to hide and to kill. I did my time and was done. Reached my limit and got out rather than re-upping."

Maybe it sounded like a line, but it wasn't. Every word rang true. He'd been raised to join the military and serve his country. There wasn't an alternative plan, according to his father. Forget college or taking a year off. They had a responsibility, and each one of them, one after the other, lived up to it.

His dad died of cancer before Andy ever joined, but the man's stern discipline and unbending belief system had rubbed off on all of them by then. It took Gabe years to break free from his father's oppressive mental hold. Watching him push Andy to the point of cracking with all those "be a real man" comments finally did it.

"How many people have you killed?" she asked, without a trace of judgment.

Still, no fucking way was he answering that one. A number flashed in his mind and he had no intention of sharing it. "It's not your turn."

He took off for the target and slid the hatchet out. He barely made it back to the line before turning and letting the hatchet fly. Didn't even look to see if it hit the circle before he started with his next question. "Who taught you that some men need killing?"

She hesitated as she stared at the handle sticking out from the target. A few seconds passed, then she looked at him again. "My father, but I'm guessing you knew that."

There might be things she could hide, but not this. Her file outlined some pretty awful family secrets. He didn't know all the details, but he knew enough. Enough to know her father killed her mother and that he should kick his own ass for asking the question in the first place.

She nodded. "Right, that's what I thought."

"Natalie."

"Technically, that was your three." She brushed her hands against her jeans and bent down to retrieve her gloves. Slid them on, one at a time, before heading for the steps.

He called out to her. "You have one more chance."

She didn't even bother to look around before she hit the door and opened it. "I'm suddenly not in the mood for games."

Yeah, neither was he.

SIX

Silence might be golden but it was slowly driving Natalie nuts. She'd grown accustomed to the bustle of the office and being on call twenty-four hours a day. Going from being needed and vital to an operation to sitting in a cabin staring at a wall made her want to claw her way through it.

Sure, she had to be on guard in case anyone came after her. Even though she now saw the futility of running from Gabe and his assistance, she wasn't the type to hide while he took the hits. Not her style at all. But in between those stark moments of tension were long periods of unending boredom that books and cards couldn't shake.

But now something else worked its way into the cabin. A heated sensation. A simmering just below the surface. They hadn't said a word since the hatchet game. Hours had passed, and they sat across from each other at the small folding table Gabe set up after he finally got bored with cutting wood.

The soup came from a can, but it was warm and it was food of some sort, so she didn't complain as she'd dumped it into a saucepan and figured out how to heat the burner. She'd had worse. In survivalist training she'd had to go days on little sleep and dig for worms. The whole deal. It supposedly toughened her, but honestly, she was pretty damn tough already.

In those moments when her confidence faltered she let the memories flood her mind. All the blood. Her mother's screaming. The knife. Amazing how that could shift her whole world back into perspective.

Despite all the turmoil of the past two months, those old haunting memories had remained blocked. She'd had enough to deal with thanks to the immediate danger. Watching her team walk into a setup on a rogue mission. Being called in to answer questions. Hunting the mole while Elijah and the rest of the team scattered, only to be picked off one after the other. She'd stepped in, thrown her weight around, took risks she never thought she'd take to save the last two—Elijah and Becca—but not before facing down another bloodbath.

It was as if death followed her. But never, during all of those dark CIA days and the ones that followed at the negotiating table, listening to Bast weave his magic with words and schemes that made her think he'd missed his calling by being a lawyer instead of an agent, had she called up the soul-sucking memories from those years before. Not until Gabe stood outside today and asked his question. Now the images ran through her mind until all she wanted to do was forget.

Done with the thin broth, she dropped her spoon next to the bowl with a soft clink and glanced across the table. "Since I cooked, you get to do the dishes."

"Technically, you opened a can." He actually grinned at her. Sent all that smoking heat in her direction.

She never knew she had a thing for beards or big men or quiet talkers until him. But the punch of that combination made her dizzy. And she didn't get breathless or silly for any man, not before him.

She cleared her throat because she had to. "Same thing."

"Not really."

A knocking sound grabbed her attention. It took her a second to realize it came from under the table where she'd crossed one leg over the other. Seemed one foot had taken to a fit of wild jumping. She rested a palm against her knee to stop it. "You're an expert at cooking, too?"

He leaned back with his arms folded behind his head. "I know my way around most rooms in the house, including a kitchen."

Prey. That was the only way to describe what set off the wild thumping inside her. She suddenly knew what a gazelle felt like the second before a big cat pounced.

She forced her voice to stay even. "You sound very domesticated."

"I am."

"You, the former sniper." That didn't make any sense to her. She pictured him going from assignment to assignment, bedding women here and there. Enjoying a country then moving on, with brief stops at what functioned as home for him before heading out into danger again.

The chair screeched against the wood floor as he sat up straight again. "Not to keep throwing the word out there, but *technically* I'm still a sniper."

The move put him closer. A table still separated them, but she was ten seconds away from flipping the thing to get to him. The answer was to circle back to a safer topic. Something mundane and not open to debate. "Well, the cooking might help if you ever decide to put the gun away and settle down to start a family, but I don't think the other skills will."

"Already did."

Words screeched to a halt in her brain. "What?"

He rested his elbows on the table and stared her down. "I have a family."

The air hiccupped in her lungs. So much for thinking anything with this guy would run smoothly.

"You mean your brother Andy?" She'd met him in the office. Actually, knew him from before, back when she knew Andy and Elijah slept together on a regular basis because Eli was on her team and her responsibility. Even knew that when Eli walked out, Andy struggled to deal and ended up in a rough place. She could understand why Gabe might be protective. It seemed ingrained in his DNA.

"I mean my son."

"I just . . . You mean . . . "

He leaned in "Yes?"

He just put it out there. No explanation or anything. Surely he was joking or she misunderstood . . . but he just sat there.

When she just sat there, he continued to stare. Finally, he spoke up again, which was good because she couldn't find the words. "I have a son."

That couldn't be right. She'd read his file and wanted to shake her head in denial, but she could see the truth in his eyes. She struggled to imagine him as a dad. Holding a kid and throwing a ball. All normal, or so she'd seen on television and in movies. Her life had never worked that way. She knew exactly what it was like to have a lethal father, but not Gabe's kind of lethal. Not the controlled kind.

And a kid meant a wife or a girlfriend. Yeah, that.

A wave of nausea rolled over her. She was going to kick his ass if he really thought she'd be some sort of vacation candy for him.

She dropped both feet to the floor, ready to shove him if needed. "You have a kid?"

"That's what 'son' means."

Wrong time to be a smartass. She still had that gun he gave her. He'd be wise to remember that. "So, you're married?"

He shook his head. "I didn't say that."

"Divorced?"

"Never."

The game of verbal gymnastics ended right now. A sudden fury on behalf of a woman she didn't know and envied in a weird way overtook Natalie. "All those passes and comments about getting me into bed—"

"Which is not something I do on a job."

"—and you have a wife." Her voice vibrated from the restraint of not launching across the table to smack his smug face.

He shook his head. "No wife."

The two words had the tension fizzling out, but Natalie's head kept spinning. Her emotions bounced from anger to relief. Fought with being ticked off for feeling either. He was her bodyguard, and an unwanted one at that. Getting wrapped up in his life, caring, all amounted to a huge mistake.

She'd seen the signs in agents over the years. They got sucked in, and their lives imploded. Of course, she'd moved past implosion a month ago. There wasn't much further for her to fall.

"I give up. You said not divorced, so is she dead?" Natalie blurted out the question because there really was no way to finesse it. Not now.

"She never existed."

Something blinked inside her brain. "I don't—"

He smiled. "You know how babies get here, right? Being married isn't a mandatory thing."

Like that, a wave of heat flashed through her. Him, in bed. Sex. Coming inside her. She was never going to survive this captivity that was supposed to save her. "I can't figure out if you're joking."

A nerve ticked in Gabe's cheek. "I don't joke about him, ever. Never talk about him on a job either, so this is new."

That sounded more like the guy she'd come to know. Dependable and clear. "Your file didn't mention a son."

"I've had some help keeping his existence under wraps." He grew even more serious. "For his protection."

"Where is he now?"

"In school."

Back to curt answers, but that one told her enough. It also deflated her all over again. "You send him away so you can play G.I. Joe?"

His eyes widened. "Wow, so many assumptions in one question."

Yeah, probably too harsh. Likely unfair. She didn't care. Not in that moment. Not when she could remember sitting in her room during holidays and having dinners with the staff. She'd been one of the charity cases that the school staff passed around because no one wanted to pick her up and take her home. She didn't really have one of those.

"Am I wrong?" she asked, hoping she was.

"About almost everything in that sentence, yes." When she started to ask more, he cut her off. "Is this some sort of payback for the comment about your father?"

The question shut down something inside her. He knew enough about her past to throw her those pitying looks. She'd experienced those her entire life and had no interest in dealing with them as an adult.

Being vulnerable sucked. "No."

"Because I shouldn't have gone—"

"I *said* no." She jumped up, needing to walk or move or at least get away from him and the table. She scooped up her bowl and held out a hand to him. "You done?"

"I'll do the dishes."

Even better. She dropped her bowl, letting it clank against the table. "Good."

She got as far as the doorway to the bedroom before his deep voice stopped her. "Natalie?"

With a hand on the frame, she stopped but didn't bother to look around. "What?"

Silence settled between them. For a few seconds he didn't say anything. "Nothing."

SEVEN

Gabe stayed outside as long as he could stand it. Walked the perimeter and re-walked it. Spent some time in the shed. Checked coordinates and the satphone for emergency messages from Andy. Nothing.

With his feet almost frozen and the cold sapping some of his strength, Gabe gave up and went back inside. Before opening the door, he knocked in the agreed-upon sequence to give her fair warning. After that dinner, she might shoot him just for fun.

He walked into the dark cabin and relocked the door. An oil lamp cast the main room in a soft light and heat poured out of the wood-stove. He should sit his ass down on the small couch and time out a thirty-minute break before he got up and took watch duty again.

He probably would have done just that if he hadn't looked into the small alcove by the front door. A doorway to the bed. The mattress just fit, with the edges touching every wall. A small bed in a small space. Going in there spelled disaster. He should walk away. Ignore the need pulling at him to lie across the bed and listen to her breathing.

As if her senses clicked on, she sat straight up. Brushed that sexy hair out of her eyes and squinted. He could see her just fine. Make out every devastating curve despite the covers she had bunched up at her waist. That thermal shirt sure didn't offer much protection. Not from him.

"Hey." That's all she said. A simple greeting.

It pulled him in close. Before he knew it, he stood in the doorway with his knees balancing against the end of the mattress. "Sorry to wake you."

"You didn't." She didn't even look away as she lied. "I thought you'd keep watch."

Before dinner he'd gone over all the procedures and the drop spots for her to get to in case danger came calling. She knew about his patrols and the perimeter defense he'd set up. She even spent time watching with her gun ready as he rested for a few minutes while she prepared the soup. He didn't need to explain what he was doing now, but he did anyway. "I'm taking thirty minutes."

"Sounds smart." She slid over, making room for him to basically fall onto the mattress.

This was the part where he should have said "no thanks" and moved on. He knew that as he took off his gun and put it on the one shelf overhanging the mattress. As he put a knee on the bed and crawled up to join her on the pillows.

A few seconds later, he lay flat on his back, staring at the ceiling. "I don't sleep very deep, so you're fine."

She curled on her side and faced away from him. "I guess that's a good trait. Having a kid and all."

This was the right time to tell her about Brandon. She talked about him like he was in elementary school and abandoned by his father, which probably made sense to her in light of Gabe's age, but didn't come close to being right. But for some reason he couldn't get the words out. Not after seeing the mix of shock and disappointment on her face.

Whatever esteem she'd had for him had fallen, and that pissed him off. He wanted to earn it back without having to give her every detail. And up until now she hadn't exactly been shy about asking him things or speaking her mind.

He turned and faced her back. Pushed up on his elbow and watched her. "Do you want to ask me something?"

"Do you see him?" she asked, in a voice muffled by blankets and pillows.

"All the time." Letting Brandon live a normal life had been a daily struggle for Gabe. His instincts told him to protect and hide, but his early years with his father had been such a shitshow that he refused to take Brandon down the same path. The kid had been blessed with book smarts and street smarts, and Gabe had to let go enough to trust those.

She rolled to her back. Didn't face Gabe but kept her eyes open as she stared into space. "So, it's not like you sent him away to a boarding school in another country."

As much as her immediate belief that he left his kid behind pissed him off, he did like the way she rushed to Brandon's defense. Didn't even know him and her first thought was to protect him. All those men who tagged her as being cold and unfeeling were jackasses.

"He's very close by at all times," Gabe said, carefully dodging the wrong words.

She glanced at him then. "Here?"

"I live in Virginia." Not that he ever divulged that information. Anything that could possibly threaten Brandon and his normal life caused Gabe to hold back. But for some reason, he trusted her to know this much.

"Your file says Maryland."

Of course it did, because that's what he let people think. "A lie."

"I'm surprised you shared that with me."

"Me, too." The place in Maryland was a real place but just an outpost of Tosh. A business property, not his house.

She laughed. "Now that's the Gabe I've come to know."

The sound of her voice was contagious. The thoughts running through his mind . . . her under those sheets . . . "Are you a danger to me, Natalie?"

"Only if you act like an asshole."

And there was the Natalie he'd come to know. "I could be in trouble then."

Her smile and her gaze skipped away from his face to the wall behind his head. "It just sucks to be sent away. That's all."

He wondered how long it would take her to circle back there. "Like you were?"

"Do you have *my* file memorized?" Her gaze met his.

"Pretty much." He reached out and smoothed the hair off her cheek. Let the silky strands slip between his fingers. "I know the basics. Your uncle got custody and sent you to a girls' boarding school."

"Right."

His fingers lingered on the side of her face, brushing over her soft skin. "I'm guessing it sucked."

Her eyes searched his. "Are you saying that because you're worried about your son?"

Now was the time. He could just set the record straight and move on . . . but the need to test her pulled at him. "The situation is very different."

"Forget I said anything."

He dropped his hand to the mattress. "I think you're disappointed in me."

"I don't know you." She looked away, but not before a shadow moved behind her eyes.

"We're in bed together." Him on top of the covers and her beneath, but the inches of material didn't matter. Being right on the edge, if she gave him the okay he might just rip through the covers to get to her.

"I thought you were supposed to be sleeping." She picked at the blanket. Folded it down and tucked it under her armpits.

The shirt outlined her breasts. No bra here. That meant no sleep for him. Blew his concentration all to hell as well. "Not really in the mood right now."

"What do you want to do?"

"Touch you." A stupid but honest answer, and it was out there now.

He started to get up, move away. Last thing he wanted was for her to worry that the threats to her safety started inside the cabin. No matter how many times he told her she held the power and he had full control over his needs when he dropped his zipper, he needed to back it up by showing her.

"Do it."

The scratch in her voice hit him first. He froze, then sank back down with his weight on his elbow. "I'm not sure that's a great idea."

"Me either, but I want you to." She lifted her hand and traced the backs of her fingers over the scruff of his beard. "Just wipe everything away."

He could give her relief. Let her find a release of some of the tension trapped inside her. She deserved that. Probably needed to find some sense of peace, if only for a few minutes. But that meant touching her, just like he'd been aching to do.

The call to forget the job and lose himself in her echoed in his head until he couldn't hear anything else. He'd taken this assignment instead of farming it out to his team because he needed a diversion. Rick kept coming around, insisting they talk. Gabe had never been a runner, but he'd needed to break away. Gain perspective. Not kill Rick even though every word he uttered begged for it.

"Here." She took Gabe's hand, weaving her fingers through his.

Her warm palm pressed against his as her shoulder touched his arm. The brush must have had her nerves jumping around because her legs shifted in a flurry of constant motion. She'd gone from stiff with an expression of deep concern, to one of wonder.

A danger sign flashed in his brain. He should drop her hand and scoot his ass off that bed. Should have done a lot of things. He picked kissing her. Not a shattering move. A simple one. Lifted their joint hands and pressed his lips to the back of hers. Licked his tongue down to her wrist.

She watched him, her gaze following every touch. "The beard."

"You don't like it?"

"The opposite." She traced a finger around his mouth. "I can't help but wonder what it will feel like everywhere."

Jesus. "You are a temptation, Natalie Udall."

And that was a fucking understatement.

He didn't hold back one more second. Shifting his weight, he leaned in, giving her all the time to pull back, slap him, hell, knee him in the groin. But none of that headed his way. If anything, she lifted her chin, bringing her mouth closer to his.

Then he was kissing her. Not sweet or lingering. No, he dove right into a devouring, oxygen-sucking kiss. Heat blasted around him as a hand slipped around her waist and tugged her in closer. Soft grumbling sounds filled the room as he crossed his mouth over hers.

Forget treading water. Hands, lips, the sweep of his tongue over hers . . . it all mixed together and combined to pull him under.

Before his brain could send a signal to his hands to keep still, they started moving.

His fingers slid under the covers. Over her stomach, learning every amazing curve. He didn't stop until his palm rested on top of her underwear. Her heat warmed his hand. Raising his head, his gaze locked with hers as he started a gentle rub, a brushing back and forth of his thumb, inching lower.

When she opened her legs even wider, he peeled away the sheets and blankets cocooning her. Pushed them to the side, freeing her.

He needed to see her, all of her. Touch her.

A sudden burst of energy pumped through him. He could feel his nerve endings snapping to life as he trailed his fingertips along the inside of her thigh. The lean muscles intrigued him, but the softness of her skin turned him inside out. The curves, every inch of her alive with feminine power.

She didn't wait for him. She covered his hand with hers and brought his fingers right to the place she wanted them—between her legs—pressing them tight against her.

He leaned down and kissed her neck. Felt the thump of her erratic heartbeat under his lips. His mouth traveled over her as his finger slipped under the elastic band of her underwear. Over the soft patch of hair. Sliding down as he drew the tip through the wetness there.

He circled and caressed as her muscles tightened. "You're ready."

"Yes." Her fingers clenched against his arm.

"This time." He kissed a line from her throat to the back of her ear and felt her shiver in response. "But you won't be in charge after this."

"Yes." She exhaled the word on a breath.

He eased his finger inside, just barely, and stopped. "Say it, Natalie."

Her head shifted on the pillow as she reached down to drag him in deeper. "Now, Gabe."

"I say when." He toyed with her. Licking her ear. Rubbing his fingertip around her clit.

A low groan rumbled in her throat. Her knees rose and her inner muscles clamped down on him.

Sweet damn, she *was* ready. Her body begged for more, and he needed to see her lose it. Watch that mouth drop open and feel her close around him. But not yet. He knew he could get her there, make them both ache for release.

He kissed her, deep and long, as his fingers slid in just a bit farther. When he raised his head, she grabbed the back of his neck and kept him close. "Gabe . . ."

"What do you need, baby?" He kissed his way back down her throat to that sexy collarbone. "Tell me."

Her back arched. "I want to come."

Good girl. He debated using his finger versus his mouth but the need to taste her overtook him. Sliding along the mattress, he took the covers with him, pushing them to the end of the bed. Of course she didn't wear pants or sweats, because then he might have stood a chance against his need for her. He sat back on his heels and took in every last inch. Her long legs carried a faint hint of a tan from the summer that had ended months ago. From the dark purple toenails to the shadow at the edge of her underwear, he loved every secret she hid under all those boring work clothes. But he had one left to discover.

He skimmed shaking hands up the outsides of her legs and up her thighs. Didn't stop until his fingers slid under the leg bands of her underwear and his palms traveled around to her ass. Firm and tight, her cheeks filled his palms perfectly. He'd enjoy that sensation another time. Now he needed her on his tongue.

He peeled the material down and off in one long, tortuous pull. Whipped the underwear behind him, not caring where it landed. With all his focus centered on her body and the peek of the flat stomach he saw beneath the hem of the shirt, he put his hands on her ankles. Pushed her legs up and out, opening her wide.

His shoulders fit perfectly between her thighs. He inched his way in as her scent filled his head. At first his finger dipped inside her. Then, no longer able to play and tease, he slid his finger deep and felt her pulse around him. His tongue danced across her clit while his finger pumped inside her, first slow then fast, then back to slow again.

Stiffness settled in her muscles and her fists twisted in the sheet underneath her. He did not stop. He licked inside her, tasting her as a tremble moved through her. He felt every pulse and every shift. When her hips lifted, he blew a breath of hot air over her that had her insides clenching.

The tension wound around them, and the room filled with a thumping sound from the leg of the bed against the old floor and the heavy breaths escaping her lungs. All those days of wanting her piled up on him. He increased the pressure, so slightly. Pressed a second finger inside her and opened them to caress her slickness with his mouth.

With the last swipe of his tongue, her body went wild. Her hips bucked and she whispered his name. Those beautiful eyes drifted shut as her chin lifted. He sat there, taking in every moment of the stunning view playing out in front of him. The long line of her body and tightening of every muscle inside and out. When she let her body go, she came with a rush and a punch of an exhale that had her dropping back into the mattress.

For a few seconds, he stayed there, with her legs wrapped around him. The temptation to get up and slide inside her nearly overtook him. But this moment was for her. She'd had her world tossed upside down, her life dissected, been pushed around and dragged across the country by him. She deserved a release of tension and a few minutes to think. He needed an ice bath.

When she tugged on his arm, he gave in. Crawled up her body, stopping to kiss a sliver of exposed stomach, before settling in beside her. Before he could roll over and away from her, she had her arm around his back and her fingers brushing over his skin.

None of that helped him restore his common sense. "You okay?"

"That helped."

He rested his forehead against hers as he struggled to keep his breathing even, or at least out of heart attack range. "Happy to hear it."

When her mouth found his again, all thoughts of work and protection slipped from his mind. Those fingers trailed down his chest, burning a path through his shirt. Much more of this and they'd both be naked. No boundaries.

Yeah, he had to sit up. Walk away. Just for a second before he pulled them past the line between professional and very fucking personal.

Even with his brain scrambled, his muscles got the message. He leaned back, trying to put at inch of space between them. No way would he be able to stand up and slip out if she continued to touch him.

"I need to . . ." Yeah, that was close enough. He didn't really have the strength to say much more.

He made it to the end of the bed and stopped. His legs better work or he'd fall on his ass. There was nothing impressive about that.

"Where are you going?" Amusement kept her voice light.

"Outside." He barked out the word as he grabbed the door-jamb and stood up. He was half surprised he didn't rip the wood from the wall.

"Gabe?"

"Huh?" He gave in and glanced over his shoulder at her then.

"Well"—she balanced her upper body on her elbows—"it's freezing."

That was the point. "I sure as hell hope so."

EIGHT

Andy looked up from the security feeds in time to see Rick barge into the communications room. Andy had given the okay for him to come into the building but hadn't expected the fire-breathing furious act that had the two Tosh tech guys clearing the room.

"Always nice to see you." Andy sat back in his chair and waited for the explosion.

It didn't take Rick long. He stopped on the other side of the table with his hands resting on either side of the video monitor. "He picked fucking Montana?"

Ah, yes. More yelling about Gabe. Just what Andy needed today. But he did have to give Rick credit for tracking down the location in record time. That shook Andy a bit more than he wanted to admit. "He likes a challenge."

"It's been snowing there like a son of a bitch for days. Getting in is not going to be easy."

Not usually one to state the obvious, Andy went ahead and did it anyway. "Which I'm assuming was the point. How did you find him exactly?"

"I only know the state. He slipped all tracking at the border." Rick leveled his gaze at Andy. "I need an exact location, even a square-mile radius will do."

Nice try, but Andy wasn't budging. "Did you answer my question?"

"Through a series of private plane movements. Gabe threw me off with a decoy. Almost thought he went into Canada. That's where the CIA thinks he is. Meaning he did buy Natalie extra time, but it will run out."

Good for Gabe. But Andy played it cool with a shrug. "Maybe he is in Canada."

"I know how he thinks." When Andy didn't say anything to that, Rick kept talking. "I'm also calling in about a hundred favors and talking to some contacts in the full-time 'getting lost' business. Repositioning a satellite and looking through top security-coded video from the day he left."

That was some serious spy shit. "What the fuck, Rick."

"I don't have a choice. I have an eight-man team running round-the-clock on this. It's taking all of us, plus outside help. You could help me cut down on how long this will take by coughing up some intel." Rick pushed off the table and stood up straight again. "Because I *will* find him eventually."

"Good luck with that."

"When do you call him next? I need to be in on that."

Finding Gabe and talking to him were two different things, and Andy was pretty sure Rick knew that. "You want to get on the line and say hello?"

His scowl deepened. "What the fuck is wrong with you? I'm trying to help him by being the one who finds Natalie and reports back to the CIA that everything is fine."

Andy had been hearing this argument in one form or the other for far too long. It was as if Rick got stuck on some sort of *sure,*

I fucked Gabe over but I really want to help now wheel. Rick messed up and somehow always found a way to blame the fallout on Gabe. Andy was done. "You mean, you've decided to step in on this job and help him after screwing him."

"Don't go there."

"Or more accurately, screwing his girlfriend." The shot landed. Andy could see it in the way Rick's stance stiffened.

"This is not your fight, Andrew."

"You made it my fight when you announced your big news at the fucking dinner table one night. You acted as if you were going to talk about some sort of life change after being injured on a covert operation we didn't even know you were on and ending up in rehab. Then you dumped that admission on Gabe. Your guilt." With a few words Rick had ripped the family apart, and Andy wasn't sure they'd ever be able to put it back together again.

Losing their mother in a freak accident when Andy was still in elementary school had been horrible. Dealing with their demanding father both while he wasted away from cancer and before that had been pretty rough. Hell, so had having the air knocked out of him when Eli walked away without an explanation. All had sucked, but no day compared to the one with that dinner.

"He deserved to know." Rick's cheeks got red and his chest puffed out. But he gave up on eye contact, which had to mean he knew the truth.

"Don't act like you did it for him." Andy had been there and heard every word. Rick created the rift then shoved it even wider by making demands.

"You know why—" Rick visibly wrestled his body back under control. "Look, this is between him and me. It's not your concern."

Andy refused to let that go. "If you really think that, you're not as smart as everyone says you are."

"You want to go at it?" Rick stepped back, showing off his two-inch height advantage and muscles honed by years of intense training. "Right now. We can have this out."

Fighting wouldn't move this argument one inch, so Andy didn't even try. He held his hands up in the air. "You've got the wrong brother."

"I will make this right with Gabe."

Andy let his hands fall until his palms smacked against the table. "You know what you need to do to make that happen, and you won't do it."

"You can't ask me to potentially walk away from the truth."

The truth that would drive them all to the brink of emotional destruction. Andy couldn't sit there. He shoved his chair back, letting it spin from the force of his push as he stood up. "You know what, Rick? I'm not asking you to do anything. Neither is Gabe. If someone needs to go out there and find him and report back, I'll do it. You can pretty up your report and—"

"No."

Andy exhaled, not holding back one bit of the frustration he held for the older brother he once idolized. "Oh, I see. You want Gabe to know you're watching over him and be the one to rescue him."

It made sense. Truth was, Rick could have turned down this job from the CIA and insisted someone else be sent out to check on Natalie. He acted now as if having his men lead on this protected her because his guys being out there might prevent a team of assassins from being sent. All true, but digging down to the core, Andy suspected this was really about Rick needing to ride in and be Gabe's savior. As if that would somehow balance the books.

"He needs to know he's not as safe as he thinks he is," Rick said.

Oh, he got it. They all did. "You've already taught him that lesson."

The red heat of fury stained Rick's cheeks again. "Fuck you."

"Good luck finding him. You're on your own." With that, Andy sat down and did what he'd been doing for months . . . pretended his oldest brother wasn't there.

Natalie stood by the woodstove but her attention kept wandering back to Gabe. To last night. To his mouth. The scratch of his beard against her inner thighs had driven her wild until energy burst through her and she could not get close enough.

She'd suspected he could back up his sensual promises with real action, but she had underestimated the man. The combination of his big hands and that tongue had turned her insides to mush. She could only imagine what other skills he kept hidden behind his spare-talking façade.

At first she thought it was probably a good thing he ran from the bed as soon as her eyes opened again. Now she wasn't so sure. The night had come and gone. So had most of today. If the man chopped any more wood, their location would be spotted because the stacks would be high enough to be seen from space.

As far as she could tell, while there were things in the cabin to keep their attention, they were running out of ways to stay away from each other. Not that she even wanted to anymore. Truth was she knew she could handle any attacker that came her way. With Gabe's help, she'd be able to take down wave after wave of gunmen sent to her door. She didn't need him for protection, but after weeks of him sniffing around and her following his every move she did need him for other things.

She glanced over to the sink and watched him play with the lid to an ancient stovetop coffeepot. Then her gaze traveled over those faded jeans and the way they highlighted his impressive ass.

Yeah, enough waiting.

"Did you actually bring condoms with you?" she asked into the quiet room.

"Shit." The metal pot bounced as he juggled it from hand to hand and caught it right before it crashed to the floor.

Seemed those hands were good at everything. "Smooth."

He stared at her a bit more wide-eyed than usual as he placed the pot on the small counter with a thud without ever breaking eye contact. "You certainly know how to open a conversation."

Then the job he'd been concentrating on so hard hit her. "Why are you making coffee like that?"

"I can't exactly go for a drive and get it." He frowned as he reached down and scooped the dropped lid off the floor and slammed it on the counter.

"There's an automatic coffeemaker in the bathroom." An odd place to put it, but she saw it every time she stepped into the claustrophobic room, so she knew.

"That's part of the homemade hot water heater." His eyebrow lifted when she didn't say anything. "It's attached."

She ignored the way he slowed down his words as if talking to a child. "Are you serious?"

"Almost always." He held up a hand. "But go back to the condom question."

Now she had his attention. Almost made her sorry the sexiest thing he'd packed for her was a thin white T-shirt and sturdy white cotton panties. She didn't know who shopped for this trip, but clearly it was someone who wanted her to stay clothed. "It's inevitable."

His frown grew deeper and deeper. "And the 'it' is . . . ?"

Looked like he wanted her to say it. Fine with her. She was a big girl and she knew what she wanted—him all over her. "Sex."

"We're supposed to be riding out danger." His words might sound tough but that look said he was turning over the infinite possibilities in his head. A small smile replaced his frown, and he took a step toward her.

"Maybe I'd rather ride you."

He visibly exhaled. "Natalie . . . "

"I'm a big girl, Gabe."

His gaze swept over her. "No argument there."

She could almost see his resistance crumble. "And I know what I want."

"I'm listening."

"Are you worried about anyone sneaking up on us or on the cabin?"

"No." He stopped in front of her, and his hands went to her hips.

The warmth from his palms seeped through her shirt and sweater straight to her skin. "I know from your lecture—"

"I don't lecture."

"—you have traps and alarms all around this place."

"Of course."

Just as she expected from his training. He had contingency plans, and plans for whatever came next if those failed. She was half surprised he hadn't figured out a way to throw a net on the whole area and hide them under it.

"I'm guessing, absent a drone flying over, we'd have warning." Her hands went to the wide expanse of his chest. Played with the black buttons on his plaid shirt. She'd never cared for the whole mountain-man, lumberjack style . . . until now.

"Even then I'd try to shoot it down," he said, in a tone so serious she almost laughed.

She forced her gaze away from his shoulders to his face. "With what?"

That small smile slipped into a full grin. "Do you really have to ask?"

"Right." He probably *would* have a rocket launcher stored around here somewhere. The man was prepared for anything. At least she hoped that was true, which brought her back to the original question. "Well, my point is that we're as safe here as we would be anywhere, so do you actually have condoms or was that some sort of guy smack talk?"

"Once you have one kid you didn't exactly plan for, you're really careful about this type of thing."

Interesting. Another tiny window into the real man behind the carefully crafted image in her file on him. She'd take a bigger peek later. Right now she had other things on her mind. "I'm hoping that means yes."

"I always bring condoms on a job." His hands slid down and over her ass. With a hand over each cheek, he squeezed as he pulled her tighter against him.

Her breath hitched in her chest, but she fought to keep her voice steady. "Even though you said you never have sex when you're working?"

"Yes."

"Interesting answer. You see why I'm confused, right?" She actually didn't know what the hell she was talking about. Not when his hands massaged her like that.

"I believe I said I never fuck on a job, and that's true. Doesn't mean I tempt fate. When I travel, protection comes with me." His head dipped and his mouth brushed over her cheek. "It's part of the go bag."

Standard operating procedure in the CIA. Apparently he followed the same rules in his security work. "Not sure if that makes you practical or something else."

A beat of silence, then another. He didn't say anything as he stood there. Watching, his breathing growing unsteady as the intensity ratcheted up.

Finally he broke the quiet, but his words only added to the growing tension. "Right now I'll be whatever you want me to be."

Right answer. Whatever silent battle he'd been waging inside him appeared to end, taking his denials along with it. "I'm willing to go into the bedroom . . . Why are you shaking your head?"

He pulled her toward the small couch. "Right here."

The lumpy cushions. The small size. Admittedly her control had reached the snapping point, but they could at least try not to make this into an acrobatics show. "Wouldn't a bed be easier?"

"I'm looking for hot, not easy."

For some reason the comment settled her jumping nerves. "So much for your idea of waiting."

"You blew past my defenses. My rules exploded the minute you mentioned condoms." And he looked ticked off about that.

She wasn't. "Good response."

"And I plan to take you in every square inch of this cabin." He let the silence play for a few beats. "Eventually."

On some men the comment would sound like cockiness. On Gabe, the words issued a promise. "Maybe you should try getting through this first time, stud."

"We'll start here, where I can see the door." He glanced from the couch to the front of the cabin. "Just in case."

"You think you're going to be in any condition to fire a gun?" She planned to have him as hot and bothered as she was.

"Is that a euphemism?"

Sometimes he said things she did not expect. "I hope you're as good as you say you are."

"I'm better." He sank to the couch and turned her until she stood in front of him, between his legs. "Want me to show you?"

She ran a hand over his hair and down the side of his head. "Was I unclear about that?"

"I want your body to tell me." With his resistance gone, his movements quickened. He pushed her sweater up past the band of her jeans and started unzipping. No fanfare or hesitating.

She loved the sure way he held his body and commanded a room. And the dirty talk. He could bring that back any time. "Then go faster."

"Quick isn't always better." He proved his point by taking an eternity to draw the zipper down click by click.

By the time he slipped his hand inside her jeans her legs shook. This time he didn't play around with touching her and waiting. His hand dipped past her underwear to her skin. His finger slipped along her, inside her.

"Your body is already talking." He whispered the comment and his breath blew over her belly. "So fucking wet."

He did that to her. The deep rumble of his voice. The intense stare. The mix of talk and touching that had her ready to go at all times. Her need for him was embarrassing, really, but she'd worry about that later. Now she concentrated on the slide of his thumb. The gentle back and forth.

The way he talked about sex she expected to be slammed against the wall and taken without much thought of what her body needed, but no. This guy was no amateur.

"Take my jeans off," she said, because she'd been dreaming about just that for weeks.

"Everything is coming off." His thumb kept brushing against her. "I want you naked when I take you the first time."

A series of images ran through her mind, each one dirtier and more graphic than the one before. "And the next time?"

"We'll have to see what we're both in the mood for, but right now I think we know."

That made one of them. She could barely think at all. "What?"

"For you to ride me." He dipped his head and pressed a kiss on the front of her underwear.

The words, that mouth, set off a tingling sensation inside her. So did the stripping as he pushed her jeans and underwear down, past her knees to the floor. When he sat up again, she wore only socks from the waist down.

Before she could say anything, he pulled her onto his lap. Her thighs straddled his legs, and the rough material of his jeans rubbed against her skin. She kissed him then, full and deep as her fingers speared through his hair. Her mouth toured his. The firm chin, the forceful lips. She loved his boldness. Loved the feel of him under her.

Sitting back as far as his arms wrapped around her would allow, she skimmed her shirt and sweater up her body and over her head. Before she even lowered her arms, his hands were on her, cupping her breasts, massaging as he ran a thumb across one nipple.

Her breath left in a rush and a sigh hit the tip of her tongue. She bit it all back as he slipped the bra straps down her arms, letting them fall. Then his mouth was on her. His tongue sweeping over one nipple then the other. He sucked and licked, not sparing any inch of skin from his mind-blowing attention.

Her head tipped back as the sensations rippled through her. "God, yes."

He mumbled something against the underside of her breast and she felt the deep voice rumble against her. She couldn't make out the words. Didn't care. Her hands pressed on the back of his head, holding him close as she rubbed her lower body up and down over the bulge in his jeans.

Minutes passed, and his clothes stayed on. But his hands moved. One swept down her body in a lazy trail. He held her hips still as a finger pushed up inside her. In and out, making her grow wet and restless with each pass. His mouth continued its massage. Every inch of her trembled from the touching and tasting.

"Everything off." He mumbled the words as he unclipped her bra and dropped it to the floor.

Before she could shift or catch a breath, he unbuttoned his jeans. His hand slipped around behind him and he pulled a condom out of his back pocket.

For some reason him being ready both warmed and amused her. "You were carrying it on you?"

"Call me hopeful."

His beard scratched her neck in the most delicious way. He turned her inside out. Made her feel raw and open, like there wasn't an inch of her he didn't intend to conquer. Not selfish. No, this was about mutual satisfaction. He primed her body until her hips bucked and she pushed down harder to feel his finger slide in deeper.

He had her wound up and ready. She plucked the condom out of his hand and ripped off the wrapper. Forget pulling those jeans off or rolling him to the floor. She did want to ride him. Hard and fast until the room shook.

The warm room kept the chill off her body. So did the big man underneath her. His finger shifted, and her breath caught. Then his mouth moved to her neck and he did it again. He touched a part of her that had her insides clenching with the need to release, and she wanted to be wrapped around him when that happened.

Unable to wait another second, she slipped his briefs down and released his impressive cock. Thick and long, just as she guessed from looking at the rest of him. She tightened her hand and slipped it up and down. Swirled her thumb over the tip before plunging her palm to the base again.

This close she could see his breathing tick faster. Feel his heavy breaths against her cheek and hair.

"Now, Nat."

Something about hearing the nickname on his tongue, so casual and sweet, had her rushing. With the help of his hand on her hips, she lifted up on her knees. He rolled the condom on the second before she sank down. His sigh sounded like a "yes," but she couldn't be sure because a haze had fallen over her and clouded her brain.

His tip pressed inside her, stretching her as her inner muscles pulsed. Tension pulled his shoulders tight as his hands gripped her back. A mix of excitement and need pounded off him. She could feel every nerve ending zap to life when she leaned down and kissed him.

"Ride me," he whispered into her mouth. His hands guided her as she took him in deeper. She heard a groan, long and gruff, and realized it came from inside her.

His body moved in time with hers. She pressed and he pushed. The bounce of the cushion underneath him added to the friction. Her breath came out in pants with each plunge inside of her. Every cell went wild. She felt his body around her, in her. His mouth traveled over her. There wasn't an inch of her he didn't touch or caress. And when his tongue licked over the lump in her throat, she lost it.

The shaking started at her toes and worked its way through her to her head. Every part of her cried out for more as she leaned back and felt him reach even deeper inside her. Her body began to buck then. All the tightness unwound and her thighs clamped against his.

As the orgasm roared through her his hold tightened. He curled into her until his mouth touched her neck and his head tucked against her hair. It was as if the shaking transferred from her to him. The quake rocked his body as a harsh moan escaped his lips.

She didn't even know he had them sitting straight up until he dropped back against the cushion, taking her with him. The move shifted his cock inside her. Already sensitive from the first round, her body thumped at the increased pressure. Every move was magnified, and intense pleasure washed through her. The trembling had stopped but tiny tremors still pulsed inside her.

"Damn." He sounded more in awe than anything else.

She surrendered to the sudden weightlessness of her bones and cuddled against him. "You got that right."

There she stayed. With other men, at other times, she'd get up, satisfied, and walk away. Not let the moment be a big deal or let it show if the sex touched her. With him, she couldn't move. Since he didn't seem ready to race around the forest either just yet, she didn't bother to play the well-that-was-good-but-it's-over game.

"I don't think I can move."

His arm fell heavy over her back. It was reassuring to know the sex affected him as much as it did her. He wasn't pretending to be all he-man and bored.

She leaned back just enough to peek up at him. "So, were you able to watch the door the whole time for intruders?"

"Hardly." His chuckle, low and deep, vibrated through both of them. "I'm pretty sure I lost the ability to see at all there for a while."

"I guess this will make you rethink your no-sex-on-the-job position." She hadn't meant to say that, but it slipped out. No way to call it back now. Whatever smartass thing he said next, she deserved. She'd opened the door.

"No." His face grew serious. "Unless the job is you."

The words fell over her, trapping her breath in her lungs. She'd almost wished he'd been a smartass. She could handle asshole men. Decent ones were not her style. "If you're looking to guarantee more sex while we're here, you don't have to try so hard."

He just stared for a second, then . . . "Neither do you."

NINE

Natalie was the prickliest woman he'd ever met. Gabe decided that the next morning, after an afternoon inside her on the cabin floor and in the shower that turned cold long before either of them came. One of the hottest women he knew, but damn hard to read.

He should be upset. Thanks to her he'd taken years of grown-up, smart, on-the-job rules and crushed them. Not that he even held out that long against her. After only a few days alone with her, he abandoned his common sense and his control. All those comments about not fucking on the job turned around on him until that was *all* he wanted to do. And he could not regret that choice. He doubted he could go back to not having her either.

The way she looked, walked, talked back to him, rode his dick. Jesus, he wasn't kidding about his vision blinking out. Seeing her naked and hovering over him twisted his control to the breaking point. But the heavy dose of denial she seemed to wallow in snapped him back to reality. Her need to put up the shield. That got fucking old fast.

Sure, he understood. He'd been wearing similar armor for years. Kept up his guard. Put Brandon first. Relied only on his brothers . . . until Rick proved that was a big fucking mistake.

But at least he'd had someone. He couldn't imagine her life and what knowing her father killed her mother must have done to her. Unbelievable shit like that had to mess with your head.

The icy top layer of snow crunched under her boots as she walked. "You're humming."

"Maybe that's frustration over your refusal to stay inside." He'd bundled up and grabbed weapons. He'd planned to forge this trail alone, but she had other ideas—booted up and followed him. It was either tackle her, shoot her or acquiesce. He picked the third but grumbled and swore about it until she rolled her eyes and followed him anyway.

"Get over it," she said, as she scanned the trees around them.

"You are not very clear on the whole concept of protection, are you?" He'd had people fight his role before. She made it a full-time job.

"And you're not getting that I'm an expert shot."

"I saw your work with a hatchet. I don't doubt it." The woman's skills surpassed those outlined in her file. The suggestion that she was soft or administrative only pissed him off. Made him want to defend her, but he doubted she needed anyone speaking on her behalf. "You seem to be good at everything, actually."

She stopped and turned to face him. "Are you talking about sex?"

Now there was a conversation jump he was happy to take. "No, but I'll talk sex with you any time."

It didn't matter that she wore a heavy jacket and gloves. That she had a plaid scarf wrapped around her neck and tucked up under her chin. Or that she was all bound up with only pink cheeks and big eyes staring out. Natalie mentioned sex and his body defied the cold. Heat crashed through him, and his mind spun to memories of her breasts and how the tips fit in his mouth.

She stole his willpower until he had to fight the clawing need to scoop her up and carry her back inside. Having sex with her only made him want to experience more sex with her. Different positions. Holding her down. Stretching her out.

So much for the idea of being civilized.

"All those comments about being in charge turned out to be bluster." She stomped her feet and caked snow fell off. "You're actually pretty unselfish."

He had no idea what the hell that meant, but it sounded kind of lame. Like, not what you wanted the woman you hoped to sleep with that night to say about you. "I'm not clear if that's a compliment."

"It definitely is."

He decided to believe her. Then he went back to walking. Standing around seemed like a good way to freeze the soles of her boots to the ground, and he had better plans for the afternoon.

"Good." But he did need her to understand a few facts about him. Better to be clear and in agreement than risk surprises. "You are wrong about one thing though."

"Which is?"

"Being in charge in the bedroom doesn't mean being selfish." He didn't know what kind of men she'd been with in the past, but he knew who he was. Sex meant pleasure. Sometimes hot and fast. Other times slow, drawing out every minute and every breath.

"Well, sure. I—"

"It's about timing."

She shot him the side eye. "Okay."

"I am going to tie you to the bed and fuck you senseless." Her breath hit the air in a visible puff, just as he'd hoped it would. "I just have to know no one is coming up behind me with a knife when I do. That means we wait to make it happen."

She tucked her gloved hands in her pockets. "I thought you were convinced we were safe here."

"I never said that." She knew better. There were too many variables. A chance that someone out there with a big wallet had made an offer Gabe could only combat with a bullet.

"You have the perimeter set up."

Motion detectors. Infrared sensors. A few traps to welcome anyone who stepped in the wrong place. The usual. "Sure, I'm not a fucking novice."

"Then?"

"Neither will the person be who comes after us." This was a game for grown-ups. He lived in a world where experts littered the ground. Finding someone to venture out here would not be a burden if someone really wanted to find her. If that happened, the cat-and-mouse chase would begin. The only way to turn this was to keep running or convince the people after her, if there proved to be any, to back off.

"You still think people are coming."

"Possibly." He kept walking and watching, doing the job he'd been sent out here to do.

"Don't." When he lifted an eyebrow but stayed quiet, she kept talking. "*No* hesitating and hiding things from me because you think that will somehow keep me safe."

Time to come clean. She deserved the facts. Her knowing would double his strength . . . and likely make keeping her there even harder. "The same biplane has flown over twice today already."

She halted at the edge of a drift with the snow piled around her, past the top of her boots. Her grim expression said she understood the potential peril. "You're sure it's the same one?"

He excelled at gathering intel. He could lie on his stomach in a swamp and not move for hours while crocodiles circled and the enemy closed in. Visually tagging a plane and marking its movement counted as child's play to him. "It's buzzing low. Doesn't have any distinguishing marks."

Skepticism showed in every line of her body and in the smirk she held back, but not by much. "And that's enough to tell you someone is coming?"

Well . . . "And Andy sent me a signal. Insists the person is not coming to inflict harm, just do a check, which is why we're walking the perimeter."

She sent him that same you're-an-idiot eye roll she'd been aiming his way since they met. "Why would someone come out here just for a check?"

"Good question." As soon as he could raise his brother, Gabe would ask. Right now they communicated through abbreviated code in an attempt not to disclose their location, because there was no question someone out there was watching. "I'm waiting for more intel from Andy."

"It might be easier to grab the person lurking around out here and squeeze the information out of him." She slipped her hands out of her pockets and acted out her words.

"I like your style." Her no-nonsense practical nature appealed to him. He'd known strong women, many agents and military officers throughout the years. He admired brains, and her beauty sure sucked him in. The combination drove him to his knees. "And that was my thought exactly."

"So, we're really looking for tracks." She glanced at the ground to the blank canvas of snow in front of them.

Good instincts but wrong direction. "Something like that."

"And while we do that, you thought it was a good time to talk about tying me to a bed?" She rubbed her hands together.

"I think about it every fucking second, so I may as well talk about it." And that was the truth. So was his need to keep her mind unfocused and off the danger. He needed her to act like a job and listen, not question if something life-threatening headed their way.

She froze. "What if I don't want to be tied down?"

No way that stiffness came from the cold. "Your eyes are all big. Not sure why you're afraid to admit you're a sexual being and enjoy sex."

"I never said—"

"You're pretty great at it and clearly like it. Seems to me, you should stop fighting it." Oh, she let go during. He just sensed that she didn't like losing control with him.

He understood the sensation of being out of control. The way he discarded every personal rule with her and felt a twisting in his gut whenever he stared at her for more than two seconds. All new, and none of it welcome. But he'd ride it out, enjoy the sex and keep her safe until he turned her over to restart her life.

"You don't know everything," she mumbled as she started walking again, taking big marching steps.

A white blanket surrounded them. The makeshift forest filled with the sounds of their thudding steps and the crackle of branches as the weight of the wet snow sent them crashing to the frozen ground.

He took it all in, the sights and echoes of the unpopulated area around them, but his mind kept winging back to her. "Tell me what I don't know."

Through the scarf, she snorted. "Forget it."

"Exactly my point."

She continued to scan the ground, careful before placing each footstep as they ventured closer to the trees outlining the side of the cabin. "You're trying to bully me into this conversation."

"I'm trying to let you know that the guy you're sleeping with gets that things happen and that life can be shit sometimes and is willing to talk it all through with you." Backgrounds usually amounted to nothing more than lines on pieces of paper to him. With her, he wanted to dig around, get to know the woman who tried to keep him at a distance even as her gaze followed him around.

"We've had sex a few times."

If she wanted to piss him off she'd found the right way to do it. His jaw tightened and his teeth clamped together as he spotted a pattern in the snow about six feet in front of them, right at the edge of the forest.

He knew he should drop the conversation and get back to work. And he would—in a second. "The number of times doesn't matter."

She broke eye contact with the snow long enough to glance at him. "You think we're dating now?"

Not that he was looking for commitment or even nights together once the assignment was over, but still. He'd used that line so many times. Having it thrown in his face made him realize how shitty it sounded. "I think I'm the closest thing you have to a friend."

She touched a hand to her hat. Pulled it down closer to the top of her eyebrows. "I don't sleep with friends."

For some reason that sent his temper spiking. "You sure do have an answer for everything."

She smiled above her scarf. "How does that feel? Annoying, isn't it?"

One point for Natalie.

Perfect time to pivot. He reached for his gun and took a step toward the spot that had grabbed his attention a minute ago. "Now we have an entrance point."

The corners of her mouth dropped. "What?"

"Do not look until we start to turn around and head back to the cabin, but we have covered tracks. No prints, but snow that's been pushed and not just fallen in that pattern."

She kept her focus on him. Didn't engage in the usual panicked rookie mistake of checking out the scene despite all warnings. There certainly were benefits to having a client who knew how the dark side of the world worked.

"Can you see anyone in the vicinity?" she asked, as she gathered her coat around her and turned back to walk directly into the wind.

He wrapped an arm around her shoulders and pulled her close. To anyone watching the move might look romantic. For him it was really about being able to jump in and shield her if necessary, though part of him wondered if she'd let him try.

"No, but I'd be real disappointed in the person's skill set if I could." He kept his voice steady and his steps even. No signs they'd found the person scouting him. Even now the person, man or woman, could be watching from nearby, and Gabe refused to tip them off.

"So, now what?" Her hand slipped into her pocket, right where she kept the gun he gave her.

He looked forward, but with each step he did a quick visual sweep of the land, looking for any sign of movement. In the trees. On the ground. The person could be hiding anywhere. But wouldn't be for long. "We set a trap."

She *hmpf*'d. "We could just shoot the person."

"While I appreciate your bloodthirsty response, we need him or her alive to answer questions." He squeezed her shoulder but doubted she felt it through all those layers. "And Andy's code said non-hostile."

"What if Andy's wrong?"

Gabe refused to let that thought snake its way in. Andy knew something. Now Gabe needed to know what. "Rarely happens."

"You'll understand if I don't trust your hopeful loyalty to your baby brother."

The same lethal baby brother who once took down a drug runner by stabbing him in the forehead. But Gabe didn't start spouting off Andy's resume or his own.

"Then trust me." He'd been nothing but straight with her, even though it cost him to admit to the attraction kicking his ass. That had to count for something.

"Because we slept together." Not a question. She said it as a statement, without judgment. Just a flat tone as she pretended to look at him but glanced past him in a check of the trees.

Part of him thought that should be enough, but he went with the more obvious answer. "Because this is what I do."

"Fine."

They walked faster, their boots clomping against the snow as he switched to a wider stride and pulled her along with him. "And, for the record, 'slept' suggests past tense, and I think we both know that's not the case."

"You're awfully sure of yourself." She matched her gait to his, never complaining, even as she grabbed on to his arm for balance.

Words ran through his head as tension built in his gut. Something was wrong. Really wrong.

He wanted her inside and behind a wall. Walking out in the open was an invitation to danger. He didn't welcome that. "The blame is on you."

"Of course it is," she said in a dry tone.

"You're the one who screamed my name the last time we were naked." The memory pricked at him, but he blocked it. Had to. He needed all of his concentration to get inside the cabin and hunker down. Regain his bearings.

She picked up her pace even more. "Go to hell."

A stray thought worked its way back into his mind, and he didn't fight it. "I'd rather go back to bed."

They reached the bottom porch step, and she practically jumped on it before turning back around to stare at him. "I have to stay alive for that to happen."

That sobered him up. "No matter what I have to do, you will stay safe."

She nodded. "Both of us."

A nice idea, but he was starting to wonder. "Right."

TEN

They'd been inside for over two hours, and Gabe hadn't stopped pacing. He went from one cabin window to another. Since there were only three, and one amounted to little more than a slit for ventilation in the bathroom, that meant he circled. Round and round until she thought her brain might explode.

Since playing the audience seemed to be her only choice, she went with that. She balanced an elbow on the couch's seat cushions as she sat on the floor and watched him stalk. That's what it was. Not walking. The intensity rose well above a mere one-foot-in-front-of-the-other thing.

She rested her chin in her palm and continued to follow his set surveillance path from her seat on the floor. "You aren't exactly inspiring confidence."

With his back against the wall, he glanced out the window, keeping his body well behind the frame. "I'm checking for infiltration."

Sometimes she wondered if he could stop a bullet with his bare hands. He came off as so capable and uncomplicated. The kind of guy with an ingrained set of rules and a theory about right and wrong that had more to do with practical life lessons than any-thing preached to him through the years.

That's why the kid thing hit her wrong. A guy who stuck to her the way he had, despite her fighting and yelling and even attempts to ignore him, ignoring responsibility? The idea of that guy dropping off his son for a semester or a year and not looking back didn't ring true for her.

Maybe the difference was cash. Powerful people paid him to protect her. People who insisted they were her friends, even though she'd never had many of those. No one paid him to watch over his son. Could be that made it easier to abandon him.

She shook her head and tried to clear the unwanted thoughts from her brain. How he treated his kid was none of her business. This didn't amount to a love affair. Their time together centered on waiting out a threat, and possibly running from one, and sex. Boredom-burning, don't-overanalyze-it sex.

And to get back to the mindless pleasure of that she needed him to step off guard duty. "No one is coming in without you knowing. Not on foot."

He leaned his head back against the cabin wall and rubbed his eyes. "We can't be sure."

The man was losing it. "You're the one who told me that." She patted her hand against the hard floor. "Come here."

He dropped his hand to his side and looked over at her. "I need to focus."

She expected a haze. She got an unwavering stare. One that told her his mind had been on something other than a potential attacker. "You can't do that here by the couch?"

"Not if I'm sitting with you."

Big tough guy wanted sex and was determined to deny it. She'd dealt with cocky assholes her entire career. Guys who thought every word and every explanation they gave came dipped in gold. Seeing Gabe fight his attraction while trying to keep her safe turned out to be pretty endearing.

She didn't do sweet or long. The last time a guy made a move to switch from convenient sex to something that included dinners and movies she cut him off. That was the right answer. Always the right answer. You stayed safe by staying smart. But the idea of losing herself in him for a few more days tugged at her. She just never thought she'd have to beg for it. Gabe MacIntosh was a mystery.

Instead of saying all of that or unbuttoning her shirt, she told the truth. One she struggled to understand because the concept seemed so foreign to her. "I trust your control."

"Don't."

He meant sex. The guy preached pleasure and could back up the words. "You don't strike me as someone who loses his way."

"Usually, no." He slid along the wall, away from the window and moved closer to her. "You're different."

If he let her she'd release some of that tension that caught him in a stranglehold. "How?"

"The competence."

Well that was . . . not interesting at all. She could almost feel something inside of her deflate. "How sexy of you to notice."

He laughed then, rich and deep, and the sound washed through the room. "It is. Trust me."

Enough dancing around it. "Come. Here."

"Why?" But he was already moving, coming in closer as his eyes flashed with an intense heat.

"The tension in here is about to choke us." Much more of this and she'd drag him to the floor with her.

"Sitting will fix that?"

Damn the man was dense today. "*I* will fix that."

"Something's off."

"What?" Whatever the sensation, it had been pricking him since they'd been outside. He stayed calm at seeing the tracks, or the not-really-tracks, but then something changed. A snap, and his mood morphed into something dark and almost paranoid.

"It's a feeling, really. Like danger is coming and I need to be ready."

She waited for her instincts to kick into gear and . . . nothing. She'd been so sure at the start of all this that the answer was to run off alone and hide. Somehow start her new, boring life that she hadn't been trained to handle. No other option made sense, and dragging someone into her mess seemed ridiculous. But here, in the cabin with him, she felt at ease. The usual panic and need to plan an exit strategy didn't hit her.

She sensed, even with someone lurking around out there, they were safe. At least for now. Which meant she needed to concentrate on him. "You can stare at the door the whole time."

He shook his head as a smile inched up one side of his mouth. "I know I've said it before, but you are so fucking tempting. You say these things and all I want to do is get you naked."

Now they were at least talking the same language.

"Then come here and let me tempt you." She glanced at the couch cushion then back at him. It qualified as the least subtle offer ever, and if he didn't take it soon she'd take it off the table.

Proving he was as smart as she thought, he started moving. Slipped the rest of the way along the wall, then to the end of the couch. He put his gun on the small table, pointed away from them, as he sat down.

"Are you going to join me?" he asked, in a voice that sounded scratchier than usual.

"Soon." She turned over and pushed up on her knees. The wood squeaked under her legs, but she ignored the sound. Gabe's gaze held her captive. The unblinking stare. And then there was the way he ran his hand up and down her leg.

When she touched his thigh, he opened his knees and she slid between. Her fingers trailed along his sleek muscles to rest on his hips. She leaned in, and he met her halfway. Without words, their mouths met and the kiss burned through her. Just like before, the touch of his lips against hers was like being thrown in a whirlwind. Energy whipped around her and waves of excitement crashed through her.

It would be so easy to lose herself, let him take over. But she wanted to lead on this. To show him that she could envelope him in pleasure.

Before he could make a move or even say anything, she reached for his belt. The buckle clanked as she opened it and pushed the ends aside. Her fingers moved to the jeans button and slid it free from the hole. Next came the zipper. His bulge grew until, with one brush against the waistband of his briefs, his cock spilled into her hand.

"Nat, please."

The temptation to draw this out, make him wait, pushed her. But she wanted this as much as he did. Lowering her head, she took him in her mouth. The first few inches slid between her lips as her hand moved up and down along his length. She lifted her head just long enough to sweep her tongue over his tip, and she felt his fingers slip into her hair.

The heat of his stare didn't throw her. She could sense his need, feel the attraction thrumming off him. When she took him deep, he groaned. The sound deepened when she tightened her fingers and licked her tongue over him. The combination of the pumping of her hand and suction of her mouth had his hips lifting off the couch.

She picked up speed, caressing his cock with her mouth. Taking her time to cover every inch of him. One hand held him still

for her mouth while the other traveled. She massaged his balls and
let her pinky finger slip between his ass cheeks. The intimate touch
might have other men bolting off the couch, spouting a stream of
denial. Not Gabe. He leaned into the touch. Let her learn what
turned his insides wild with desire.

With each plunge of her mouth his body pulled taut. He wound
her long hair around his fist and held her there. Looking down
the length of his body, he watched her. Saw every puff of her
cheeks and lick of her tongue.

When she swallowed him to the base one last time, he started
to come. His body shook, and low, guttural sounds rumbled in
his throat. She could feel and hear him shift as those fingers tightened against her scalp.

"Jesus, Natalie." The whisper floated through the room as his
hips continued to shift. "You're amazing."

She swallowed and sat back on her heels. Tried to regain her
usual even breathing as she took in the sight of him in a half-naked
sprawl. He'd slouched down until his head balanced against the
cushions, and those sexy dark eyes stayed shut.

Her legs ached and she needed to stand up. She was about to
when his eyes popped open and he looked at her.

A smile formed on his lips. "Your turn."

She thought he'd never ask.

An hour later Gabe slipped around the left side of the
cabin at the point farthest away from where he'd seen a break in
the trees. Another few steps and whoever was out there would
have tripped a sensor. A bit to the side and he would have snagged
a wire and been hanging in a net from a tree branch.

The tracker seemed to be too smart to get caught fast and clean.

Erasing the footprints showed serious training. Gabe would have made the same move but done better. The trick is not to make the trail too perfect. That operated as much as a giveaway as leaving the footprints.

After years of building his skills and refining his craft, he didn't get thrown off easily. In stepping outside, he'd blocked Natalie from his mind. Pretended he couldn't still feel her mouth on him or remember the feel of her skin under his fingertips. He needed focus and clarity.

All good things, except for the fact that he could smell her. That shampoo he'd purchased and thrown in her go bag before taking off for Montana smelled like the beach. Recalling her blond hair and that scent, his mind wandered, and that could not happen now.

He glanced over his shoulder and saw her creeping up behind him. She'd been quiet, even managing to keep her footsteps from crunching in the icy snow. He glared at her anyway.

When she fell in behind him with her body almost touching his, he whispered. "I told you to stay inside."

"Outside of the bedroom you aren't the boss of me."

Fucking damn. "We're not talking about that now."

"What are you looking at?"

He hesitated, convinced the answer was to shoo her inside. Not that she was a *shooing* type of woman. "Around the back of the cabin to our eleven o'clock."

She eased her way to the end of the cabin wall and peeked out. Her eyes went to the ground then lifted before she turned to face him again. "In the tree."

"Good catch." Not that he was surprised. She might have spent the last few years riding a desk and commanding from headquarters and behind armed guards, but she understood how the game worked and didn't show fear.

"Has he moved?"

Despite the stress of the moment Gabe had to smile at that. "You think he's dead?"

"No, genius. I'm wondering if he possesses your stalking and waiting skills." She took out her gun and checked it.

Watching her hands move, those fingers sliding over steel, mesmerized him. "Possibly."

"What's the plan?"

"We're not shooting him." Though part of Gabe did think that would be the most efficient solution. Dump their tail then move on. Maybe to somewhere warmer this time.

"I think that should be Plan B."

Since she sounded so serious, he decided she probably was. The snow had begun falling again. The watcher was about to get cold and wet. As much as he wanted her out of this, grabbing the watcher's attention now might be the best way to shake a few answers out of him. Then he could talk with Andy at the prearranged time and report in.

That meant subterfuge. Gabe would bet she excelled at that, too. "Since you're out here, we'll flush him out. You create a distraction, and I'll bring him down." With a shot, if the guy even thought about raising a weapon in Natalie's direction.

She nodded. "Sounds good."

"Walk around the front. Carry the hatchet or something that suggests you're gathering wood or whatever. We'll have only seconds before he realizes I'm not with you and we lose our edge."

"Then you'd better run fast."

"I aim to impress." He didn't hear what she said after that because she turned around and headed toward the front of the cabin, but the mumble sounded like "You do."

Gabe slipped to the corner of the cabin where the side wall met the back and hunkered down. His timing had to be perfect. One second off and he'd be spotted, and the guy could bolt. One second too early and there could be gunfire. Gabe was up for both options but secretly hoped this went according to their informal plan.

From this position he couldn't see the cabin's front and watch whatever Natalie was doing, but he trusted her to follow through. He focused all of his energy on movement in the trees, looking for any sign the other guy got up or moved. The world around him fell into a still silence as he concentrated. He took the small magnifying lens out of his pocket and watched.

After a few seconds, the surveillance paid off. An arm shifted and the guy's weight moved forward. He stayed on his stomach, but he'd switched to alert. That could only mean one thing: Natalie.

Gabe didn't wait. He took off at a flat-out run, ignoring the way his boots slipped against the snow. The depth of the pile slowed his movements, but he stepped as lightly as possible, careful not to sink.

By the time he hit the clearing where the open area met the edge of the trees, the guy was already climbing down. Gabe jumped over the trap he knew lay right there and jumped deeper into the thick woods. Out of the corner of his eye he saw Natalie running toward him.

"Match my steps." It was all the warning he could get out before he picked up the pace. All of his attention stayed on the guy bounding down the tree with an ease that almost suggested he'd been raised in one.

The guy let go of the last branch and Gabe leapt. Hit him square in the side and knocked them both off balance. They flew, falling to the ground. Rough rocks and broken tree limbs poked into Gabe as they rolled. The other man, younger and lighter, used his legs and hands. He was fast, but Gabe had the weight edge and a load of fury fueling his movements.

They ended their sparring with the guy's back on the ground and Gabe straddling his hips. The guy kept moving. Reached for a knife in a holder by his waist. Might have gotten off a swipe if Natalie hadn't picked that moment to step up.

She aimed her gun at the stranger's head. "I'd stop moving unless you want us both to shoot you."

While she covered him, Gabe sat back and caught his breath. A second later he searched the guy for weapons. Slid his hands into pockets and conducted a pat down. Unpacked two knives and two guns and figured he'd missed a few before getting up to stand next to Natalie.

Out of patience and pissed off at being in wet clothes again, Gabe launched right into threats. "You have ten seconds to tell me who you are and why you're here before she uses you for target practice."

The guy kept the back of his hands flat against the ground by his head. Smartly did not move even as his gaze went back and forth, and fear showed in his eyes. "Just scouting out the area."

That just made Gabe ache to shoot. "Eight seconds."

Something in his tone or about the situation must have broken through, because the guy dropped the scared innocent look. A calm washed over him as his gaze bounced to Natalie then back to Gabe. "This isn't about you."

"Six." Gabe took off an extra second just because the guy looked at her.

She sighed, clearly done with the testosterone show. "Just tell him."

"Can I sit up?" the guy asked.

Gabe wanted to say no but Natalie beat him to the answer. "I'd do it slow and keep your hands up."

The guy obeyed but once his ass hit the cold ground he winced. "I was sent to watch over you both."

"Watch over?" Natalie repeated the words slowly, drawing out the last syllable.

The guy's gaze flicked to Gabe. "By someone concerned with your continued safety. Someone in the business who's worried you're in trouble."

The motion was enough to clue him in. He didn't lower the gun because the news didn't do anything to lessen his shoot-first instincts. "Ah, fuck. Rick sent you."

"Rick, as in your black-ops brother Rick?" She shrugged when Gabe stared at her. "What? I told you I read your file."

The guy on the ground cleared his voice. "Can I get up?"

Since he delivered shitty news, Gabe thought no. "Is Rick in Montana?"

For a second the guy didn't say anything. Then Natalie gave his upper thigh a kick with the snow-covered toe of her boot. "I'd answer if I were you."

"No."

She frowned at the guy. "You don't sound convincing."

"My orders were to watch and report back. Not make contact." Rick's man dropped his hands to the ground but didn't make a move toward any part of him that could hide a weapon.

"You failed on that score," she mumbled.

They needed to collect as much information as possible, so Gabe focused on that rather than Rick. "Where's the plane?"

"Belongs to a local."

She blew out a long dramatic breath. "A well-paid one, I'm assuming."

That explained the informal checking and how he got in so close despite there not being a single cabin nearby. The closest one sat miles away, which in this weather and on foot could amount to a ten-day trek.

Not that the guy was staying.

Now that Gabe knew he couldn't, or shouldn't, kill the guy, he went with the next best thing. Made him a messenger. "Your job is to go back to D.C. and tell my big brother to fuck himself."

Natalie smiled then. "Probably won't do much for this poor schmuck's job security."

"As if I give a shit." Gabe didn't. That would teach this guy to throw in with Rick.

"Report back that we're living in a cabin," Natalie said as she took over. "Not in contact with anyone. Not hurting anyone. Because all of that is true."

The guy started shaking his head before she got all the words out. "Can't."

Now that was irritating. Gabe tightened his grip on the weapon. "I'm still holding a gun."

"You're not going to shoot him," she said.

"I never promised that."

The guy must have sensed his death sentence had been commuted because he stumbled to his feet. "I sit here and do my job and we all get to go home faster. Easy."

"Your job is to contact Rick. Tell him I spotted you and that everything is clear here." Gabe refused to budge from that position. "Then tell him to fuck himself. Don't forget that part. It's important."

"Gabe—"

"That's as nice as I can be." He slid a hand under her elbow and started to walk away. He turned back and glanced around the ground by the guy's feet. "And I'd be careful where you step. It would suck for you to step in the wrong place and die for Rick and one of his operations. He's not worth it."

ELEVEN

Natalie knew her skill set. Handling touchy males about even touchier subjects with any degree of tact was not one of them. Still, Gabe needed something, and for whatever reason she wanted to help. Blame the close quarters, or maybe the waning resistance to him the more time they spent together.

He stormed around the cabin and had been doing so ever since sending their watcher away. First Gabe washed the dishes. Actually, that came second. He had to create dirty dishes first and accomplished that by making coffee and oatmeal and not touching either.

The answer probably went something like: gently nudge him into conversation and, once he relaxed, circle around and ask him the more direct questions. Screw that.

She sat down on the couch's armrest. "So, I guess Rick is a dick."

Other than the brief stiffening of his shoulders, Gabe didn't show much of a reaction to the comment. "Understatement."

Since that didn't work, she circled around and tried again. "You seem close to Andy."

"I am."

At this rate she'd run out of questions in about two seconds and he would not yet have said ten words. Men at work used to whine about difficult women all the time. Talk about a pot-kettle situation.

She sighed because it was either that or yell, and she guessed that wouldn't help the situation one bit. "Talk to me."

He turned around and faced her then. "About what?"

Yeah, no question about it. He was in full-on showdown mode. She hated the curt answers, the barely talking thing he did in general. The scruffiness, the rough hotness—forget all of that. Right at this moment his mood struck her as especially annoying. "Don't be an asshole."

He didn't even blink. "It was a legitimate question."

Right. "You and your brother Rick work in the same field and—"

"Wrong."

Anger radiated off him. She knew it was directed at some feud with his brother but still felt caught in the crossfire. Whatever plagued him now and drove him and Rick apart qualified as the type of thing that should have been in her file on him but wasn't. That meant the fight was new or so deeply personal that no one talked. Both options piqued her curiosity. "Correct me then."

"He's on the government payroll." Gabe leaned against the counter and gripped the top on either side of him. "I'm not."

She knew all about Rick and his black-ops career. The guy had a go-to operation for off-the-book infiltration and extraction jobs. Nasty stuff. Not something a guy with deep emotions and a bright-line sense of right and wrong could pull off. Word was Rick didn't let either get in his way. He'd been seriously injured about eighteen months ago and came back twice as lethal.

"Is that why we hate him? His job choices?" she asked, trying to make light of an obviously heavy subject.

Gabe's grip tightened until his knuckles turned white. "No."

Could be Rick's mind-set and personality clashed with Gabe's. She could see that. Gabe talked tough and absolutely qualified as lethal, but something about him said bone-deep decency to her. He'd followed orders and gotten the job done, killed when necessary, but she had a hard time imagining him torturing someone under the guise of information-gathering and enjoying it.

But then this kid issue hovered. She didn't get that part of his life at all. Abandoning a son he never disclosed in the first place didn't fit in with the guy she thought she knew, so maybe she didn't know anything at all.

Except the stubbornness. He didn't bother hiding that trait. "Gabe, honestly, it would be easier to talk with a tree."

He shrugged. "Maybe I don't want to talk."

That would be consistent with his personality. Still, she didn't intend to let him get away with the lame excuse. Not when they had days, possibly weeks, to get through with nothing but each other and a few elk for company. "We're stuck in here. We may as well burn through some time."

For a few seconds he just stared at her. Stood stock-still and toured his gaze over her, his frown deepening with every second. "Do you want me to fuck you? Is that what this is about?"

The icy words crashed over her, and she held back her flinch. She morphed from half-amused and wanting answers to fighting off the urge to punch him. Hell if he didn't deserve it. "I don't know Rick but from your description of him it's starting to sound like you're a lot alike."

Gabe pushed off from the counter and came toward her. "Sorry, do you want me to use a prettier word?"

Every syllable slashed into her. Ripped and tore until she expected to see blood puddle on the floor. She shouldn't care. She had protective walls to keep shit like this out. But something about him attacking, about him using sex and what they'd shared as a weapon, struck against something deep inside of her.

"I want you to drop the attitude." That qualified as an understatement, but she went with the comment anyway. Much more and the tension would skyrocket.

"We are not friends." He took another step.

She refused to get up. To show any sign that the words landed with the force he intended. "True."

"If the plan is for me to spill my guts for your entertainment, forget it." He stood right in front of her, blocking the light behind him and looming over her seat.

"Understood." He could not be clearer, and she could not hear one more thing.

Fighting with her need to battle back, she stood up. If he wanted to piss all over someone, he'd need to find another target. He'd slipped into nonsense mode, and she refused to follow right behind him. It was as if he thought no one else got the crap stick when it came to family. Wrong.

She got up and snagged her jacket off the peg by the front door. Her palm touched the knob before she felt him behind her, bearing down, breathing hard and filled with fury.

With a hand on her arm, he turned her around to face him. Grabbed the coat out of her hand and threw it over the couch. "Where are you going?"

"Wherever you're not."

His head snapped back and his eyes grew wide. "*Now* you're sensitive?"

"What the hell does that mean?" She sensed the load of sarcasm headed her way but pushed. If he had something to say, he should just say it.

"You played the cold fish for weeks before we got to this cabin. You'd barely look at me." His eyes flashed with fire. "Now we get here and you get bored. You figure out there may be a division between the MacIntosh brothers and you move in."

She put a hand on his chest and shoved. Used all her strength and barely moved him. "I think you have cabin fever."

"Maybe this amuses you, but I'm not an assignment." He pointed his finger right in her face. "You are. You are the file. My personal life is off-limits."

She slapped his hand away. Seriously thought about kneeing him in the groin. Maybe that would put his life and this fight back into perspective for him. "You think you could be blowing this out of proportion?"

"You know what? You stay in here." He reached around her for the doorknob. "I'll head out for a few minutes."

She stepped away. Let him open the door before she took the shot. "And people think I'm the runner."

The door slammed shut with a loud whack as he turned around to face her again. "What did you say?"

"You heard me."

"Tread carefully, Natalie." His voice stayed deadly soft.

He needed a wake-up call, and she decided to be the one to deliver it. "What are you going to do? If you think I'm afraid of you, sorry." She shook her head as much to make her point as to drive the horrible memories of her past away. "The days of me cowering in a corner for any man are over."

He went still. "What does that mean?"

Her words ran right over his. "Honestly, I will shoot you before I let you physically hurt me."

"I would never do that. You have to know—"

"Stop talking." A swirl of energy caught her. She felt a great crashing inside her. It was as if the emotions she had long suppressed—fear, frustration—boiled up and spilled over, wiping out everything else. "I've been terrified by the best of them, and you don't even register on the scale."

The color drained out of him. Shock and something that looked suspiciously like guilt moved behind his eyes. "Your dad."

Wasn't that convenient. "Oh, I see. My personal life is open to interrogation but yours isn't."

"Natalie." He reached for her.

She took a step back, just out of touching range. "Don't."

"Fine." He held up both hands. "Tell me what to say. What you want me to do."

"Nothing." And she meant it. He couldn't reach back and erase the words or stop the firefight he'd set off inside of her. But he could redirect it. "Actually, one thing."

Her fingers went to her belt and the button underneath for her jeans. He didn't comment. Didn't try to stop her or help. Part of her wondered if he knew what she wanted. That she needed him to help burn off the raging inside her.

She just said it. "Sex."

No feeling, no emotion. She craved bodies sliding against each other. Friction. A true burn-off of energy and a few minutes to forget everything.

She got her zipper down and reached for his pants. With a finger tucked in the waistband of his jeans, she pulled him closer—brought his body right up against hers—and he didn't fight her.

Forget smooth. Her hands jerked and tugged until she had his pants open. The whole time he stood there, letting her undress him. When her fingers slipped into his briefs, he put a hand over hers. Before she could say anything, he stepped away from her.

The move had her falling back against the wall as rough breaths rocked her body. Her mind went blank. She forced it to stay that way before feelings of vulnerability and failure seeped in. She'd made a pass, a serious one, and he was pushing her away. In terms of ego, this amounted to a killing blow.

Then he was in front of her again, pants still open, holding a condom. "Tell me what you need."

Relief whooshed through her, almost dropping her to her knees. "You. Inside me."

"Done." Instead of ripping at her clothes, he dropped to his knees.

The jeans slid down, and her underwear went with them. When he stood again he lifted her now bare legs and wrapped them around his body, low on his hips. Tore the condom package open with his teeth then held it out to her.

"I've dreamed of fucking you against the wall." The scratchy edge to his voice suggested he wasn't kidding.

Good, because neither was she. The need swamped her, and it took all of her control not to press him against her, condom or not.

She forced her breathing to slow. She wanted to draw out every second and knew once he slid inside her the world would flip and her brain would shut down. "Make it happen."

He smiled as he placed the condom in her palm and went to work moving her thighs as he tugged and shoved his jeans and briefs, finally getting them down far enough to release his cock. He put his hand between them and rubbed his hand up and down his length, letting her watch as he grew thicker, longer.

Forget control and common sense. She wanted this to happen. Anything to wipe out the argument of the last few minutes and the black memories of all that came before.

She removed his hand and slid the condom over him. Took her time even as her insides screamed to hurry. The pleas echoed in her head but she didn't say them out loud. Not when he felt so good. Not when his finger slipped up inside her.

But she didn't need foreplay. She wanted fast and hot and sweaty. Tugging on his head, she pulled him in for a kiss. Their mouths met, and light exploded behind her eyes. All the aching crescendoed and her body melted into his.

He balanced her back against the wall as a hand went to her thigh and held her legs still. When his other palm slapped against the wall, he started pushing into her. Not sweet and not gentle. No, this was a taking. He went from letting her lead to overwhelming her. His scent, his breathing. The strength of every muscle and all that attention focused on her. It all ramped up as he plunged in and out, rubbing their bodies together until the friction had her fighting for breath.

Still, he moved. In and out until her shoulders knocked against the wall. Her vision blurred, so she closed her eyes and let the sensations wash over her. His rhythm didn't falter. He pounded forward, and her body took off. She met every thrust. Dug her fingernails into his back and held on for the amazing ride.

When his chest shuddered she knew he was close. In her mind she wanted the spiraling to continue. To ride out this euphoric feeling. But her body had other ideas. The pulsing started and her hips shifted forward. Right as his orgasm hit, he skimmed a hand down between them and rubbed on the spot sure to make her control implode.

One touch and she joined him. Her breathing ticked up and her chest heaved. Every muscle moved without a signal from her brain. Instinctive and freeing. She dropped her head back against the wall and let the tremors jump through her. She could hear his low moan and feel his body lean heavier against her. She knew he'd found his release. She still rode out the thumping aftermath.

Minutes passed. She opened her eyes, and slowly the room

came back into focus. Her muscles had turned to liquid. His body anchored hers to the wall or she would have fallen onto the floor in a pathetic heap.

The sex didn't erase the harsh words or violent memories, but something had changed. The air buzzed with attraction rather than anger. The aftereffects of sex left a charge running through her body but the instinct to run away, to strike back, had disappeared.

"I was in the room." Her words slipped out. She half hoped he was too far gone to even hear her. But then she realized that's not what she wanted. Something inside her drove her to tell him her secrets. To open the door, just a bit, and let him peek in. Not long and not forever, but for a second. So he'd understand. "When he killed her."

Gabe exhaled and his warm breath blew across her neck. "Fuck."

That might have been the perfect response. No pity, and he didn't launch into a game of Twenty Questions. Instead, he lifted his head and looked down at her with clear eyes.

"He was evil and dangerous. Spent his life hurting her. Liked to do it in front of me—said it would teach me how to be an obedient wife one day." Without even trying Natalie could call up her father's grim voice and all those lectures.

"Sick fucker."

"He was that." Natalie let her legs slide down Gabe's until her feet touched the floor. But she didn't let go and he didn't step back.

"You tried to protect her."

"Yes." She knew he'd get it. With who he was and how he stepped forward, he would have done the same thing, even as a kid. She was sure of it.

His hand cupped her cheek and his thumb traced her mouth. "And he punished her for that."

Natalie tried to swallow, to say something, but couldn't. She just nodded. The guilt knocked into her and her knees started to buckle, but the weight of his body resting against hers held her up.

"The police report said you were asleep upstairs," Gabe said.

Because the officers on the scene protected her. Engaged in a conspiracy of silence meant to quiet the whispers and keep her from the torment of hours of interrogation and all the second-guessing that would follow.

She didn't share that piece or how she'd come to understand that gift as she got older and tried to repay it once or twice in her cases. Skipped right to his ability to read between the lines of her official report when no one had ever done that before. "But you knew that wasn't true. That I'd seen more."

Gabe nodded. "You would have heard the noise. You would have investigated and rushed in." He kissed her forehead then let his rest against hers. "Is the scar on your stomach from him?"

She didn't even know he'd seen it. Time had faded the angry red to a soft white. Low on her abdomen. A slice that spilled blood and marked her forever. "From that night."

Gabe lifted his head. His gaze searched hers. "Did you kill him?"

No judgment. He asked it like he might ask what she wanted for breakfast. The question should have shocked her. With anyone else she would have rushed to deny and change the subject. But the way he held her, looked at her, wrapped her in this cocoon of safety . . .

For the first time since that night, the words spilled out of her. "I had to make him stop."

Memories flashed in her mind. Red splashed everywhere. Her mother's sobbing as she tried to reach for the cord and bring the phone hanging on the wall crashing down. Her father's shouting about how her mother deserved this. How he should let her die.

Then the knife was right there. Natalie remembered looking

down and curling her fingers until the handle pressed tight against her palm. The first slash made his eyes pop open wide. The next one drove him to his knees. All while her mother begged her to stop.

She didn't know she'd been lost in the whirl of the past until Gabe gently touched her. Placed a palm against each cheek and lifted her head so she could see directly into his eyes.

"Yes, you did," he said, as if willing her to believe.

The words didn't make sense at first. "What?"

"We're the same on that score. We don't kill lightly, but sometimes we have to." Then he kissed her. A soft peck on the mouth, likely more for comfort than anything else.

"Yes." Exactly that.

"But the haunting never stops."

He would know. He'd killed. In the name of God and country, maybe, but he'd still taken lives and he wore that with a dignity she appreciated. "But the pain did."

He shot her a lopsided smile. "Good. Some of it."

The sounds of the cabin and forest came roaring back to life. The hum of the lights and the knock as the wind hammered a loose shutter against the outside wall. The strangeness of the moment hit her. The smell of sex still lingered in the air. Gabe's strong hands and sweet touches. Both of them basically naked from the waist down.

A rational conversation about a horrific event. It was surreal and healing. The way he pressed his lips to her eyebrow then her cheek cleansed her.

She held on to his shirt. Curled the material into balls in her fists. Stood there and rode out the last of her memories. Their fight fell into the forgotten category. He wrestled his own demons and she would try to help him through that, even if he didn't want to open up. But until then, she closed her eyes and held on.

Her bodyguard.

TWELVE

This qualified as the shittiest meeting ever. Andy looked around the conference room table. His older boneheaded brother standing by the door was bad enough. The other two guests almost sent Andy's temper skidding over the edge.

Elijah Sterling, former CIA agent and the guy Andy once pegged as the love of his life. Tall, lean and hot as fuck with a hint of Japanese heritage showing in his black hair and dark eyes. He carried his body with confidence. Then there was Wade Royer, the guy Andy hated on sight—from his muscular build to the short light hair—because he was the one guy Eli *could* make a commitment to.

Wasn't this just a fucking fantastic way to spend an already busy afternoon packed with work and intel and meetings.

Rick finished his call and slipped his phone into his pocket. Coming around the side of the table, he took the chair at the head. Of course he did. Only he would see the open seat as an invitation.

He glanced around, glaring, then pointed to Wade and Eli. "Why are you two here?"

To prevent the bloodbath Andy sensed coming, he jumped in.

"Eli works for Bast—Sebastian Jameson, Natalie's lawyer." That was the easy introduction. "Wade is basically here because he hates me and wants me to stay away from Eli."

Wade nodded. "That about sums it up."

Rick being Rick, he skipped right over the personal stuff and started scowling as he focused in on Eli. "You're a fucking lawyer?"

"Hell, no." Eli looked appalled by the idea.

Andy couldn't imagine Eli arguing points in a courtroom. The guy liked the outdoors and guns and shooting things. He made a life out of chasing people the CIA determined needed to be chased. He acted as a human weapon. Point and fire.

But that suit and the blue tie. Goddamn. "You look like one."

Eli frowned at Wade. "Why didn't you tell me that?"

"You look good in the suit." Wade shrugged. "Sue me."

Rick sat back in his chair in one of those dramatic movements usually meant to draw attention and put the focus back on him. "I don't have time for games with the little league."

"Uh, Rick." Looked like his big brother missed a few pertinent facts in whatever file he used for Natalie's case. He'd been out of the country when the Eli relationship imploded, but Andy assumed he'd caught up. Apparently not.

"No, really." Eli held up a hand without ever breaking eye contact with Rick. "Let him continue."

Andy saw Wade smile. Heard Eli's cool tone. For whatever reason Rick goaded as if he wanted to start a fight. Andy wasn't in the mood for any of it.

"This is a grown man's game. Go back to your law office and file your briefs and lodge your complaints." Rick took the phone out of his pocket and started scrolling through messages. "Actually, I don't care what you do so long as you get out of here."

As far as exit lines went it was a pretty good one. It also showed that Rick had no understanding of his audience. Andy did, so he sat back and let this play out. Eventually they'd get around to why Eli wanted the meeting and insisted Rick appear.

"Are you done?" Eli asked.

Wade shook his head. "For the record, *Rick*. That tone, all flat and low, is a very bad sign."

Yeah, forget waiting it out. Andy didn't want to wipe up the blood from this massacre. "Rick, Eli is former CIA. Some of his black-ops job make yours look like kindergarten recess time. He used to work for Natalie. Now he works for Bast."

Rick hesitated. He got that look on his face that said he was performing a few mental calculations and realizing the scales weren't quite as unbalanced as he had assumed. He turned to Wade. "And you?"

"Consider me the criminal element."

"He used to be an enforcer for some unsavory types." Andy knew because he'd investigated the guy right after finding out Eli had moved in with him. Wade had gone legit, but he hadn't started out that way. His experience with weapons and death likely rivaled Eli's, and that was saying something.

"That's a pretty way of putting it." Eli brushed something off his jacket sleeve, though it didn't look as if anything was there. "Point is your blowhard asshole act doesn't impress us. You want to compare gun sizes, I'm in."

"Don't let the nice suit fool you," Wade said. "He will kick your ass."

Rick slipped his phone back into his pocket. "Why are we all here?"

"My boss is not happy." When Rick started to talk, Eli spoke right over him. "There's a deal in place, and you sending people to stalk Natalie and Gabe violates it."

Rick's expression went blank as he turned on Andy. "You told them?"

Not a surprise he got dragged into the middle of this. Andy expected that. Rick had been trying to put him in the middle of the private battle with Gabe almost from the beginning, make him choose sides. Why should work be any different? "Gabe reports to Bast. Eli reports to Bast. You can see where those dots connect."

Rick swore under his breath before looking at Eli and Wade again. "Look, I can't talk about this. Suffice to say, I'm watching out for them."

"Now *you* sound like the lawyer," Wade said under his breath.

Not one to be quiet, Rick upped the volume. "I have this under control."

"No, you don't." Eli leaned forward, balancing his elbows on the table. "See, if we—Natalie's side—complain about the surveillance, your cover is blown. That's not a big deal in this case, other than the twisted part about tracking your own brother, but I'll let you figure out how to deal with that at the next holiday dinner."

"But once Eli and Bast report back to the CIA, the people who hire you will know you blew this operation," Wade said, taking over. "That sort of things tends to make you not be the first guy they call when they need help in the future."

"Are you two threatening me?" Rick sounded honestly stunned at the idea. No one questioned him. He'd risen to the top in record time. People depended on him for both his skills and his anonymity.

But Wade clearly wasn't impressed. He just stared back. "Yes."

"The deal is simple, call off your guys. Report back to whatever piece of shit is paying you that all is fine and Natalie is not a security risk." Eli laid it out then sat back in his chair. "Then you can go back to playing, what was it you called it? Big boy games."

"Fuck you."

Wade winked. "Sorry, he's taken."

They made a good team, Eli with the calm delivery and Wade as the backup. Andy hated noticing that.

Rick thumped his fingers against the table. "Gabe is screwing her."

The news didn't exactly surprise Andy, but he wasn't sure it needed to be broadcast. "This might be family stuff."

Rick's gaze shot to Andy. "What does that have to do with anything?"

"As enjoyable as this sick peek into your family dynamic is, let me get to the point." Eli shifted in his chair and all eyes went to him. The move and the deadly cold tone assured that. "Bast negotiated a deal for Natalie. Part of which promised a release of information that makes the NSA digging into the public's phone records seem like a good government idea if anyone went near her."

"You think people will believe you have that sort of intel?" Rick shook his head. "It's only leverage if you can prove the information exists and Natalie has it."

"Last I checked, the CIA wasn't supposed to be sneaking around, checking on U.S. citizens. Natalie has some files that suggest that's happening on a regular basis. And the citizens in question, some of them, are connected and will get really pissed once this news is out." Wade held up both hands as if in mock surrender. "Just saying it sounds like pretty good leverage to me."

Eli nodded. "If whoever hired you continues to track Natalie, the subjects of the surveillance—the entire public—will see internal documents, and those suits at the CIA who are so worried about Natalie's location right now will be more worried about finding their own places to hide."

Wade cleared his throat. "The public hates this shit."

The double-team impressed Andy. "You two sure you're not lawyers?"

"We prefer to work outside of the law." Eli kept his focus on Rick. "You might want to keep that in mind."

Something in Rick's affect had changed. He no longer looked ready to rip the walls down. "They're safe. Gabe spotted my man and tried to scare the piss out of him."

Wade glanced at Eli. "I like Gabe's style."

Eli nodded. "It's a shame Rick here still hasn't said what we need to hear."

Rick ignored the byplay. "Fine. I'll talk to my people about Natalie's supposed leverage and how, if it truly exists, it might be time to rethink tracking her down in any way."

"Your people?" Eli shook his head. "It doesn't make you throw up a little in your mouth to say that?"

Rick stood up. "I need a secure room."

"You know where it is." Andy almost hated to add this part: "Take Eli with you for confirmation."

But Rick didn't balk. Phone in hand, he walked out with Eli trailing right behind him. That left Andy alone with Wade, a combination Andy did not like one bit. And he could sense Wade knew that.

Better to jump to the offense, or at least Andy hoped that was true. "You know I'm not going to make a move, right?"

"On Eli?" Wade scoffed. "Fucking right you're not."

"So, you can drop the jealous act." Though Andy couldn't blame him. Despite the sometimes surly mood, there was something compelling about Eli. Something that reeled you in and made you want to know more. Those quiet moments, the ones that provided a promise of more. Andy had bought in. Eli told him not to, but turned out Andy didn't have a fucking choice.

Wade leaned forward and tapped an abandoned pen against the table. "I've been where you are."

Since he lived with Eli, and Andy never got the opportunity, Andy doubted it. "Oh, really?"

"It's easy for me to say, and God knows I couldn't do it, but you need to move on." Wade looked up and pinned Andy with a serious gaze. "Take my advice. Find someone else."

"I'm not still hung up on him."

Wade shook his head. "Yeah, you are."

"You don't—"

"You need closure. I'm giving it to you." Wade stood up. "It's over."

"Confident."

"I'm not letting him go, Andy."

He knew that before Wade ever said it. Andy had checked up on them, asked around. Eli looked as domesticated and assured as ever. People, mostly Bast, said that came from Wade. Still, Andy could hope. "You could fuck up."

"Probably will, but that won't create an opening for you because I'm the one he wants." When Andy started to talk, Wade talked right over him. "Not trying to be a shit here. Just being honest. You can get all twisted up and act like Rick or move on. I'd move on."

The words left a hollow pit in Andy's stomach. "Thanks for the advice."

"Take it."

They ended up on the floor.

Gabe lay there on his back with Natalie cuddled half on his side and half on top of him. He loved this position. Loved being wrapped up with her, with her leg lying over his. The softness of her skin.

They both wore their shirts and sweaters but their pants sat tangled in a jumbled mess by their feet. Soon the stove would need stoking and a chill would fall over the room. He saw it all coming but couldn't move. Not after the sex against the wall and another round with her riding him on the floor.

Not after her admission about her father. The idea of her living through that hell made him sick. What happened explained so much about who she was and how she handled crisis. She grew up to be the one who carried the gun. The person who gave orders. Her need for control, the way she protected herself and fought off too much hovering over her, all fell into place in his head.

It bordered on a miracle that she trusted him enough to even spill what she did. She didn't have to. He was being a complete dick. He'd been spun up about Rick and lashed out at her. She should have kicked him, thrown him outside . . . something. Instead, she fought with him, pushed and then opened up.

"I was an asshole." It was a flat-out truth he couldn't deny, so he said it.

"Absolutely." She didn't open her eyes as she mumbled the word against his skin.

"Like, a totally fucking asshole."

"I'm not disagreeing."

"Rick is a touchy topic for me. I . . ." Every time he thought about the fracture in their relationship he got hit with that same raw, inside-out sensation.

She leaned up on her elbow and looked down at him. "Because?"

"I don't want him in my life."

But that was only half true. They'd all been close—had to be, with their dad. Gabe had depended on Rick to steer him away from anything that would earn their father's disapproval. They bonded, stuck up for each other. As they got older, Gabe spent a lot of time watching out for Andy both because he was younger and because he was gay, which made him a target until he got too big and too good at self-defense for that bullshit. Gabe missed the guaranteed family safety net. He still had it with Andy, but he missed the rest.

Natalie's fingers brushed over his chest. "Your file doesn't mention a rift."

He slipped his fingers through hers and loved when she grabbed on. "That's a nice word for it."

"Okay."

That's all she said. No questions or nagging. She acted like she'd let it end there if he needed it to. After all his blustering and the shitty things he'd said to her, after she opened a window into her world, she still didn't make demands. Not that he could walk all over her, because he couldn't. It was one of the things he found so damn sexy about her. That inner toughness.

The way she reacted made it all seem so easy. The secret he'd kept locked inside. The one only he and Andy and Rick knew. The allegations that tore him up every time he looked at Brandon. Gabe let it all spill out. "He had sex with my girlfriend."

"Rick? Oh, God." She made a face as if she'd tasted something spoiled. "I don't have a sibling, but that has to break some sort of brother code."

"Shredded it to pieces." And that wasn't even the worst of it. The ripple effect swallowed up so much more. "Brandon's mom."

Natalie's mouth dropped open. "What?"

"He slept with my son's mother." His own brother. Gabe couldn't find a way out of that haze. The whole time he'd been making plans and thinking he was in love, Rick had been screwing him. "I didn't know at the time. Didn't know for years. The admission is pretty new."

"So, Rick isn't why the two of you aren't together?"

Gabe understood the confusion. He still hadn't cleared up her misconception about Brandon's age. Now might be the time, but on top of every other thing she was hearing, it might not even sink in.

"We haven't been together for a long time. Probably shouldn't have been in the first place. Not that I regret it, since the relationship gave me Brandon."

"Of course."

"Linda didn't want a kid. Didn't want a guy who traveled a lot either." Which would have been a good thing for her to tell him *before* he joined the Army. "But I was able to convince her to carry Brandon to term. She took some money and signed an agreement where she gave up parental rights. I took full responsibility, so she wouldn't get stuck with child support."

"She sounds kind of awful." Natalie shook her head. "Really immature."

Gabe went out of his way not to say what he wanted to say about Linda in front of Brandon. He knew the basics, but Gabe made sure that while his son knew he hadn't been planned he knew he was absolutely wanted. Gabe fought like hell for the kid. "She turned out to be, yeah."

"Brandon doesn't see her?"

"Never met her." Never asked, which made Gabe's life easier. He didn't have to track Linda down. He could have but vowed only to go down that road if it was important to Brandon, and so far it hadn't been.

Natalie winced. "Is Rick still with her?"

"Nope." But they could have each other as far as Gabe was concerned.

She squeezed his fingers and brought their joined hands closer to her mouth. "What aren't you telling me?"

Smart woman. He knew she'd put the pieces together and find one missing. "Rick has decided he's really Brandon's dad."

She made a strange strangling sound. "What the hell?"

"I used stronger language. Also kicked him the hell out of my house and banned him from the office." Gabe wrapped his arm tighter around her. "Andy has been stuck in the middle ever since."

"Does Brandon know?"

And that was the fight. The point he debated with Rick over and over. "Not about any of it. He thinks Uncle Rick and I had a work argument. They're still in touch but not much."

She pulled their joined hands closer in to her body until they rested against her chest. "Doesn't that worry you? Like, that Rick will go behind your back and tell Brandon?"

"Scares the shit out of me. But the one promise he gave me, and I made it clear I would kill him if he broke it, was that he wouldn't tell Brandon on his own."

Gabe didn't fully trust Rick's word. It was hard to after everything that had happened. The only thing that made it possible for Gabe to keep moving and not spend every day paralyzed with fear was that Andy joined in the threat. Rick would literally lose everything, including possibly Brandon, if he pulled some reckless stunt. Still, tired of waiting, Rick had given Gabe a deadline and it was coming toward them pretty fast.

"And you would." Her hand dipped into his hair and she nuzzled his chin with her nose. "Go after Rick, I mean."

"No one hurts Brandon." That was a fucking vow.

She lowered her head until it fit in the crook of his neck. "No wonder the idea of Rick sending someone here made you hostile."

"Understatement."

"Why would he get involved in this?" She touched his knuckles to her lips.

"I know you're thinking sabotage, but no." His lips brushed over her hair. He took a second to inhale, breathing in that scent he now associated with her. The one that stomped all over his self-control. "More than likely he thinks he's helping. He does this work and is trying to put the power of his business between us and the person at the CIA who is determined to cause trouble for you."

She groaned. "Please don't try to make your brother out to be the good guy after telling me what he did to you."

The automatic acceptance. He wondered if she even knew she did it. She liked to fight with him about details, but they generally agreed with each other on most things. And her trust in him after such a short time, knowing her past and who she was, humbled him.

"That's just the thing, he was. For a long time." Rick had helped Gabe raise Brandon. Stepped in when work intruded for Gabe or Army travel pulled them apart. That's what made the breach of loyalty such a deathblow. "He got this idea in his head, and now he's pushing it. I blame the injury. It's as if it turned him around and has him going back over every mistake in his life and trying to set them right."

She rubbed her fingers over his chin. Back and forth over the stubble and through his beard. "Don't get pissed off here, but is there a chance he is Brandon's dad?"

He sensed the question before she asked it. He would have been disappointed if she didn't raise the issue, not with her curiosity and tendency to solve problems. "They were having sex back then, so yes. Biologically."

"Okay, God. This just gets worse."

Gabe shifted, because suddenly just lying there made him twitchy. He needed her to know how strongly he felt about this issue.

He lifted his shoulders off the floor, and she inched up just far enough that her face hovered in front of his. "He's my son, Natalie. I don't give a shit who provided the sperm."

She didn't say anything for a few seconds. Just stared at him, as if waiting for him to say something else, but he'd made his declaration. His point was that simple. Brandon was his son. Period.

A sexy smile broke across her mouth. "You know, you may act like an asshole sometimes, but you're actually a very good guy."

With that, the tension building inside him and the charged energy zipping through the room changed into something very hot and, if he was lucky, a little naughty. "Don't tell people that. I'll never get a protection job again."

She lowered her head and put her mouth by his ear. Licked the outer rim as she talked. "How about if I just whisper it?"

She crashed through his defenses. Made him want things he hadn't wanted in so long. He'd closed some parts of himself off. Enjoyed sex and moved on. Concentrated on Brandon and work and keeping them all moving forward. Then she walked into his life. At first all haughty and demanding, cool in a blue business suit as she fought off any hint of vulnerability underneath. Now, tough and sure, even as her world collapsed and her future darkened. She was the most competent woman he'd ever met . . . and the sexiest.

"That works, but I bet I'd hear it better if you got on your hands and knees." He drew his finger down her neck and under the band of her sweater collar. "Without the shirt."

She flattened a palm on either side of his head. Straddled his hips with her knees. "Yes, sir."

So fucking hot. "You're going to say that a lot before we're done."

"I'm counting on it."

THIRTEEN

The next morning Natalie stood sipping her coffee while Gabe banged together the two pots they had as he made breakfast after a long night of bedroom activities. She gave him credit for trying. Gave him credit for a lot of things.

She couldn't imagine raising a child, only to have a sibling threaten to take it all away. It seemed incomprehensible. Also made her rethink her theory about Gabe abandoning his son. A guy who begged a woman to keep his baby, who worried about protecting him and keeping him close, would not just throw him away when he became inconvenient.

And that reimagining scared her. The son piece provided her with a protection against him. It was the one fact that made Gabe less appealing. The one part that reminded her to keep vigilant and not be thrown off by his smooth words and those hands that drove her wild. If he truly was exactly who he seemed to be, the last of her shields would fall.

She'd already shared parts of her past with him that she kept buried from everyone else. Those horrible moments she tried to forget and, in her most desperate times, pretended didn't happen.

Joining the CIA she'd been subjected to all kinds of questions and daylong lie detector testing. All those questions. The insinuations that she was holding back. She knew the game but did fear her inner thoughts gave her away. The CIA needed to know about her past and if she could be trusted. They did not need to know she was the one who used the knife that night. She repeated that refrain every time her name got chosen for random testing.

The facts she'd hidden for so long were now out there. Gabe could turn around and use every sentence as a weapon, but she knew deep in her soul he wouldn't. There was no escaping the truth. Something about him pulled at her and quietly shifted every rule she'd made for her life.

Stay detached and tamp down her emotions. A good plan. One she followed for years only to have Gabe blow it apart in a matter of weeks.

"Oatmeal?" Gabe's deep voice cut through the cabin.

She glanced over her shoulder and saw him shake a packet of instant chalky-tasting food at her. She had no idea how he managed to stand there in a thermal Henley and jeans and look so adorable. He could shoot, stalk, hide, cook and make her body tremble from the inside out. His skills crossed the spectrum, and as someone who benefitted she appreciated them all.

"Sounds delicious." She totally didn't mean that but didn't want to see his smile fall. But, really, the thrill of oatmeal had worn off on day two of being on the run.

He winked at her. "Liar."

She glanced out the cabin's front window then did a double take. There, at the edge of the trees, right before the open area of packed snow, stood a man. She could only tell that much from his build. Broad through the shoulders with a hood pulled tight against his face. High boots and a gun in his hand.

He stared at the cabin and didn't move. His presence could be random or just a matter of a local passing through. Then her gaze went back to the weapon. No, this wasn't someone stopping by to say hello—at least she hoped they and this guy were not that unlucky.

Shock grabbed her. Her body went numb, and the mug slipped from her hand. The metal clanged against the hard floor and hot coffee splashed up her leg.

Before she could blink Gabe was at her side, guiding her away from the spill. He stepped in front of her. "What's wrong?"

"Someone breached the perimeter." The alarms didn't ring, which only highlighted the danger.

Her mind blinked in and out. This couldn't be the guy who watched before. That man would not be so stupid as to take the risk of closing in a second time. And to stand there? No, this person wanted to be noticed. Probably welcomed a fight.

"Impossible." Gabe stepped in front of her. A gun appeared out of nowhere. That lazy satisfied-from-sex expression disappeared, and he switched to protector mode.

Not one to wait behind she grabbed her gun off the table and joined him by the window. "How did it happen?"

"Fuck me."

That struck her as the right reaction. She just wasn't sure what it meant. "What?"

"He's not inside the perimeter."

She looked again. Maybe her eyes played tricks on her, but he seemed to have cleared the trees.

"I can't see . . ." Her voice trailed off as she took a good look at Gabe. Watched every muscle stiffen. He knew something, and it was not good. She'd bet money on that. "What is it?"

"Rick."

That guy was a pain in the ass on every level. "Another one of his men?"

"No, I mean actually Rick. He's here."

The words rang in her head. She tried to make sense of why that would happen or how Gabe could know. She'd seen his brother's photo. Finding intel on him proved tougher thanks to his black-ops work. He knew people who could bury his information and keep him off the grid to aid in his work. But she'd seen early ID photos.

That's what confused her now. With the hood and jacket she couldn't even tell what color this guy's hair was. "Do you recognize the coat or something?"

Gabe checked his gun as he grumbled under his breath. "The cocky way he's standing there."

"That's not enough." When Gabe didn't answer, she tried again. "Right?"

Could it be? She tended to study people, looking for identifying traits. With all her training even she couldn't see through inches of down and make out a face intentionally covered. Certainly not from a distance of fifty plus feet away.

"For better or worse, he's my brother. I can pick him out of a crowd." Gabe didn't stick around and debate the point. Didn't even put on a coat. He unlocked the door and opened it.

A rush of cold air blew over her. White flakes danced on the air as a new round of flurries swirled. She reached out to grab his arm but missed. He moved fast and sure. Lunging steps took him to the small porch then down two steps. The cold didn't affect him at all. He tightened the hold on his gun and fended off the wind with a shirt meant to layer under things.

She started after him then stopped. Scrambled to find her boots. Shoving her feet in them, half turning her ankle as she tried to stomp her right foot in over the stiff material. Then she was off, trying to keep up.

Gabe might be sure about their newest watcher's identity but she wasn't. Not yet. Until a lightbulb turned on for her, she planned to keep her gun close and be prepared to fire. If that guy—whoever he was—lifted his weapon, she would blow a hole through his hand. That would teach him to sneak up on people.

She hit the snow and her boots sank up past her calves. She immediately regretted not grabbing her coat and thicker socks. The delay would have limited her time refereeing this showdown.

Not that Gabe acted as if he needed any help. "Hey, wait."

He didn't even spare her a glance. "Get back in the cabin."

No way was that happening.

She kept making her way, ignoring the burning cold assailing her limbs. With each step the walking got harder, but she pushed on. Catching up proved tough, but that ceased being a problem when Gabe stopped ten feet away from their unwanted visitor and aimed a gun at the figure bundled in a jacket.

This close she could see the man stood right on the edge of the safe side of the perimeter. She had no idea how Gabe had spied that from the distance to the cabin. Eyesight issues aside, she did understand how the protection barrier worked. Gabe said he'd set traps and warning sensors a certain number of feet apart, all around the cabin right where the wooded area broke open. The guy's foot had to be near the line. Natalie half wished he'd touch it.

"Gabe, no." The man didn't put the gun away, but he did reach for the string keeping his hood tight against his head and shoved it back on his shoulders. "It's me."

Gabe didn't lower his weapon. Kept it leveled right at his brother's head. "I know."

So much for the concept of brotherly love. Not that she could blame Gabe. Not after what he'd shared.

The informal ID proved correct. Natalie really didn't need an updated photo to confirm this one. Rick and Gabe looked alike. Rick was a bit slimmer with more of a lean runner's body. A narrower face and lighter hair, but the same stern expression and a familiar way of standing.

She decided to try to slice through the suffocating tension. "Why are you here?"

Rick finally looked at her. His gaze traveled over her then over Gabe. "We should go inside before you two freeze."

Not a bad suggestion, but she didn't want him inside or anywhere near the place where she'd been staying with Gabe. Welcoming Rick felt like a betrayal even as her toes began to tingle.

She tried a more tactful approach, though she had no idea why she bothered. If these two planned to kill each other, she'd stand back and watch . . . then jump in to save Gabe. They had reached that point. The one where she couldn't stand to think of anything happening to him. Damn him.

"If you step across that line you run the risk of—"

Rick cut her off while his gaze traveled back to Gabe. "It's a warning perimeter. You have weapons set up to fire at other spots, but not here." The man had the nerve to smile. "I'd say someone taught you well, but since most of that came from me, I'll refrain."

She made a mental note not to call Gabe a dick again. *This* guy was a dick. "How subtle of you."

"I have never been accused of that, sweetheart."

Make that a sexist dick. She started to wonder how Rick and

Gabe came out of the same household. "Well, *sweetheart*, even without traps, Gabe and I still have guns."

"Gabe might be pissed, but he won't kill me."

"I will." She didn't regret the comment. She meant it, and when she saw Gabe smile out of the corner of her eye, just for a second, there and then gone again, she relaxed. Rick might think he controlled the situation but he was dead wrong.

With a heavy exhale, Rick tucked his gun behind him. "I came to check on the two of you."

For some reason that annoyed her. Everything this guy said had her wanting to punch something. "We're fine. Now, leave."

Rick's eyebrow lifted. "I see why you like her."

No, he didn't get to engage in light banter. Didn't get to joke with Gabe. Not on this topic or any other. Not while she was around. "You want to date me, too? Or maybe hitting on Gabe's woman once was enough."

Gabe nodded. "Yeah, she knows."

Rage pulsed off Rick. His mouth fell into a flat line and tension almost had him puffing up. "What the fuck, Gabe? You won't tell Brandon but you tell her. You sure work fast. Screw a woman for a few weeks and she comes running to your side."

Gabe took a warning step in Rick's direction. "Her name is Natalie, and she is under my protection. One more wrong word and I will give in to the clawing inside me and wipe you off the earth."

The man just got more and more attractive. She decided to thank him for that later. After she let Rick know how little she thought of him. "But, really, keep being a condescending ass."

"It's too cold to stand out here without the proper weather gear." Rick kept falling back on that argument.

The guy wasn't wrong. Not about this. The cold seeped through her sweater and into her bones. Much more time out here and her teeth would start chattering. Her words would slur. With a lower than normal body temperature she'd always been susceptible to cold, and today she could not afford that weakness. "We can go back inside."

"I'm going to follow."

Maybe it would be faster to shoot him. She was starting to wonder. "You are such—"

"Enough." Gabe finally lowered his gun. He nodded toward the ground in front of Rick. "Take a giant step, about three feet and slightly to your left."

Rick scoffed. "That's a bit dramatic."

"Teacher or not, you missed a trap." Gabe swept an arm out to the side. "If you don't believe me, step wherever you want."

Score one for the middle brother. "You shouldn't have told him."

Gabe kept talking. "We go inside and you have ten minutes to tell me why you've been sending men after us and what the CIA hopes to accomplish with this bullshit."

Before he finished Rick started shaking his head. "You know I can't—"

"That's the only deal to make here, Rick." Gabe shrugged. "My terms or you crawl home."

Rick looked from Gabe to her and back again. "Fine."

Part of her thought Gabe had let his brother off too easy. The other part understood the garbled it's-confidential talk. She'd been trained in CIA-speak for years. Punishment for divulging details came swiftly and hard.

Since Rick worked outside of the CIA, had his own company, the rules might be less strict, but he had to sign an oath. Had to make promises. Had to have a special clearance and pass through a bunch of crap before he could look at one file. His livelihood and those of the people who worked for him depended on him never showing his hand. On him being willing to take a bullet if that's what it took.

She tried to drum up some sympathy for the position Gabe put him in now. Tried and failed.

She glanced at the cabin, and when she looked back again Rick had crossed the danger line. They all took off for cover. No one talked. The only sounds came from the sway of the trees and crunch of the ice on top of the snow. The thumps of their footsteps echoed around them. Their strides outpaced hers so she hurried to keep up. No way was she getting left behind by these two. By the time she got the door open she'd likely have a bloodbath on her hands.

After making the trek and pounding their boots on the porch to knock off as much of the snow as possible, they walked inside. Gabe slammed the door behind them and turned on his brother. "Talk."

Rick's gaze went to the coffeepot sitting on the burner then to Gabe's hand. "Maybe you can lower your weapon."

She didn't even notice Gabe still covered Rick. Seemed like a smart idea to her. "If he does, I'm still keeping mine right where it is."

Rick unzipped his coat as his stare stopped on her. "I've been hired by a group within the CIA that's concerned about your loyalty."

"That's bullshit," Gabe said. "She hasn't shown one sign of disloyalty or breaching her extraction agreement."

"I happen to agree. It's why I took the job, so I could control the reports back to the concerned party and keep you both safe from some trigger-happy assassin sent out here in my place."

She didn't buy it. Rick was setting himself up as some sort of avenging angel. Him, the guy who had his hands all up in his brother's business. He was supposed to be the one to save them all? No way. "So, you're my savior now?"

He exhaled as if to say he was bored with her questions. "I'm trying to help."

Gabe walked around the room until he stood near the kitchen.

This time he lowered the gun, but it remained in his hand. "That's new."

All traces of lightness left Rick's face. "Do you want to have it out right now?"

"There's nothing to fight about. You fucked the woman I was seeing. Didn't care what she meant to me. Then when you hit some sort of midlife crisis brought on post-injury—"

"Watch it."

"—you decided to have a kid by taking mine."

Of all the things that could tick Rick off he picked a shot at his age. She would never understand men. But focusing on his comments proved easier than thinking about Gabe's. *What she meant to me* . . . The words had the gears in her mind spinning. For whatever reason she hated hearing about this other woman, the one who held two MacIntosh men enthralled.

"You telling me you wouldn't try to find out if a kid you thought was yours actually was?" Rick asked, in a low, soft voice that carried a note of threat with it.

"Not if he was my nephew and was doing well and loved." Gabe's shoulders fell. "Goddamn it, Rick. Why would you put him through this?"

"You mean you. Why would I put you through this?"

Gabe threw up his hands. "Okay, fine. Why do this to me?"

"That's the point, little brother. This isn't about you."

Gabe moved like lightning. He flew across the room. Gun gone, he grabbed Rick by the throat and pinned him against the back of the door. "Your time here is up."

If she hadn't been standing there she wouldn't have believed the change. So primal and unexpected, yet not a surprise the longer she thought it through. The man who held her while she unburdened about her father vanished. Turned into a giant ball of fury. Looked ready and quite able to kill at any moment.

Rick didn't panic, but he did try to break Gabe's hold. Clawed at the hand tightening on his neck. "Let go."

"No."

Rick dropped a hand to his side. Moved it around to his back.

That's all she needed to see. She whipped her gun up and aimed it.

"I wouldn't do that." She moved to stand next to Gabe. "See, he's related to you. I'm not."

"I don't get it." Rick tried to shake his head but Gabe held him steady. "You sat in an office all day. What's with the sudden need to rush to Gabe's defense?"

"Please test my skills. I'm begging you." Not that she would do anything in front of Gabe unless he was threatened, but Rick didn't need to know that.

After swearing under his breath, Rick dropped his hands to his side. Lifted his chin. "I'm actually trying to get the CIA totally off your backs."

Gabe hesitated a second before letting his vise grip go. "Since when?"

"I was threatened to make it happen or else."

She didn't get the comment. "What?"

"Your lawyer sent Elijah Sterling to see me. That guy's record . . ." Rick blew out a long, ragged breath. "It can't be real."

Leave it to Eli to swoop in and provide backup. "I ran his team. It's real. He's that scary."

"Thanks to some well-placed comments by him, I have something to work with. I'm going to push back on the people who hired me," Rick said to Gabe. "Make it clear Natalie's leverage and this hidden information she compiled is not something you play around with. Buy a bit of room, let them see everything is okay, or at least convince them that they have a lot to lose if they don't ease up."

"How much time will this take?" Gabe asked.

"A week?" Rick shrugged. "Hell, I don't know."

"Good."

The word clunked in her brain. An unending run away from some unseen threat? No, thank you. "How is any of what he said good?"

"Rick is going to handle his end, which will support all the threats Bast is making on your behalf." Gabe talked slowly, emphasizing each word. "We'll lay low while all of that shakes out."

She knew he was trying to tell her something, but she didn't get it. Didn't really want to. They were talking about her life like it was nothing more than a cheese sandwich to be bargained for and discarded. She expected that from Rick. Not Gabe. "You trust him? You think whoever is paying him will just back off because we're all waving threats around?"

Gabe nodded. "Yes."

"Of course," Rick said at the same time.

They seemed so sure. Both stared at her with an annoying stop-worrying expression. As if she was the one out of line here. "Up until right now I thought you both were pretty competent."

Gabe stared at her for an extra beat before turning to Rick. "It's time for you to go."

"A storm is kicking up." Rick touched the tab to his zipper as he glanced out the window.

"Then you should move fast."

"Gabe." Even she thought that might be taking the vengeance angle too far. If something happened to Rick out there, Gabe would not forgive himself. Forget how mad he might be, this guy was his brother, and Gabe had proven over and over again to be decent.

"I don't believe for one second hanging out here for the rest of the day and tonight was his original plan. He has a plane waiting or some mode of transportation." Gabe shot his brother a skeptical look. "I'm just wondering why you came all the way out here to deliver this news yourself."

"Didn't think you'd believe one of my employees if I sent him out here, talking in code and shouting about Bast's arguments and Natalie's leverage."

"True, but Andy can reach me."

This time Rick zipped his coat. "He hasn't been all that helpful to me on this operation."

She knew she'd liked Andy. "I wonder why."

"I'll walk you out. Make sure you leave." Gabe grabbed his jacket with one hand as he shoved his brother toward the door with the other.

Somehow they made it out onto the porch. The snow had started to fall, a bit harder now than earlier. Gabe knew because he'd spent the early morning walking the area around the cabin, looking for tracks or any other signs of life. If he had known he could have stayed in bed with Natalie a few more minutes and let Rick come to him, he would have.

Natalie. Gabe shook his head. Fought off a smile.

She'd been on his side through this battle. Got all furious on his behalf over Rick's choices about Brandon. Gabe often wondered if the world flipped upside down who would defend him. Now he had an idea. Had no clue what to do about it or think about her, but her loyalty meant something.

If a man could wrangle her into a relationship, she wouldn't cheat. That might be a low bar for some men, but not him. Combine that with her resilience and sexiness and he was having a hard time thinking about anything but her.

Rick turned right before starting down the porch steps. "She's not your type."

True in some ways but not in others. The main difference is that with other women, Gabe had counted the days until it ended. With her he dreaded the day it would. "You don't know anything about me."

"Come on, Gabe. I told you the truth about what happened in the past because I thought you deserved to know."

He didn't pretend to misunderstand. This wasn't about Natalie or work. "You told me because it was expedient to get what you wanted. Brandon."

"I love that kid."

The word grated across Gabe's nerves. Before the admission and epic fight a comment like that would have filled Gabe with pride. It would signal that Brandon would always have family. Now everything Rick said came delivered with two edges, both sharp and dangerous. "So do I. Try to take him away from me and you'll see how much."

"You think he'll love you any less if he finds out you're his uncle and not his father?"

That question played over and over in Gabe's head. Had for what felt like forever. "We will never know."

"I need this, Gabe." Rick blew out a long breath. "I'm not letting this subject drop."

There it was. The constant threat that sucked the life out of everything else. "And I'm done talking. Have a nice hike."

Gabe turned around and shut the door before Rick could say anything else. But one day, soon and before he was ready, Gabe would have to hit this horrible issue head-on. Then he'd see how much blood mattered.

FOURTEEN

Gabe shut the door, blocking out the cold wind and every memory of his brother. Inside meant Natalie. It was just the two of them, safe and warm. No new threats. No realities to face. And if Gabe guessed right, at least until Rick landed back in D.C. and delivered his report to whomever needed to hear it, very limited risk of attack.

That meant no more kissing Natalie while a warning light flashed in the back of his head to be careful. He'd told her he needed to watch the door and have a gun nearby. All true, up to a point. Now, not so much. And as soon as he burned off some of this anger toward Rick, he'd touch her. Really touch her.

She'd taken her boots off and stood up from her position kneeling on the couch where it looked like she'd been on some sort of guard duty. Her approach was cautious. She fidgeted as she rubbed her hands together. "Are you okay?"

"Sure." He would be. He just needed a few more minutes, but staring at her helped.

Damn, but she was pretty. That face, round with big eyes. A

body that left him breathless and a soft southern accent that appeared and disappeared depending on her mood. That part proved to be one of his favorite things about her.

"Gabe, please." Her head tilted to the side and her soft hair fell over her shoulder. "I can see the distress in every line of your body. Hear it in your voice."

"I can't pretend he's not trying to rip my life apart." But he could focus on something else. Something clean and light and full of energy—her.

"Of course not. I wouldn't expect you to, but why let him get away with bullshit answers and send him away?"

Now he understood. It made sense that she'd want concrete intel and promises in writing, though the ones she had didn't appear to be all that rock solid. "Because he will make the report to the people who hired him. He'll make it clear that they are engaging in a game of mutually assured destruction if they continue."

She shrugged. "I'm not convinced that will be enough since they've known I held the leverage all along. Bast used it in the negotiations."

"Clearly they thought that was a bluff or that they could take you out before you could use your leverage."

"Idiots."

"And none of that matters because by the time Rick gets back home we will be moving again." He probably should have led with that. By this time tomorrow they would be out of here. Rick could send all the men he wanted to watch over them. They'd be staring at an empty cabin.

"What?" She said the word nice and slow, as if trying to figure out his plan.

Gabe didn't see a reason to make her guess. They were talking about her life. Her safety. "We're leaving here."

"That sounds better than hanging around depending on your brother for help."

"That's not happening, ever." Even before the fight Gabe didn't operate that way. He'd long moved past the time when he needed his big brother to swoop in and take over. In fact, the idea of it pissed Gabe off. As an adult and successful businessman, he was in charge. Always and completely.

"Any chance you can pick a beach area next time?"

Tempting, but Gabe already had a destination in mind. "We're going to my house."

She stilled, every muscle frozen in place. "The fake one in Maryland?"

"The real one in Virginia." The words came out before he could mentally weigh the pros and cons and find more cons. Taking her breached his personal vow to keep his work world and private world separate. Truth was, bringing her to his most sacred place, the house he shared with Brandon when he wasn't off at college, meant something. He didn't want to examine what, he just knew it was the right answer.

And the things they could do in his big bed. His feelings for her went beyond sex, but the fantasy had been working in his head. He looked forward to the live version.

She sat down hard on the armrest of the couch. "You often take people you're protecting to your private home?"

"Never." He slipped off his coat then kicked off his boots. The move gave her a little extra time to process, which she seemed to need since she just stood there.

Her eyes finally narrowed. "Why me?"

The simple answer popped into his head and he said it. "You're special."

She shook her head. "I'm not."

Damn it, someone did a number on her. Her idiot father or some loser she dated. Somewhere along the line she'd learned the lesson that she didn't matter except for what she brought to the job. Even that got trounced by the men in her office who insisted on taking credit for her ideas. He'd seen the evidence in the research file he complied for this job and heard about the annoying tendency during his talks with Eli and Bast about her.

"I'm going to show you." Not that she lacked confidence. She just funneled it all to the CIA and her abilities there. Not to who she was as a woman. And that part of her appealed to him on a very primal level. "Do you remember what I told you around the time we got to Montana about liking to be in charge?"

"I don't know what you're—"

"Right." He didn't believe her. Her eyes and the faint color on her cheeks said otherwise. "I'm going to tie you down."

"There's no headboard."

Always so practical, but interesting how she'd already done the math on that one. "I'll improvise."

Her mouth broke into a sudden smile. "You're not going to watch the door this time."

He liked this side of her, playful and sexy. When she let go and allowed this part of her personality to come out it was pure magic.

"The only thing I'll be looking at is you." He started unbuttoning his shirt. "Consider it a good-bye gift to the cabin."

"Does the sex end in Montana?"

She had to be kidding. "No."

He didn't even want it to end in Virginia. That was the problem. The way she wound her life around his without even trying. Maybe without intending to.

Scary shit.

She nodded, clearly unaware of the thoughts in his head. "Good."

"Take off your clothes." This time he wanted to see all of her, take all of her. It would whet their appetites until he got them back to Virginia. "All of them. I want you naked."

She didn't fight him. Her fingers went to the hem of her sweater. She lifted it up and over her head. Shed the bra next. Her body trembled in what he hoped was excitement as she moved. The flush of her skin suggested yes. So did the way her nipples stood in stiff peaks.

The temptation to touch her, run his hands over her while his mouth went to work tasting her, kicked strong. He held it off. This time he would give her pleasure the way he needed it. In control. He liked when she touched his dick or licked her tongue over him. She could initiate sex any time she wanted and he was in. But this time would be about a mutual satisfaction brought on by anticipation.

When she continued to stand there, with her hands at her sides, he pushed a little further. "The pants, Natalie. Don't make me wait."

Her hands went to the buckle of her belt. With aching slowness, she opened the clasp. The zipper came next, ticking down with a sound that vibrated in his head. This sexy woman knew how to play him. Knew exactly what it took to rev him up until he itched with the need to touch her,

But not yet.

"Keep going, baby." He lowered his gaze to her legs. "Off."

She shimmied then. Rocked her hips from side to side as she peeled the slim jeans down. Hands down the hottest striptease he'd ever seen. Heat flushed through him, and he had to force his body to remain still. When she stood back up, completely naked, he almost lost it.

He had to swallow before issuing the next command. "Get on your back on the bed. Fingertips against the wall and legs open."

This was going to kill him. No question about it. Just watching that high, firm ass walk across the room had his erection thumping. And she knew it. She worked that walk. The gentle swing of her hips. The way she glanced back at him over her shoulder, as if to tease and lure him in.

Here he thought he was in charge. Truth was all the power lay with her. She said yes or no. She turned him on. When she harnessed that feminine strength he turned to mush. It was fucking embarrassing, but he was starting to get used to it.

Now he just had to survive the next hour. He stepped into the bedroom doorway. Neither one of them could hide in the small space. She didn't even try. She sprawled out on the bed, that skin gleaming in the soft white light. When she spread her legs, taking her time and stretching out the process, he had to remember to swallow. He was pretty sure he'd stopped blinking, too.

As he stood there, she lowered her arms. "No, hands against the wall."

"There's nothing to tie me to."

Goddamn. "Then you'll have to be a good girl and keep those hands up."

She shifted her legs from side to side on the mattress, blocking his view but enticing with every move. "You don't want them on you?"

He heard a screeching sound in his brain but ignored it. "There will be time for that later. After."

He wanted her this way first, open and free. Following his commands as he walked her through each step and brought her body to the brink. The question was whether he could survive this. He'd been dreaming about her, thinking about her, for so long. The sex they'd had before now only stirred his cravings. He wanted more.

He slipped his shirt over his head and reached for his belt. When she flinched, as if wanting to join in and help, he stopped. Dropped his hands to his sides and lifted an eyebrow. She quickly got the hint. Those palms pressed tighter against the wall.

"Nice." And he meant all of it. Her body glowed. Every inch firm and lean, toned from exercise and all of her training, which she never gave up even once she exchanged the streets for a desk at Langley.

The pants came off next. Something inside him drove him to rip them off. He fought the sensation, choosing instead to strip them down, watching her as she watched his hands. The boots, the socks, nothing stayed on. This time would be their bodies with no barriers other than a condom.

The reminder had him picking up his jeans and digging the one out of the pocket where he had put it this morning. He clenched it between his teeth as he crawled up the bed. He would have smiled as she opened her legs to make room for him but his nerves had his body pulling tight and his emotions raw.

Settling between her thighs, he could smell her, see how wet she was before he ever touched her. This woman matched his needs so perfectly. Looking at her made him hard. Stripping for him got her ready.

He put a palm on the inside of each leg and pushed them open a little wider, inhaling her compelling fragrance. He ran his tongue along the fleshy high parts of her thighs, stopping to kiss and nibble on her skin. With each pass of his tongue her body pulled tighter. He glanced up the length of her, saw her head tip back and her shoulders fall against the flat pillow.

He blew a cool breath over her and felt her tremble. A soft moan filled the room. She was better than any drug.

"Hands on the wall." As her body fell deeper into a sensual haze her fingers dropped. And he could not allow that. Not this time.

She immediately listened, stretching her body even longer as she placed her palms flat against the wall. He wanted to praise her, but the need to taste her took over. He swept his tongue along her seam then dipped inside her. He licked around her clit until she squirmed. Heavy breaths punched out of her, and he could see her chest rise and fall.

If only he had a tie, something to hold her arms down, but this would do. He could drive her to the brink of madness just like this. Both of them, actually.

His tongue went back to work and she swelled under his mouth. When his finger slipped inside her, a tiny growling noise, almost like a low hum, rumbled in the back of her throat. He didn't let up on the pressure. His mouth and fingers took turns. A lick and a thrust, he rotated, touched her in every way at both times, until she soaked his fingers.

When her hips lifted off the bed he stopped. Her body froze except for her head, which lifted as she glared down at him. "What are you doing?"

"You're not ready."

She looked ready to pounce. "I am."

She was. Every cell in her body sang for him. He could feel the gentle shake in her muscles as she strained to keep her legs open. Loved the way her chest rose and fell. And that's what he wanted. To kiss her everywhere before he entered her. He'd hoped to make this last longer. To make her come then start all over again, but his control waned.

He wanted her. All of her.

Taking his time as much as he could stand it, he walked up the bed on his hands and knees. Let his body brush over hers. Felt the friction of skin against skin and the sharp intake of her breath. He didn't sit alone on the shaky edge of control. She was right there with him. Proving even more the power she held over him.

He could usually go at this for hours. Enjoy being with a woman until they both were left wrung out and weak. With Natalie, he got to that point so fast. When he'd said she was special, he meant it. He hadn't totally and completely figured out where she fit in, but she did. Had even back when she was ordering him around and he spent most of his days pretending to ignore her.

His elbows rested on the bed by her neck and his fingers slid into her hair. He reached one hand up and slipped his forefinger into her half-closed palm. Her fingers curled around his one in a loose hold. Still, it was a bond of sorts. One he didn't want to break.

He fumbled with the other hand to get the condom wrapper open. She watched with a knowing smile on her face, but he did not ask for help. Not this time. After a few false starts he got it open and tugged it on. Still, he didn't slip inside her. His mouth went to her breasts, and he wondered why he'd let this part of her body go unattended for so long.

He sucked the peaks into his mouth. Slid his fingers through hers as his mouth traveled from one breast to the other. He kissed and sucked. Took her soft skin into his mouth and rolled the nipples between his teeth. By the time he stopped, her ankles pressed into the back of his legs and her grip on his hand tightened to the point of snapping.

Not that he cared. He'd take whatever she wanted to give. He only wished he could survive hours of foreplay. Maybe next time, after he worked her out of his system. After he sheathed his body in hers and let go.

With his hand wrapped around his stiff cock, he started to enter her. Slow at first, then pushing in one long thrust. Her insides clamped down on him. He could feel her closing around him, clenching him as she pulled him in tighter.

Energy welled inside of him. He could barely breathe as he pressed in and pulled out. Then something primal took over. He stretched his hand and touched the wall by her hand. The shift

gave him leverage, let him plunge deeper inside her. The bed
rocked and sweat broke out along his shoulders. He could feel the
wet smoothness of her skin under him. The chill of the room
evaporated and heat poured over them.

He kept moving. Pushed faster. The tempo picked up, and his
nails dug into the wall. He could hear her palms slap against the
wall close to his with each thrust. Feel the grip of her legs bind
around him.

Every thrust, every breath, centered on bringing her pleasure.
He didn't hold back. One hand roamed over her as the other
braced against the wall. He hovered right on the brink of something amazing. He'd abandoned his control and let the energy
sweep them both up in its wake. Now his body bucked without
any signals from his brain. He moved on pure instinct. In and out.

His hand slipped around her body to land on her ass. He
cupped her cheek and brought her in even tighter against him.
The move had her body jerking. She started to chant his name as
an orgasm ripped through her. He could watch it play in the puffs
of her cheeks and flush of her skin. She closed her eyes and let her
head fall back. Her arms stiffened and her hands curled into balls.

The stunning display could have lasted seconds or minutes. He
couldn't tell, but he watched it all. Envied every inhale while he held
back. This time was about her, but his body had other ideas. As
soon as the pulsing died down inside her, his ticked up. The tightening finally snapped and he let go, biting back a groan as he came.

His palm slammed against the wall right as her arms dropped
next to her head. It was as if her muscles lost their strength. Being
inside her zapped his. He felt both weak and strong as his orgasm
raged on. When he finished his arms wobbled. He didn't have the
strength to balance above her.

To keep from crushing her, he rolled to the side and took her with him. There, with their arms curled around each other in the darkness, she cuddled in even closer. He remained lodged inside her and didn't care. She felt so good. So fucking right.

She kissed his throat. "That was impressive."

He laughed because he couldn't hold it back. The sudden happiness inside him seemed to swamp him. "I think you stopped my heart."

She placed one last kiss on his chin then settled in against his chest. "I can only imagine what you'll do when you actually tie me up."

His body jerked as visions from his dreams ran through his head. "Soon."

"I'm holding you to that promise."

"I always keep them." And he would keep this one, too. Trust and honesty mattered to him. Except for some omissions about Brandon, he'd never lied to her, and he wasn't about to start now.

FIFTEEN

Natalie wandered around the cabin in a daze the next morning. Her body still hummed from the lovemaking the afternoon and night before. When Gabe felt free to explore, he did not hold back. That might be her favorite new thing about him. That and his mouth. Lord, the man could use that mouth.

She stood over her small duffel bag where she'd opened it on the bed and tried to think of what she was forgetting. Not that any of the items in there, in Montana, truly belonged to her. Gabe had picked them all out, which explained the slim-fitting T-shirts for under the bulky sweaters. She was pretty sure he was a breast man. At least he seemed to be last night.

She almost turned around but then she heard footsteps. His footsteps. They thundered except for those instances where he wanted to sneak around. It was an impressive skill.

Arms wrapped around her from behind and his chin rested on her shoulder. The move struck her as so normal it almost freaked her out. She didn't do dating and ordinary. Just the thought of it made her flinch inside.

But something about Gabe smoothed out the usual rough spots. Things that had her twitching and panicky with other men barely registered. With him, life zipped along in a way she hadn't experienced before.

She chalked the feeling up to her current place in the world. Nothing stayed certain. She didn't even know what she could do now and where she should start. She ruled out Montana as her new home base thanks to the snow, but that left a lot of options. Every time she tried to run through them in her head she thought about Gabe and Virginia.

Now she thought about his strong arms and all the things he could do with those fingers. She had to say something or risk dragging him back to bed, and that sure was a tempting idea. "What's happening today?"

"A plane crash."

The words sank in and she spun around to face him. "What?"

He rested his hands on her hips and stared down at her. "Not a real one."

"Okay." He sounded so serious, as if she thought he might really bring a plane down with them on it. Though there was a tiny part of her that did wonder if he could actually pull that off and have them all walk away safely—not that she intended to find out today. "Well, I guess that's good news."

"Andy and I set it up."

"When?" And why hadn't they filled her in?

"It was in our list of potential plans. We decided to set it in motion because of the Rick piece and the obvious fact someone you used to work with wants you, at the very least, followed and your movements analyzed."

"Aren't you enterprising." If she'd had more people like Gabe working for her she might not be in this mess. She'd only landed on everyone's radar this time because of a rogue agent under her watch. She'd raised concerns but no one listened. Then when everyone overreacted by trying to neutralize the rest of her team, she stepped in. Thanks to that she didn't have a career or a clue as to how to lead the rest of her life.

"He'll have footage and reports. Photos of a plane and, I'm afraid, your body. Well, one he produces."

"But not a real person." She sure hoped that was true.

"That's up to him." Gabe shrugged. "Either way, it will look legitimate to most people and provide cover."

"This is to throw the CIA off?" Because she couldn't imagine that. A good forensics team would see through the ruse, and it would take weeks of planning and a whole host of trustworthy staff to really pull something like this off. They didn't have the time or the resources.

"They'll figure out it's fake. The point is to show them you have every intention of disappearing. Of not being Natalie, one of their star agents, anymore. Apparently Bast has been doing a lot of yelling. This venture will support his claims about you."

It was the right answer, but it chilled her insides. The idea of pretending to plunge to her death and doing it so she could walk away into . . . what? That's where she kept getting tripped up. All of this, the hiding, the bodyguard, the players, the negotiation, all of it led to a place where she could have a new life.

The amount of work that went into the setup and execution awed and humbled her. She couldn't even figure out a way to express her gratitude now that she'd stopped feeling so sorry for herself for being thrust into this situation. But what now? No one seemed to be able to answer that question. Not even her.

Gabe rubbed his hands up and down her arms. "What are you thinking about?"

"The future." Which wasn't a lie, except for the fact that she didn't really have one.

He gave her forearms a squeeze before dropping his hands to his sides. "Let's concentrate on today."

An idea popped into her head. A view of the bigger picture and the consequences he kept ignoring. "Some of the people who hired Rick are going to be ticked off that you're doing this."

"I've decided that crowd is never happy. They don't want you at your desk. Don't want you away from it. Want you dead then alive. No, dead." He rolled his eyes. "It's exhausting."

She couldn't miss the humor in his voice, and it helped. He wasn't making fun of her, but he tried to take some of the pressure off the situation. That she understood. The faking of her death she liked a little less. She'd lost her family long ago and didn't collect friends, but there were other people invested in her life, including the people who insisted she be protected right now like Bast and Elijah and a few others.

"Is this like witness protection and—"

"Anyone you want to know you're alive, will." He cupped her cheek in his palm in a gesture so reassuring she almost sighed. "This setup is purely for cover for those in your old office most prone to panic."

She snorted. Couldn't help it. "So, most of them."

"Yeah."

"Thank you." The words came out softer than she intended but the feeling behind them was heartfelt.

After she'd nearly driven him mad with her stubbornness he should rightly hate her. She pushed and denied right up to the point where he drugged her and got her on the plane. Not her finest moment, but the lack of trust came from a very real place.

A shaky one that wanted life to shift back to normal, even though she knew that could never happen. She'd made that decision the day she opted to keep her people safe over covering her own ass.

Before he could say anything to ruin the moment, she rushed to set some emotional ground rules. "And don't say you're only here because you're being paid. I mean, I know that's true and all."

"Natalie."

He stared at her until the heat bore into her and she looked up. "Yes?"

"I am here because I want to be here. You are going to my house in Virginia because I want you there."

The words washed over her. She turned each one over and around, looking for a hidden meaning, and didn't find one. He wanted to be with her. Her, little Natalie from the trailer park. Little Natalie who killed her father and couldn't save her mother.

Emotion clogged her throat. She knew she should say something profound but nothing came to her. Her mind got stuck on the beautiful comments he made. The ones she'd hug close in the future when and if her new life fell apart.

She settled for expedient. "Then let's go crash a plane."

He held up a finger. "Fake crash."

"Yeah, let's definitely do it that way." She glanced around the tiny bedroom and looked into the family room beyond. "I'm going to miss this place."

"You're kidding, right?"

The words finally came to her. Stuttering and a little disjointed, but the idea behind them stuck with her. "Actually yes, since I'm taking the one thing I would miss along with me."

He nodded. "The shampoo?"

"You."

. . .

Andy didn't even look up from the file in front of him when Rick walked into his office. He'd insisted on being buzzed in five minutes ago. Andy seriously considered pretending not to be in.

This is why he preferred being in the field. No one just stopped by out there. No one annoyed him with mindless chatter. He had no idea how Gabe tolerated running this place and managed to do it without killing anyone. That was some impressive personal strength right there.

Andy kept flipping pages even though he had read through this operation report several times already. "You're starting to be here a lot."

Without any introduction or hello Rick dropped into the open chair across from Andy. "My guy was right. They're together."

The next thing on the agenda was to remove that extra chair. Maybe making people stand would usher them out of his office faster. But first he needed to figure out what mess Rick had created now. "And you know this how?"

"I went to Montana."

Of course he did. Hopped on a plane, flew to an area where no one lived except militia members and off-the-grid types and bothered Gabe. Andy thought there had to be a better job out there than the family business. He thought maybe he and Gabe should take it. "Now there was a terrible idea."

Rick slouched down in the chair and crossed one leg over the other. "Gabe didn't exactly welcome me to the place."

"You thought surprising him out there, in the middle of nowhere . . . the guy who's an expert shot, by the way, was a good idea." It was a wonder they weren't planning a funeral right now. "You're lucky to be alive."

"Natalie wasn't exactly happy to see me either." Rick frowned. "Threatened to kill me more than once. Seemed mighty connected to Gabe."

"Not a surprise." At least not the first part. Natalie might be on the run, but that woman was capable. She also had a loyalty streak that rivaled Gabe's.

But the last part piqued Andy's interest. Gabe's attraction to her wasn't exactly a secret. He took this assignment, one he would normally outsource to someone on the staff. He insisted he be the one to communicate about Natalie's case. That he be the one to run this operation. The guy practically drooled when she walked in the room.

While Andy liked to see a spark of life in Gabe, that road could lead to some very dark places. Andy knew from experience. His feelings for Eli once had him so wrapped up that when the guy left, Andy checked out. Literally. Had to go away for a while. The whole scene knocked him sideways. He saw hints of the same thing between Gabe and Natalie.

"But dangerous," Rick pointed out.

Andy couldn't argue with that, so he didn't really try. "So was going out there without any warning."

"I needed him to know where we were."

"Uh-huh." Now that sounded like nonsense. It ignored pretty much every rule of surveillance. Also skipped over the part where Andy could contact Gabe. Rick didn't need to take this one on personally and fly back and forth to Montana in something like eighteen hours.

"What's the matter with you?" Rick asked, but there was no real heat behind his words. Not this time. Not like usual.

But that didn't mean Andy thought they'd worked through their issues. A battle loomed and he dreaded its coming with every cell inside him. "I'm just waiting to see what you say next."

"He's still pissed off about Brandon and my request for a DNA test."

There was no way a trained operative, a guy who could read people and interrogate in ways Andy didn't even want to think about, could be this clueless. "Now there's a surprise."

Rick shook his head. "I don't understand why you two don't see how important this is to me."

And that said it all. That was the part about being a father by blood only that Rick could not ferret out and deal with in any real way. "You mean to Brandon."

"What?"

"Yeah, that's what I thought." Andy closed the file and put it on the stack on the left side of his desk. "Look, you did your duty by Gabe. I'll take over now."

"Fine." Rick stood up and headed for the door. Didn't actually get there but stood nearby, as if ready to bolt any minute.

But the concession came too easy. Andy had never known Rick to agree and walk away. Just to be safe, he poked around. "Did you contact the CIA as you promised you would?"

"I have a meeting scheduled this afternoon."

Andy wasn't convinced they were saying the same thing. He'd call Eli and Bast just to be sure they kept applying pressure. He'd take care of the subterfuge on his end. Fake a plane crash, because how fun would that be. He'd faked a lot of things, but never this.

But Rick still needed to play his part. "Be convincing."

Rick nodded then turned to the door. His hand slid off the doorknob as he spun around to face Andy again. "Gabe is gone, isn't he? He took Natalie and left Montana already."

Now there was the smart, quick-thinking brother he knew. "Wouldn't you have done the same thing?"

"Yes."

"I guess you guys still have something in common." Andy wanted to say that showed some hope, but he knew it didn't.

"This assignment still could go sideways on Gabe."

Andy knew what Rick was saying, but there was no way he'd ask for help. Gabe would kill him. "I'll make sure that doesn't happen."

"And if you can't?"

Andy went with the stark truth. "I've never let him down before."

SIXTEEN

Gabe had dealt with jet lag on a regular basis for most of his life. He could get off a plane and go right to work. He didn't need time to acclimate or whatever regular people did. But he must be getting old, because the only thing he could think about once the wheels touched down at the private airstrip in Virginia was hustling Natalie back to the house and into bed. Or maybe that meant he was still young. He wasn't sure.

He reset the alarm as soon as they stepped into the foyer. He expected her to say something. When he told her he lived in a log home in the woods of Virginia, she'd winced. Tried to hide it, but he saw. She likely feared a lack of running water and a water heater partially constructed with a coffeepot. Fair enough since he forgot to tell her the place constituted a fortress.

It could not be described as rustic. Built into the side of a mountain and surrounded by a motion-sensor-activated fence, it had four thousand square feet of stone and wood aboveground. A place designed to his specifications with big rooms and high ceilings. Stuffed with comfortable furniture and housing a state-of-the-art kitchen. An indoor theater and a game room rounded out the specialty items.

He didn't exactly skimp when it came to his home life. He liked to pretend it was all for Brandon, but truth was Gabe liked toys, too. That explained the hot tub and pool out back. Not that she could see either right now since he used the program on his phone to keep the place, including the grounds, dark. The contained and secure work area and communications center downstairs would also remain a mystery for a bit longer.

Then there were the photos all over the house. Those posed a problem. As soon as she looked at them she'd know Brandon was not some elementary school kid. That would lead to a discussion, possibly a lecture, and he'd never get her into bed. And that was the goal—her hair fanned out across his sheets. That needed to happen now.

Right now she stood at the edge of the flagstone entryway and stared into the great room. She seemed frozen in place.

"You okay?" he asked, knowing he wouldn't like the answer.

She glared at him. "Did you forget to mention something?"

Everything. The whole place. The reality of the normal life he tried to live outside of the office. The seven televisions spread through the rooms so Brandon never missed a second of a football game. Well, that was mostly for Brandon.

Gabe went with an abbreviated response. "No."

"Well, Mr. Mountain Man." She took one step down into the great room. Then another. "You said you lived in a cabin."

He didn't bother turning up the lights. She could wait and explore tomorrow. He was fine to leave the arguments and debating until then. "I never said that. You assumed."

Her eyes widened. She looked fully awake now. "You let me."

"Okay, yes. That might be true."

Dealing with her had been a lot easier when he drugged her to fly. Not that he would do that again. She'd never let him get away with that move a second time, especially now that the reason for it had disappeared. She'd long stopped fighting with him about sticking close.

She squinted and headed to the fireplace. He knew he had to stop her. The mantel served as a showcase for Brandon. Kid photos, prom photos. Gabe didn't exactly hide Brandon's life inside these walls.

"I know you want to look around." Which was just about the last thing in the world he wanted, so he hooked her arm and turned her around until she faced him. Ran a mental inventory, trying to remember where all the wall photos of Brandon were in the house.

"Yes."

He wrapped his arms around her waist and brought her in closer. "We should sleep."

"I'm thinking about kicking you." But her hands went to his chest and she didn't fight back.

He frowned. "I'm not really into that."

"You're loaded."

"You say that like it's a bad thing." When she snorted he tried again. "I work hard, to the extent that makes the bank account fatter, so be it."

"I had visions of her and your son living in this tiny two-bedroom." She started telling a tale straight out of Dickens, complete with begging for food.

Gabe decided he probably needed to trim the beard and buy something other than a plaid shirt. Clearly he came off as if he made six cents per year, which was not really the look he intended. But he did get her theory. It wasn't far off from the life they led in the beginning. Being an eighteen-year-old father didn't exactly make a big house and fancy cars a possibility at first. Even now he kept that sort of thing to a minimum. Except for the house. He loved the house.

"Honestly, we did struggle for a very long time." And he'd vowed to make things better for them and worked his ass off until he did. "I don't come from money. I don't flaunt what I have now, but I earned it all. Legitimately, I might add. Since I deal with stress, this is the place I come to burn all that off."

She tapped a finger against his chin. "I feel like you're leaving something out."

That list was so long, but there was only one item on it that he cared about at the moment. "Did I mention my big bed?"

"About a thousand times on the flight here. Even the pilot of that private plane heard you."

Gabe hadn't been going for subtlety, so that wasn't exactly news. Plus, the guy worked for him. Mostly contract work, but his piloting skills weren't up for debate. Gabe paid what needed to be paid to secure his services and his loyalty, not to mention his dignified silence.

"Want to see it?" With the hope of winning her over, Gabe started kissing her neck. Hell, they could make out on the couch for all he cared, but later.

"This conversation isn't over." But she tilted her head to the side to give him greater access to that soft skin.

Relief washed through him. "Of course not."

"I'm going to figure it out."

"I'd rather you spend your time studying me." He lifted her off her feet.

On cue, she wrapped those long legs around his hips. "Naked, I presume."

Now they were back on track. "Definitely."

SEVENTEEN

The man exhausted easily for someone who spent most of his military life waiting in fields for the enemy to arrive. But Gabe being asleep provided Natalie with the perfect opportunity to wander. She refused to hang around in bed, staring at him until he woke up.

Though that did have some benefits. In sleep, some of his rough edges smoothed out. He didn't look so stern and couldn't sound unbending with his mouth closed. And that dark beard against crisp white sheets was something to behold. But curiosity with a side of hunger called, and she planned to answer.

She slipped across his big bedroom—emphasis on big—and stopped at the dresser running along the side wall. Not to be confused with the sitting area or the couch or the connecting room she could barely make out without the sun rising or a light on, but it looked like a deep cave. The walk-in closet, she presumed.

She picked up the T-shirt he'd abandoned on the floor. Held it to her nose and inhaled his scent. Something spicy that reminded her of the outdoors. Not being one to stumble around naked in strange houses, she put on the shirt and it dropped to her upper thigh. Very upper.

For some reason being clothed, at least a little, made her snooping feel a bit less sleazy. Not that she planned on looking through drawers and cabinets. This really was a what-does-this-place-look-like run.

She slipped into the hall and for a second debated looking around on the upper floor. She decided that great room had to lead to a kitchen and she'd start there first. Her feet thudded against the shiny floor. She smiled at the contrast between her pale skin and the dark hardwood.

She'd probably be able to see her nearly white legs in the dark but she didn't need to rely on that. The pale gray morning, just before dawn provided a dull splash of light as she rounded the first set of stairs and hit the landing to the next. He had carried her up those without breaking a sweat or starting to pant. The man sure did impress.

The steps emptied out into the great room. The space was aptly named. It stretched across a good portion of the back of the house. Outlined by glass doors, it had an open feel. The soaring ceiling and two seating areas did the rest. And she didn't even know what to think about the massive television over the fireplace. The thing looked six feet long, but she doubted that could be right.

She might have done the calculations and measuring if she hadn't spied the photographs all lined up on the mantel. So many of them. Her eyes refused to adjust so she stepped closer. Tiptoeing for some reason she couldn't really explain. It wasn't as if she was doing anything wrong.

She'd wound her way around to the back of the large sectional. There was something odd about those photos. She needed to get closer to see.

"Good morning." The deep, booming male voice rang out in the quiet room.

She nearly jumped out of her skin. She spun around, her hand going to her hip for her gun but she grabbed nothing but cotton. And not much of it.

She had no trouble focusing now. The last traces of sleep vanished. She stood facing the shiny sprawl of the kitchen with its light gray walls and stainless steel everything. That and a kid, but not a kid. An almost-man. One right on the verge where his body had just transitioned from gawky to muscular. Tall with a sleepy look on his amused face.

The black hair and blue eyes might be different, but the way he held himself. His mouth. "Brandon."

She actually might shoot Gabe. He let her think that his son was young, really young. That he got shipped off and forgotten. None of that appeared to be true.

"I know you didn't expect me to be here." Brandon sipped on a cup of what looked like coffee.

The smell hit her. Then she took in the light and the toast on a plate in front of him. How had she missed all of those signs on her laser-like walk to the fireplace? "That is only the start of my confusion."

He smiled, and the rest of the resemblance fell together. "Okay."

She tried to do the math in her head. She sucked at guessing people's ages. She knew Gabe's—thirty-six—but no way was this kid only thirteen or whatever would make sense in terms of Gabe raising him.

She tugged on the hem of the shirt again, which seemed to be getting shorter by the second. She wanted to run back upstairs and find pants. Maybe punch Gabe, but no way was she giving this kid a show of her ass. "I'm not sure how to play this."

He laughed. "Me either."

That didn't make much sense. He must have been here before, meeting a woman who clearly spent the night with his father. Bumbling his way through the awkward morning-after introductions. "Why?"

"Dad doesn't bring women here."

Her response, anything logical or smart, slammed to a halt in her brain. "He . . . oh."

Footsteps sounded right before Gabe stepped into her line of vision, holding something in his hand. He winked at her, then went right up to his son. "Look who's home. This is a surprise."

"Clearly." The smile that broke over the kid's face looked genuine and warm. "Hey, Dad."

Gabe wrapped an arm around Brandon's shoulder and pulled him in close. Touched a hand to his hair in a gesture that struck her as almost reverent. Like something he'd been doing forever, to build the bond between them.

She didn't understand this type of family. She knew about fear and carefully chosen words. No one surprised anyone. Her mother never raised her voice and her father always did. He screamed about everything. Seeing the kitchen a mess with a butter knife sticking to the countertop and crumbs falling on the floor would have set her father on fire. Days later they'd all be paying for not cleaning up that one time before he came downstairs earlier than usual in the morning.

Not here. Gabe held up the knife with two fingers and dumped it in the sink as he lifted an eyebrow at Brandon. The kid shrugged. Even grumbled when Gabe reached over and took a big bite of the toast sitting there.

Gabe dropped whatever was in his hand on the countertop as he chewed then swallowed. "Forget to tell me something?"

"That's what I was thinking," Brandon said after a quick glance in her direction.

As if these two cornered the market on shocks this morning. "Me, too."

"Eyes stay up." Gabe ended his point by rolling his.

Brandon nodded even as he struggled to follow that order. "Yes, sir."

With an ease that came from living together, Gabe reached around Brandon and grabbed the coffeepot. They worked in sync, shifting this and moving that until Gabe held a mug. "In case you skipped over the introductions or shock held your minds captive, Brandon, this is Natalie. Natalie, my son, Brandon."

He made it all sound so light and carefree. Never mind that they'd been holed up in a cabin in the packed snow, fighting with Rick and threatening the man's employees. She had to question if Brandon had any idea about the danger his father wallowed in every day. Kind of made her wonder why Gabe took the risk.

She shook her head to clear away the haze descending on her. She had so many questions and knew now wasn't the time for any of them. Then she picked up on the silence. Noticed them both staring at her.

She tugged the edge of the shirt a little harder. Bent over just a bit more to hide whatever needed hiding. "What?"

"You did know he had a son, right?" Brandon asked.

"I thought you were eight." She just sort of blurted that out. Once she did there was no way of calling it back.

His eyes widened. "Sure, ten years ago."

Gabe leaned in, brushing his shoulder against Brandon's. "She's doing the math."

"Everyone does. He was seventeen when my mother got pregnant. Eighteen when I was born." Brandon balanced his palms against the counter and smiled at her. "He's been giving the condom speech ever since."

"You're lucky I love you." Gabe ruffled Brandon's hair before tipping his mug in her direction. "Coffee?"

At this point she might need something stronger. Images bombarded her brain. She'd paged through Gabe's file so many times. Nothing she saw now, the house, Brandon, the easy camaraderie between the two, fit with the lethal man the government had trained as a weapon. The juxtaposition was surreal.

And she was almost naked, which made the situation even weirder. "I think I should—"

Before she could even finish Gabe leveled a finger in her general direction. "Do not even think of leaving that spot or going upstairs and putting on clothes."

Brandon hissed as he winced. "Wow, Dad."

"Or jumping out a window," Gabe added.

She had to give him credit for understanding her, because the thought did run through her mind. "I need clothes."

"We'll debate that later, but I doubt you want to walk up stairs in that short shirt while we stand down here and watch." He slipped the ball of material from his side of the counter to hers. "Lounge pants. They'll swamp you but they're good enough for now."

"I'm one of his cases." For some reason she felt the need to explain that to Brandon. Ignoring the shirt that was obviously not hers and the total lack of a bra and underwear, she was here for a reason . . . sort of.

Brandon cleared his throat. Did a pretty sucky job of hiding a laugh behind a fake cough. "Really?"

"Well, okay. There's more happening." She wiped a hand over her face, half hoping it would make her disappear. When it didn't, she practically jumped into the pants then held them up before they could slide back off her waist again. "I really think I should go upstairs."

This time Gabe pointed at the empty barstool on the other side of the counter from the males of the household. "Sit."

Demands. Really not her thing. "Your son is standing there, so I'm going to let that slide."

"Ha! Good for you." Brandon took the cup out of his father's hand and started pouring. Instead of giving it back to Gabe, he set it in front of the seat Gabe told her to take. "Black or do you want something in it?"

She debated bolting or toughening it out. Decided sitting down would make it easier to keep the oversized pants up. She could hide part of her under the counter while she silently cursed Gabe for his tendency to tell half a story.

"I think I need full strength this morning." She slid onto the stool and ignored Gabe's satisfied smile.

Once everyone had coffee, Gabe leaned his hip against the counter and faced Brandon. "Spill it."

She had no idea what was happening, so she just watched. Waited to see if the nasty side of Gabe, the side she'd never seen, came flying out. If it did she didn't know what she'd do, except put her body in front of Brandon's.

He shrugged as his gaze went to the countertop, then into the great room, then across the kitchen to the refrigerator. Everywhere but his father's face. "I wanted to come over and say hello."

"Nope." Gabe broke eye contact to glance at her. "When a teen boy leaves college on a weekend and heads home, he wants something."

Good to know. "Like what?"

She understood what motivated people—greed, revenge, honor, a cause. Kids were like a science experiment to her. Their minds seemed jumbled, and little they did made sense to her. Except for those in countries who were trained to fight or acted the part of terrorists, and those kids had ceased being kids long ago, she didn't get them.

Brandon tried the same tact. "A few hours with my dad."

Even she knew that wouldn't fly. The kid had an obvious tell, or three. He also had spunk, but lying straight to his father's face seemed to be a problem for him. She guessed in the world of parenting, that was the equivalent of a superpower.

Gabe downed the contents of his cup and set it down on the table. "Nice try. You knew I was away."

"Which was why I was a little surprised when I heard you come in last night."

Gabe frowned. "Why didn't you say something?"

"Well." Brandon's gaze flipped to her then back to his father. "You seemed busy."

She felt a rush of heat on her cheeks. This kid had her struggling to remember what happened when they walked in the door last night. How much and what he could have overheard. Something withered inside her at the thought.

"This just gets better and better," she mumbled under her breath, as she hoped she'd disappear in a big puff of smoke. If only her CIA cronies could see her now.

"I think he figured out we're having sex," Gabe said in a dry, let's-be-serious tone.

Talk about oversharing. She wrapped both hands around the mug and held on for dear life. "Are you guys always so chatty in the morning?"

Brandon shot her an apologetic smile. "You're embarrassing her."

"Which is weird." Right when she was about to ask what the hell he meant by that, Gabe turned back to Brandon. "So, a party? Was that the plan?"

"No."

"Money . . . oh, wait." Gabe started nodding. "The car."

That fast, Brandon switched from seemingly mature and in control to babbling. "Look, it's no big deal. It really isn't." He was pleading now. "I just want it for a few days."

She took in the byplay and tried to figure out what Gabe had said to trigger this reaction. The side of Brandon that was not quite adult and more focused on his needs came roaring to life. Natalie liked the reaction, because it made the kid, who up until then had come off as almost too perfect, seem pretty normal. Whining she understood. Didn't love the sound and she never got away with it as a kid, but it fit.

But Gabe was having none of it. "No."

"I'll bring it back next weekend." Brandon's voice got a bit more singsongy.

"Still no. College freshmen don't have cars."

The math still astonished her. She couldn't imagine Gabe at Brandon's age, with a baby and no wife. She tried to image what kind of life that must have been then gave up and went with a question that had to be easier to answer.

Gabe didn't ask so she did. "Why do you need one?"

He snorted. "I'm guessing a female is involved."

"I didn't want to go to the movies by bus," Brandon said in full whine voice.

"If you knew how little sympathy I had for you on this issue." Gabe smiled as he said it. "How did you get here?"

Brandon sighed and his shoulders dropped. He wore the look of defeat. "A few friends were going to D.C. this weekend. They swung by and left me off about a half mile away. I walked the rest."

"A half mile?" She thought about the snow and tried to remember if there was any on the ground here. "How big is this spread?"

Brandon held his arms out wide. "Big."

"Okay." Gabe shook his head as he reached for the coffeepot again.

"I get to take the car?" Brandon asked, almost painfully hopeful.

"No, you get to live."

"Funny." The kid performed the perfect eye roll. "Fine, do I at least get to stay or am I cramping your style?"

"Don't push it."

But she didn't sense any tension. They weren't fighting. They were discussing. Gabe handled most of it with a firm hand and a bit of humor, something that must have felt familiar to Brandon because he didn't balk. Didn't make a scene. Natalie found the whole thing fascinating . . . except for the part where they talked about her and she still wasn't wearing any underwear.

"Let me go make a call about needing a ride back tomorrow." Brandon rounded the edge of the counter then stopped before smiling at her. "Nice meeting you."

"You, too." Strangely, she meant it. The insight into Gabe's home life provided a pretty big window into Gabe, the man. She scowled at him anyway.

He peeked at her over the rim of his mug. "What's that look?"

"You're kidding, right?" This guy could win an award for subterfuge.

Gabe shrugged. "*You* assumed he was younger."

Oh, no. She was not letting him bury the truth under a pile of that crap. "You let me think that."

"In my defense, you've only known I even have a son for about six days. It's not like I've been hiding his identity from you for years."

"Is that really the argument you're going with?"

"You seemed determined to think the worst of me."

Fair enough, but still. "I wonder why."

"It ticked me off that you thought I could abandon my kid."

"Apparently, I was wrong." And the relief nearly crushed her. Leaving Brandon off somewhere was the one piece of Gabe's personality that didn't fit. Now she knew why.

Gabe set his mug down against the counter with a click. He followed Brandon's route and rounded the long counter. Stopped when he got right in front of her. "So, that's Brandon."

And she liked him. Liked the kid and liked the dad. Too much. "Not a little kid."

Gabe shook his head. "Not little at all."

"You know what I think?"

His eyes narrowed. "I'm afraid to ask."

It was the one thought that kept running through her head. Seeing Brandon and Gabe together. Walking through this house. "Your brother Rick is an asshole."

A smile broke across Gabe's face. "That deserves breakfast." He tilted his head to the side. "Oatmeal?"

That was enough to kill her hunger. "Never again."

"I knew I liked you."

EIGHTEEN

Gabe adjusted the photos on the fireplace mantel. No question Natalie had been looking through them. He'd watched her earlier from his position on the stairs. She'd pick one up and smile, then move on to the next. Sometimes she'd trace a finger over something she saw in a picture.

It struck him as such a private moment that he didn't intrude. True, the photos documented his life with Brandon, but he understood that for someone who knew so little about true family ties, the photos might mean even more.

Somewhere after a shower and a long lunch where Brandon regaled them with campus stories, some of which made Gabe want to call the administration or at least stop payment on the tuition check, maybe get in touch with a few parents, she slipped away. He knew she needed alone time and gave it to her. Now he wanted to know where she'd run off to. Maybe fit in a round or two of touching.

"So, you brought a woman home." Brandon made the comment as he slumped down on the oversized sectional. He put his feet up on the coffee table and knocked the remote to the floor.

From experience Gabe knew it would sit there until Christmas unless he picked it up. His kid was smart but could be so lazy.

"Careful," he said, both about the coffee table and the subject matter.

"What?" Brandon shrugged but overplayed it a bit. "I'm just saying."

"Right." Not one to ignore a father-son talk when the kid looked for one, Gabe sat down on the end of the couch and waited.

"It's not normal. You know, for you."

There it was. Didn't take Brandon long to weigh in on his private life. Gabe guessed he'd already texted Andy to ask about Natalie. That's how the communication string worked in the house. Nothing stayed private for long within the inner circle. "I've been with women, Brandon. You do understand how you got here, right? We've had that talk."

Brandon's smile fell. "I'm good on the safe sex chat. Please don't launch into it again."

But it was so much fun to see the kid's face. "You sure?"

"I'm talking about the fact that you brought a woman to our house. That never happens unless it's a woman from work and it's only for a work thing."

Gabe toyed with how much to say. He wanted to be honest but not scare his son. They'd been playing this game since he was a kid. First came deployments then in-the-field assignments. Finally Gabe transitioned to the role of boss and kept to the administrative side, mostly for Brandon's sake.

"We had some trouble on the assignment." Compared to others, this one had gone well, but there were issues.

Brandon sat up straighter. "Are you okay?"

"I'm good. I promise." Gabe reached across the top of the

couch and let his hand rest near Brandon's shoulder. "You know these days I mostly sit at a desk. No danger there."

Seemingly satisfied with that explanation, interest flared in Brandon's eyes again. He liked the strategy part of the job. Putting pieces together. He'd gone to school to become an engineer but could switch at any time. "Well, what happened?"

"Your uncle showed up."

Brandon groaned as he dropped his head back against the cushions. "Rick, right?"

Gabe blamed himself for that reaction. There was no good way to hide the internal fighting from Brandon. He'd been there when Rick left a holiday dinner early and under a cloak of silence. He knew when Rick stopped coming around and from the heated phone calls. Gabe finally had to fess up that they had a disagreement and were trying to work through it.

Not that Brandon accepted that excuse or liked it, but he did keep his distance from Rick, as if trying not to take sides. And how ironic was that.

"Yeah, the point is our safe house location was compromised." The comment sufficed to give Brandon the flavor. Gabe decided he didn't need to know everything.

Brandon smiled. "She really is a client?"

Leave it to him to focus on the important part of what he'd learned today. "Yes."

"But you're sleeping with her."

Gabe tried to be open with his kid about sex. He was desperate for Brandon not to make the same mistakes he did and grow up too early. Still, even Gabe squirmed when the talk of his personal sex life hit the table. Happily, it didn't happen all that often. "Yes, and before you say it, I know that's not normal for me."

"Right." Brandon hummed. "You like her."

Talk about drilling down to the heart of the issue. "When do you go back to school?"

"She's pretty."

"Yeah, I know." He did have eyes and had a very hard time keeping them off her.

"Like *whoa* and *damn* pretty."

The kid had good taste. "I get it, Brandon."

"She watches you. You watch her."

"You make us sound weird." But Gabe liked the idea of the attraction running both ways.

At first he figured he was convenient for her. She needed to gain control and burn off some energy. He was right there when no one else was and happy to volunteer. But somewhere along the line whatever arced between them morphed into something else. He could feel her watch him when they were back in the cabin. He planned to make it clear she could watch, touch, do anything she wanted, as soon as Brandon went back to the dorm.

Maybe that way he could keep whatever sparked between them on a sex-only level. He'd been trying since day one, before he ever touched her to get there and failed. He'd known back then that a certain energy hummed between them. He didn't want it to mean anything, yet here she was. Sitting in his house. Meeting his kid. Knowing about his past and about things no one else knew.

She had his trust. He had no idea when or how it happened but it all felt pretty committed to him. He hoped to figure out why as the days went on.

"Grown-ups are weird. All old and boring." Brandon tapped the toes of his sneakers together in a clapping sound.

"Happy we settled that."

"I'm just saying that if you brought her here she means something to you. She's not just some woman." Brandon stopped staring at the black screen of the turned-off television and looked at Gabe. "Right?"

Gabe refused to answer that one because the potential answer was starting to scare the shit out of him. "That psychology class is paying off."

"And if she means something, that's okay with me. It's great, actually." The kid's devilish smile came back. "Good to see you getting a little action."

"Honestly, Brandon." Gabe rubbed a hand in Brandon's hair and ignored the slick of gel that now stuck to his fingers. At least he'd moved on from the rancid-smelling aftershave or whatever it was that had followed him senior year in a tiny cloud.

Brandon stood up. "I'll let you go find her."

"Where is she?"

"Last I saw she was wandering in the backyard, sticking close to the house like I assume you trained her to do."

"You just know everything today." But Gabe appreciated the information. It would cut down on his hunting for her.

Brandon spun around and his sneakers squeaked against the hardwood floor. "One more thing."

Gabe braced for whatever came next. With Brandon, the leaps of logic and conversation topics could be big. "Yeah?"

"Uncle Rick keeps texting."

Gabe felt everything inside him fall. Just crash inward until he consisted of a hollowed-out pile of nothing. "Okay."

"He says he wants to come to Charlottesville and take me to dinner." Brandon put his hands up before he even finished the sentence. "I know you guys are still fighting and thought maybe you wouldn't want me to."

Gabe wanted to shout no, but he choked the words back. This should be about what Brandon needed. "Do you want to see him?"

"I do miss him. You and Uncle Andy suck at fishing." He wiggled his eyebrows.

Gabe wondered for about the thousandth time in his life how he got so lucky with this kid. Everything should have gone wrong. They were set up to fail. Now they just had to survive Rick's admission.

"Then we'll make it happen." It hurt to say the words, but Gabe spit them out.

"Thanks, Dad." Brandon slipped the phone out of his back pocket and started punching in something as he left the room.

Yeah, that's what dads did, biological or not. They coped. Gabe just wished it wasn't so damn hard.

He suddenly needed to find Natalie.

"This place is pretty spectacular. I've only ever lived in condos." Natalie made the comment as she closed the French doors and stepped back inside the great room after looking out over the rolling hills and lush green lawn that stretched as far as she could see. She glanced up, took in Gabe's drawn face and came to a halt. "What's wrong?"

He plastered a fake smile on his face and came around the sectional to meet her halfway into the room. "Nothing."

That he thought he could still fool her, or that he needed to, frustrated her a bit. She got self-protection, but they'd shared so many secrets that they had to be past some of the basic stuff.

"Something." She put a hand on his chest. Let it trail down until it rested on the top of his jeans.

His hands came up to rest on her waist. "Rick has been in contact with Brandon."

Rick wasn't even in the room and he changed the mood to

something dreary. The guy needed to back off. She wished she was in a position to tell him. Frankly, if he were standing here she would. Forget protocol and manners. He acted like an ass and deserved to be treated like one.

Since Gabe didn't seem to be in the mood for an it's-not-that-bad speech, since it clearly was, she went with reason. "Doesn't that violate your informal agreement that he not talk to Brandon directly about what's going on?"

She could have Bast there in ten minutes to straighten it all out. Maybe not that fast, but he'd hammer through a real deal. The problem was, no matter how she turned this problem over in her head, at some point Gabe was going to have to concede to the DNA test. He could only run from the truth, whatever it was, for so long.

"Rick isn't exactly one to follow the rules," Gabe said.

He managed to say it in a nice way, so she followed his example. "Apparently he's not a boundaries type of guy."

Gabe exhaled and his head fell forward. He rested it against her cheek and just stood there. "He wants a DNA test, but I guess you figured that out."

"Seemed logical under the circumstances." She caressed his cheek because nothing she could say would bring any comfort.

"He wants it now and has given me a deadline to agree. I have a week or two left. He promised not to bring Brandon into this directly right now, but who knows."

She hesitated for a few beats before talking again. "You should be the one to tell him."

Gabe lifted his head and looked at her with eyes filled with pain. "That's not a conversation I ever want to have."

She felt sick for him. His love for Brandon, biological or not, shone throughout the entire house. She couldn't walk into a room or down a hallway without seeing a reminder of some piece of family history. Photos from rafting trips and baseball games. Little Brandon and Brandon as he was now. The photos showed so much.

But photos were about memories, and they had a real-life crisis to deal with. She brushed a hand over Gabe's hair. "What are you going to do?"

"Let it happen. Maybe try to control the conversation a bit. Brandon wants to see him."

She'd meant the DNA test, but he clearly was talking about a meeting between Rick and Brandon. No question he wasn't ready to deal with the big picture yet. "That sounds like a nightmare."

Gabe lifted his head then. Sadness vibrated through him and tugged at the corner of his eyes. "That's what all of this is, Nat."

"That boy loves you." She knew that. Could tell from ten minutes with the kid.

"I know."

At least he had that. She'd been raised without any sense of love. She envied Gabe for his certainty even as she worried about the weeks ahead and how he would get through them. "You aren't going to lose him."

Gabe exhaled as his expression visibly changed. It was as if he pulled himself back from the emotional abyss. "Hey, we're supposed to be worrying about your safety."

She glanced out the glass door then looked around the comfortable room. "I feel pretty calm here."

"Me, too." His hands slid a little lower, past her waist. "Bought the land when the only thing here was a falling-down shack of a two-bedroom cabin."

"Ah, now I see where I got that idea."

"We struggled and built it up."

She tried to imagine those years and couldn't. The strength it must have taken. The perseverance. She admired him so much, but another emotion snuck in. One that had her feeling light from the inside out. She didn't analyze it and vowed to ignore it. Underneath all the gruffness he was a good guy. That's what she was reacting to. Nothing more. Well, that and great sex.

"How exactly did you handle a baby when you were barely an adult yourself?" She'd once decided not to get a cat for fear she'd forget to feed the thing.

"That's just it. Rick and Andy helped. It was a family effort. Neighbors stepped up. The Army had some programs that provided assistance. We somehow made it through without me dropping him or forgetting him at school one day."

Which only made Rick's deception and demands now more painful. She got it. "And now that the hard part is done, Rick wants to swoop in and play dad."

"That's how I see it." Gabe nodded. "He got injured, took a shot to the back that should have paralyzed him, and came out of rehab with this need to be closer to Brandon."

She could see the entire scene playing out. "He had an epiphany."

"You'd think that would be a good thing." Gabe groaned. "Hell, maybe it was for him. I don't know."

She slipped her hands up his chest and around his neck. Laid her head against his shoulder and smiled at the sound of the strong heartbeat thundering under her ear. "Let's just stand here."

He rested his chin on top of her head. Kissed her hair. "And do what?"

"For the first time in my life, nothing. I guess I should get used to it." But she didn't feel sad or upset. She'd actually found a sense of peace. In his arms, in this place.

They swayed in time to whatever music must have been playing in his head. "You're going to find your way."

This time she didn't rush to deny the claim. She'd been so programmed to fire back a snotty response that it had become routine, but with him it all fell away. "You did."

"We all do."

"We'll have to see what the next few days bring." She knew reality would come crashing in. She'd have to make decisions. They'd have to figure out if she'd finally gotten to the point where she was safe to move on. Then she'd have to force herself to do that.

"While we—"

"Wait." She lifted her head and looked up at him. "Are you about to mention your bed?"

"Hell, yeah."

She almost laughed at his enthusiasm. "Your son is around here somewhere."

"When he leaves tomorrow, you're mine."

She didn't hate the idea. "Deal."

NINETEEN

Gabe somehow made it through the day without jumping on top of her. He wasn't a fucking animal but sometimes he felt like one around her. She listened, she held on to him. His blood raced.

He'd almost thrown Brandon in the car and drove him back early. Well, he thought about it. He'd never actually do it, but it was the first time in his life the idea tempted him. The two cold showers today helped a little to take the edge off. He was still recovering from the one he tried after they all sat around watching an adventure movie. For some reason just having her next to him on the couch, so close with their legs touching, did it for him now.

Maybe he was an animal after all.

Night had fallen and Brandon ventured off to his room to spend some quality time with his computer. Gabe decided he didn't want to know what that meant. In the old days he'd use the time to play video games, but the kid was old enough to find and watch all kinds of porn now. Gabe just pretended he didn't.

He'd reset the property alarm and checked every door. Standing in the middle of his bedroom, he found only one thing missing—Natalie. He had a feeling he knew what was happening.

Throwing on a T-shirt to go with his faded jeans, he stalked down the hall. Past Brandon's door and the steady thump of the bass from some song he couldn't recognize. Kept going until he got to the room at the end of the hall. The guestroom Andy didn't use. The one actually for guests, which meant no one ever stayed in there.

Gabe knocked once then threw open the door. He caught Natalie in mid-squeal as she made up the bed. He asked anyway. "What are you doing?"

She glared at him as she held a folded sheet to her chest. "Getting ready for bed."

She still had her clothes on. She'd only managed to wrestle the bottom sheet on. There was still hope he could turn this around.

"Not in here." Gabe didn't bother lowering his voice. He wasn't really in the mood for this or for hiding. He was a grown-ass man and he paid the mortgage on the place. He got to say who slept in which room, and she was with him.

"Excuse me?"

She could save the indignation and grumpy tone. They'd moved on from that, at least he hoped so. "You're sleeping with me."

She got up on her toes and looked like she was trying to peek around him. "Close the door."

He ignored the order and kept staring. "What?"

"What do you mean *what*?" She shifted around him and closed the door for him.

He thought that amounted to a waste of energy since they'd be leaving the room soon. Or that was the plan. Since they clearly had a communications problem he was no longer so sure. "I have a big bed. It will fit us both."

The argument seemed reasonable enough to him. He didn't

even understand why they were having it. She'd become a bit shy. Okay, he could adjust to that. For now. No screaming. No tying to the bedpost. All that could wait. Holding her, touching her. Nope, he wanted that back on the agenda immediately.

"Your son is right there." She pointed in the general direction of the hallway behind him.

"So this is a proximity issue?"

"You can't be this clueless."

Apparently he could be. "He knows we're having sex."

She dumped the sheet on the bed. "That doesn't mean we need to rub his nose in it."

"I'm not sure you're using the right metaphor, or whatever that is."

She actually growled. Made a rumbling sound and sounded ready to launch a smackdown. "My point is that we can wait until he's gone."

Damn kid. "No."

"Whatever happened to me getting the choice?" She laid it out there then raised an eyebrow at him.

That shot landed. Gabe could feel it all the way to his gut. "That's not fair."

She shrugged as she held her hands out to the sides. "Your words."

If she wanted to fight dirty he would join. She could not win this game. Not against him. "Fine, we'll stay in here."

The amusement left her face. "You're not getting this."

Oh, he absolutely was. He stepped up to the bed and tucked the end corners in. Snapped open the sheet she'd left in a pile and threw that over the mattress. "There."

Admittedly it was not the most inviting bed he'd ever seen, but it had a mattress. Unlike the cabin, it also had an inch of breathing room around it. Even being the smallest bedroom, this one measured sixteen by sixteen. Hardly small, and the perfect size for what he had in mind.

"Go back to your big bed." She whispered the comment, but those sexy eyes widened.

He had her intrigued. Exactly as he wanted.

He kicked off his shoes and sprawled across the bed on his side then patted the open space in front of him. "Have a seat."

She took a step closer. Her knees actually knocked against the side of the mattress now. "Your son will hear us."

Brandon wore headphones half the time and kept his music cranked up to deafening levels, so Gabe doubted it. Still, if she needed the reassurance, he'd reluctantly give it to her. "We're not going to have sex."

"No?" She almost sounded disappointed.

That made two of them. "We're going to sit and then I'm going to head back to my big bed for a lonely night of sleep."

"You poor thing." The tone suggested she thought he needed to get a clue.

He refused to take the bait. She was an expert at sidelining them into a conversation he didn't want to have. One that postponed what he actually wanted to do with her. "I know, right?"

"You could go now."

"Oh, I don't think so." He reached out and ran a hand down her outer thigh. Felt her lean in, just a bit, to his touch.

"What are you planning?"

Now who was clueless? Rather than keep her guessing or risk having her be wrong, he gave her a pretty big hint. "It involves striping your pants off and touching and licking you until you come."

Her knees buckled, but the mattress stopped her fall. "That's sex."

"Don't have a condom on me." He hadn't put one in this pair of jeans. Didn't think he needed to since he expected her to follow him back to the bedroom. Didn't look like that was going to happen, so he went with improvisation.

"That's not the test."

He had no idea what she was talking about, so he kept on his subject. "There's only one thing we need to worry about."

"What?" She rested a knee on the bed.

He decided to take that as a good sign. Still, he waited. She needed to come to him. Once she raised the *I decide* question, there was no way he was moving until she did. "You're a screamer."

She shook her head. Looked half ready to slap him. "Shut up."

"I'm not lying. You'll need to cover your mouth or yell into a pillow."

"Maybe you won't excite me enough to scream." She had both knees on the bed now as she sat back, just inches away from him.

"Challenge accepted." He reached out and touched her hand. Laced her fingers through his and gave a little tug.

She tumbled onto the mattress then turned around until she lay down beside him. "I didn't mean—"

He cut off the comment with a kiss. His lips met hers, and everything else fell away. His resistance shattered. When he felt her hands slide up his back he knew hers had as well.

In all the rolling her shirt had balled up around her midsection, treating him to a view of her stomach. He flattened his palm against her warm skin. "Still think you won't like this?"

Her breath caught on a sharp inhale. "I know I will."

"Then it's your job to stay quiet." He undid the button and zipper of her jeans and slipped his hand inside.

"You're awful." But her eyes glazed over and she relaxed into him.

"Do you want me to stop?" He needed to know. Had to hear her say it.

She pressed her hand against his through her clothes. "No."

He could feel the heat pouring off her. "I'm thinking you mean that."

"Enough talk." She pulled his head down for another kiss. This one lingered as her lips danced over his. When he opened his mouth and deepened the touch, she fell back against the mattress and dragged him on top of her.

Tonight was for her. The touching, the tasting—he would love it all, but this was about her pleasure. He plunged his hand deeper into her pants, past her underwear to skin. His fingers went to work, preparing her body for his mouth.

He stared down at her. Brushed the hair off her cheek. "I like a woman who knows her mind."

She shifted her legs. "That is not the part I'm thinking with right now."

Green light. That was all the encouragement he needed.

He slid down her body, taking her jeans with him. He left the underwear in place because he wanted to strip that off with his teeth. When he settled again between her legs, that familiar scent hit him. This was not all he wanted tonight but he wasn't about to complain.

He lowered his head and nipped at the front of the material covering her. Her body jerked at the contact and her hands knotted in the loose sheet.

She didn't make a sound, but he teased her anyway. "Quiet."

She pressed her heels into the mattress. "Do it."

He hadn't even touched her yet. Not really. He skimmed his fingertips over the elastic band by her leg then caught it between his teeth. With a slow and steady pull he stripped them off her. Over her and down to the tops of her legs. He had to sit up, put her legs together, to peel them off.

When he was done he opened her legs wide again. The back of her hand covered her mouth.

Now he'd make her scream.

His fingers touched her, and her back arched. He dropped down on his elbows and placed a kiss on the very center of her as his fingers slipped inside. No sound ever came from her but she grabbed a pillow. He sensed she would not lose this challenge. It didn't matter, since in his mind he'd already won.

He'd gotten the girl.

An hour later Natalie walked around the house. She knew this was a bad idea. Like, on a scale of one to ten, it ranked as a hundred on the do-not-do-this side. Still, she had to help and this was the only way. A backdoor way of finding out.

Gabe insisted on control and depended on family. As a third party she could step in. Call in a few favors through Eli and Wade. Get the answer that plagued them all.

The plan was simple. She and her teams had done versions for years when it came time to collect blackmail material. She'd snagged an extra toothbrush from the hall closet. The thing had more supplies than some pharmacies. After a quick trip downstairs, she had the rest of what she needed for tonight's adventure. The plastic bags and the will to follow through.

Gabe would be furious. She knew without asking him, not that she wanted to ask. He'd see this as an interference. But, really, she took this risk for him. For his family. The ripping and tearing wouldn't stop until they had answers. Pretending the problem didn't exist or that it would go away hadn't worked. It was time to face it head-on.

In her life she'd always found knowing was better than not knowing. At least people could move forward.

With quiet steps she opened the door to the bathroom off the bedroom Gabe said Andy sometimes used when he stayed there.

This room and Brandon's shared the same bath. Peeking through from one door to the other, she could see the one to Brandon's room stayed open a crack. Her gaze zoomed past the opening to the lump in his bed. Thanks to the darkness she couldn't make out much else.

Careful not to make noise or drop anything, she reached across the counter of the double sink. Her gaze stayed locked on the unmoving figure asleep in the bedroom, but she kept going. She snagged the toothbrush and dropped it in a plastic bag, replacing it with the new one. Same color and same type. She hoped he didn't figure it out.

Sneaking back around the corner she made it into the empty bedroom without getting caught or having alarms flashing or sirens roaring. She rested her back against the nearest wall and let out a quiet sigh as she struggled to bring her breathing back under control.

She was partially done. With Brandon headed back to school tomorrow, she'd had a relatively small window within which to act when it came to getting something with his DNA. Collecting Gabe's would be much easier.

Now to get back to her bedroom without being seen. She had no idea what kind of security Gabe had in the house. Well, some idea. She'd staked out the place earlier, checking for cameras and such. She knew what she could see, but he would be just paranoid enough to own some new technology that she couldn't even pick out when looking at it.

She slid into the hallway and tiptoed back down toward her room. Right as her hand touched the doorknob she heard a sound. Turning around, she watched as Gabe's door swung open.

With only seconds to make a decision, she pitched the closed bag into her room, hoping it landed somewhere easy for her to find and hard for Gabe to see. Frozen by the soft creak of the hinges, she stood there. Gabe appeared in the opening. Even in the low light from the rooms behind each of them she could make out his frown.

He took a few steps and got closer. That's when she realized he wore only a pair of boxer briefs, and those were on kind of sideways with the seam running at an odd angle. The man clearly slept naked and rushed to put something on.

"Why are you up?" she asked, dreading what he might say.

"I heard a noise." He rubbed his head. "Why are you walking around?"

She thought through every possible answer and decided to go with the true one. "I was hoping the offer to share that big bed was still open."

She'd grown accustomed to sleeping by his side, to the noises he made. Being in a strange house, in a strange room had her on edge. So did her mystery project.

But he didn't invite her in. Instead, he stood there watching her.

Finally, he held out his hand. "You should consider it a standing invitation."

She was down the hall and by his side in two seconds. Forget the DNA test she planned to run and all the other barriers in their way. Forget climbing into bed without him. After that comment she doubted she'd ever be able to sleep again.

TWENTY

Andy walked into his office in the morning and came to a stop. Almost dropped his beloved coffee and the briefing file in his hand. There sat Rick, in the big chair with his feet up on the desk and arms folded behind his head. It was enough to make a guy want to reach for his gun. Andy refrained, but he did plan on firing someone for this. No one got in here without his permission, and Rick certainly did not have permission.

"Move." The tone worked, because as soon as Andy barked out the word, Rick's feet dropped to the floor. It took another minute and some glaring to get him up and on the right side of the desk.

Rick didn't bother to sit down in the visitor's chair. Just hovered at the edge of Andy's desk. "As suspected, they left Montana."

"And good morning to you." Andy set his cup down. A guy should have at least five minutes of breathing room in the office before dealing with yelling. He planned to institute that rule right after he finished with the firing.

"They took off."

So much for pleasant conversation. Since he knew who the "they" were and wanted this over before it became a scene, Andy answered. "Their plane crashed . . . or don't you watch the news?"

"The subterfuge angle. Damn it, Gabe." Rick started pacing. More like walking in circles as he muttered under his breath.

"He's not even here and you're swearing at him."

This was new. Not the anger. Andy had witnessed more than enough of that in the MacIntosh family over the years. Something else plagued Rick. His normal detachment slipped.

"They're definitely together. Very cozy," Rick said, as he massaged his temples then stared at the floor.

Not a surprise to Andy. He'd seen the way Gabe looked at her, the way Natalie looked back. Heated and a bit uncomfortable to anyone watching, so Andy had tried not to. Just accepted that Gabe felt more than protective toward Natalie. But who knew what the hell was going on in Rick's head. "Does that piss you off?"

He stopped stomping around and shot Andy a confused glance. "Why would it?"

The easy answer proved to be a little too easy in this case, so Andy let it drop. "Honestly, I've given up trying to read you."

"I cared about her, you know."

It took Andy's brain a second to catch up. When he did the emotional shields slammed down and his hands came up. "No way."

Rick frowned. "What?"

The last thing—absolute fucking last—Andy wanted to hear right now was some convoluted explanation for why Rick thought it made sense for him to poach from Gabe all those years ago. "You are not unloading on me. Whatever you have to say about Gabe's ex, you say it to him."

"I didn't mean for it to happen."

Hell, no. Andy sat back in his chair to keep from coming up out of it swinging. "Your dick just slipped? Admittedly, I don't date women, but I know how the body parts function."

"You're not funny."

He wasn't trying to be. Andy wanted, no needed, for Rick to understand how his words made it all worse. Maybe then he'd stop with the same tired refrain and take some responsibility. "And you can't sell this as a mistake."

"I don't see Brandon that way." Rick's voice flattened and his mouth pulled tight at the edges. While he fought and engaged in what amounted to just the newest round of posturing, he looked different. Haggard. Exhausted, as if he aged in rapid acceleration the more he stood there.

Andy refused to give credence to any of it. "Truth is you went after Gabe's girlfriend, slept with her, lied to him and created a mess. You did that. Not him."

"I didn't force her."

As if that was even up for debate. Andy knew where to place the blame, firmly on Linda and Rick. Both of them. Together, their actions created the black hole that sucked Gabe in. "Is that really your defense for screwing over your brother?"

"I'm stepping up and helping now. Isn't that what you want to hear?" Rick came to the edge of the desk. Something new moved into his expression. A note of desperation, maybe?

Andy leveled the one thing that stood a chance at mending the breach. "Then drop the talk about the DNA test."

"Would you?"

That one was too easy. "I would never be in this position."

"Because you're gay."

Rick could really be a clueless jackass sometimes. Andy did

not love this side of his big brother. Those blinders. The denial. "Because I would never go out of my way to hurt Gabe."

Rick shook his head. "It wasn't like that."

"It looks exactly like that, or are you trying to say you were a twenty-something in love with a seventeen-year-old?" Andy picked up the file on the fake crash aftermath and started blindly paging through. He'd had enough of this conversation. Enough personal stuff for seven o'clock in the morning.

"I have an appointment with my clients." Rick leaned against the side of Andy's desk, trapping a short stack of files under his thigh. "About this situation."

This he could handle. Andy lowered the file to glance at Rick and gauge his sincerity. "You mean with the CIA assholes tracking Natalie."

"I never actually admitted that was happening." He shrugged. "Deniability."

Right. There were limits to what he could share. Andy got it. He worked in this area as well, but he didn't pretend to be stupid about reality. "Didn't have to."

"I'm trying to clear this up so she can get on with her life." Rick's voice dipped low and what little emotion remained in it vanished. "If that includes Gabe, fine."

That was the least sounding "fine" Andy had ever heard. "You don't sound too excited about that."

"Do you think she's his type?" Rick winced as if the words tasted bad in his mouth. "Linda was quiet and sweet."

Talk about revisionist history. Andy had to bite back the smart-ass comment on his tongue. "And cheated on him."

"Natalie is kind of . . ."

"No." He shut this down. Had to, because if Gabe came back

and heard Rick bad-mouthing Natalie, that battle they'd been promising each other would happen. Life would break out into a holy war with no survivors. "You might want to choose your words carefully."

"Now you're her defender, too?"

"I like her." Andy thought about the words as he said them. They were true. Natalie had been dealt a shitty hand all around. She could have hid and played the victim but never did. He could see where Gabe might find that interesting.

"Why?"

"She's tough and smart. She won't take Gabe's shit and can handle his moods and work demands." Simple words but they worked here. "She's not my type, of course, but I can appreciate a hot woman when I see one."

"He needs someone who isn't so damn difficult."

That sounded exactly wrong to Andy. "See, it's that type of comment that makes me think you don't know Gabe all that well anymore."

"Oh, really?" Rick stood up, full battle stance and sharp tone back in place.

Whatever had weighed him down when he walked into the office seemed to be gone. Andy hoped Rick hadn't released the guilt, because he deserved to wallow in it a bit longer. He also owed Gabe an apology and Brandon a life that didn't include doubts and huge changes.

But Andy went with the most obvious point, the one he thought he could sell. "What our brother needs is a challenge, someone who equals him. Pushes him."

"Sounds exhausting to me."

"And I bet he likes that, too." Not that Andy wanted to spend one second thinking about what Gabe and Natalie did together in that department.

"What happened to the whole loner act?"

"Maybe he was just waiting for the right woman to wander along." Worked as good as any explanation, but the truth probably had more to do with the work and the energy needed to raise Brandon alone and in safety.

Rick actually sneered. "Oh, come on."

The men in this family needed some work on the romance front. Gabe was wounded and pretending not to be. Rick was . . . who the hell knew. And Andy had to admit that he still had a thing for a guy who had moved on. *Fucking Eli.*

"I guess we'll know soon enough," Andy said, because that was easier than launching into a statement about how they all sucked at this.

"Which brings me back to my point." With each short sentence Rick banged his fist against the corner of the desk. "The men I work for do not like being threatened. Your fake plane crash worked to the extent that it convinced some she wasn't looking to be out in the open, causing trouble. Others remain skeptical. Those two factions are fighting it out right now."

"I'm pretty proud of that operation." He'd never staged something so elaborate in so little time. The number of moving pieces was staggering, but the photographs and press coverage impressed him.

"Just knowing Natalie is out there and has damaging information on them is making those last few doubting holdouts twitchy. They should back off but there are contingency plans in place for another course of action."

The men she once worked for continued to underestimate her. Andy had no idea how that was possible. "Do they want her to release the intel?"

"I think they're trying to figure out how to find it before she can. They view this as a race."

No way. But that meant it was up to Rick to convince them otherwise before someone did something really stupid. "You said you were doing this for Gabe."

Rick shrugged. "Yeah, so?"

"Handle it." When Rick just sat there, Andy doled out a bit of truth. "Redemption is a bitch."

Gabe couldn't put his finger on what he enjoyed more, watching Brandon settle in at home and eat everything in sight or the look of horror on Natalie's face as she watched it happen. Either way a feeling of calmness settled over him. This, them together, struck him as right. Not really a guy to seek out or depend on comfort, he appreciated it all the more when it blanketed him without warning.

Natalie inched closer to the opposite side of the counter from Brandon with every mouthful he swallowed. He stood over the sink, not even bothering with a plate as he feasted on a piece of chicken. He held a napkin and ate with a bit less than his usual gusto, so Gabe let it go. He picked his battles, and a chicken leg wasn't one of them.

She put her palms on the edge of the counter and rested a foot on the bottom bar of the stool next to her. The move pulled her slim jeans tight across her ass. Gabe tried not to notice but his gaze kept bouncing. He had eyes and a functioning dick. No way could he ignore the way she looked, all casual and cozy, in his house. Made him extra happy he'd asked for her sizes before hunting down clothes for her for the Montana trip.

"You eat enough for three grown men," she said with more than a little awe in her voice.

Brandon took the time to wipe his face and finish chewing before answering. "You sound like Dad."

"He drinks a gallon of milk every three days." Gabe's grocery budget expanded and groaned every time the kid came home.

Natalie kept frowning. "Maybe we should check him for a tape-worm."

"Wait, what?" Brandon froze as he stood locked in a staring contest with her. "How would you do that?"

"You don't want to know." But Gabe was pretty tempted to explain how it all worked just to see Brandon's face.

Brandon dropped the chicken leg. "Sounds gross. I'll pass."

Damn, he missed his kid. The semester had only started a few months ago, but that didn't matter to Gabe. Not having Brandon around after having him underfoot for so long tugged at him.

He'd thought he'd be the tough dad who appreciated his son's maturity and let that satisfaction be enough. Instead, he'd spent every night of the first week sitting on Brandon's bed glancing around the room. Pathetic stuff but Gabe didn't fight it. Brandon meant everything.

"You sure you don't want me to drive you back to school?" Gabe didn't mind, and Natalie might like the diversion of mindless sightseeing through the countryside and being on the move might be safer for her than being still.

"Nah, my friends are coming through." Brandon didn't even look up as he dropped his backpack on the counter and started loading it with boxes of crackers and protein bars.

Natalie glanced over her shoulder at Gabe. "They come here?"

"No." Not until he checked them out and knew they were safe. None of these kids rose to that level yet.

Brandon headed for the pantry. "Not even close."

"So, we just drop him off on the side of the road somewhere?" That judgment moved back into her voice.

Gabe decided to ignore it. "Tempting, but there's a cabin."

She rolled her eyes. "Of course there is."

Gabe knew she thought about the one in Montana with the homemade water heater, but this was not that. The structure functioned as a guardhouse of sorts but didn't look like one. Two floors and two bedrooms. Where he and Brandon lived while the main house was being built. The same place Andy tried to claim before Gabe set it up as a security feature.

"It sits on a plot of land and looks like that's it. Just the house and some yard." A place with sentimental value. Watching Brandon move around the kitchen, acting as if it were a grocery store, the memories hit Gabe. "We take him there and wait. If everything looks fine, he goes, but he carries a tracker and some other things on him at all times."

Natalie smiled. "How very covert of you."

"You're not the only one with training."

Brandon's hand dropped to his side, the water bottle in his palm all but forgotten as he stared at Natalie. "Wait, you're an Army sniper, too?"

She snorted. "Lord, no."

That seemed like a bit much to Gabe. "I'm going to pretend you didn't sound appalled by that possibility."

"I used to work in intelligence."

Brandon's eyes grew wide and stayed there. "Computers?"

They'd be at this for hours, going round and round. Gabe cut it off with a simple comment. "Spy shit."

"Gabe—"

"Cool." Brandon made the word last for three syllables. A new expression crossed his face. A mix of respect and curiosity.

Gabe couldn't blame his son. He felt the same way every time he looked at her, which was about every two seconds. His usual I've-got-this reserve slipped around her.

Seeing her in the hallway last night had almost done him in. Took every last ounce of control he had not to scoop her up and drop her on his bed. Instead, he went with holding her. The cuddling thing was new to him, but he didn't hate it.

"Brandon learned long ago not to use my job or the jobs of some of our friends and family to impress his friends." Gabe meant it as much as a hint to Natalie as a reminder to Brandon that dads remembered every last thing.

She picked up on something, because she turned back to Brandon with a look of curiosity that rivaled his. "What did you do?"

"Told some people at school," Brandon said with a shrug. "Maybe took one of Dad's guns in to show it off."

Natalie's sharp whistle cut through the room. "I bet that went over well."

And those were memories Gabe preferred not to take out and examine. "Which is why we no longer live in West Virginia and haven't for more than a decade."

Brandon nodded but kept his head down. "Right."

Turned out Gabe wasn't quite ready to let the topic drop. Not while Brandon did all that squirming. "Don't let the hunting crowd fool you, they do not like guns in the classroom. Lots of ticked-off parents in West Virginia. Hours of explaining without really saying anything."

"That happened years ago. Let's move on." Brandon tried to wave it off with a flick of his hand.

Gabe didn't buy that. "It's cute you think it works that way."

"We really take him to this empty cabin and—"

This woman had him justifying everything. Gabe wanted that

part of their relationship to end. "Stop being offended on his behalf. He might act like it, but he wasn't raised by wolves."

Brandon was smiling now. Clearly having the attention shift did wonders for his ego. "Not entirely."

"An older family friend, also Army, lives there and watches the place for me. Brandon only uses it as a meeting place for people he doesn't know that well or is just learning to trust."

"So, at some point you are allowed to bring friends here?" she asked.

Gabe wondered if she knew how insulting some of these comments really were. "It's not a prison."

"It wouldn't be if I had a car." Brandon mumbled the comment loud enough for the next town over to hear.

Natalie sat down hard on the barstool next to her. "Wow, he never stops."

"And this is him on his best behavior."

Her gaze went back and forth between Brandon and Gabe. "Because I'm here?"

"I don't want to mess it up for Dad."

Her attention shot back to Brandon. "What?"

"You."

"We're not dating . . ." Her gaze kept bouncing around and finally landed on Gabe. "Say something."

Since he'd only decided just that second that they actually *were* dating, or the kind of dating people like them did—in the shadows, hot and heated, always together—he wasn't sure what she wanted him to say. "I'm waiting to hear what you come up with next."

"Sex here. You being invited in. You're dating." When Natalie made a strange noise Brandon nodded his head and kept talking. "Hey, I approve. I just don't want to scare you away before Dad can."

Gabe eyed the sack by Brandon's feet. The one previously filled with nothing but dirty clothes now held snacks and what looked like a load of clean laundry. "I wonder if you'll fit in that duffel bag."

"Not after I take the rest of your food."

Gabe didn't fight it. Pay for the food here or at school. Didn't matter to him. "Grab whatever you want."

He was about to help empty the rest of the cabinets when Natalie slipped off the stool and grabbed his arm. Pulled him into the great room, just a few feet away.

"We're not dating," she said in a desperate whisper.

The denial was starting to get annoying. Sure, he would have backed her up just yesterday, but now . . . no. "You sleeping with someone else I don't know about?"

"My life is a mess."

"No question about that." Seemed to be an affliction of almost everyone he knew.

"The plan is to placate the CIA and start over."

The words, however smart and right, grated on his nerves. "Where?"

"I have no idea."

Relief smacked into him. From the wild look in her eyes he got the sense she wasn't lying. She'd planned out so much of her life but now she was winging it. And Natalie was not a winging-it kind of woman.

He knew the changes, the uncertainty, had to be ripping her apart. She had mad skills but no place to use them. She'd served with distinction and was being hounded and followed. The whole thing pissed him off on her behalf.

So did the idea of her panicking and running away. "Then, for now, you'll stay here."

She held up a finger in front of his face. "Not dating."

He folded his hand around it but didn't push the topic. Not yet. "Call it whatever you want, but you're sleeping in my bed tonight."

"You're mighty sure of yourself." But she didn't jerk away from him. If anything, she moved in closer, lowering her voice with each sentence.

No woman had ever wreaked havoc on his senses like this one. She had him thinking things, wanting things. Breaking promises he made long ago to stay unattached.

But one fantasy had been playing in his head almost from the start and it was time to bring it to life. "Let's just say it's time I follow through on that promise to tie you up."

"Your son is right there."

"And he'll be gone tonight." For once Gabe didn't hate the thought of Brandon heading for school. Not when he remembered what waited for him at home. He leaned down and whispered into her ear. "Be ready."

TWENTY-ONE

The man kept his promises.

Stretched out on Gabe's big mattress, Natalie breathed in, letting the last of her worries morph into excitement as Gabe walked around the bed. Naked. He didn't wear a thing. Neither of them did. Except for the red ties in his hands and the soft white sheet underneath her, not a scrap of material threatened to get in their way.

She'd been in this position, arms above her head and legs spread wide, for what felt like an hour. After stripping the clothing off her piece by piece, he positioned her there. Waiting. Then he performed an excruciatingly slow striptease. When the last of his clothes hit the floor she almost jackknifed off the bed to get to him but she clamped down and waited. The tension rose, and her stomach churned with each passing minute.

Those long, lean thigh muscles brought him around to her side of the bed. Her gaze traveled over the flat stomach to his broad chest and the sprinkling of dark hair there. Up she continued, to his bulging biceps, then farther until she met him gaze for gaze. The intensity in his dark eyes nearly had her turning away. But she couldn't. Wanting him, needing him, entwined until she craved the touch of his hands and mouth.

He had her wound up, fighting against her own shaky control. She wanted to move, to squirm, but she stayed still. Every cell waited for his next move. Even the air in the oversized room felt thick. The overstuffed couch, the soothing medium blue walls. She ignored it all and focused on him. The one man whose memory danced in her head from the first minute they met.

At first, months ago, he'd said very little, almost nothing, as his gaze followed her. She'd pretended he repelled her and tried to boss him around. Insisted she didn't need his protection and would be fine on her own. But everything about him, even from that very first day, intrigued her. Made her want to know more.

All that strength. The command he held over his body. His competence. The scruffy beard that drove her wild. Her hands balled into fists as she forced her arms not to move.

The mattress dipped from his weight as he sat down next to her. Facing her. He put his palm on her stomach and his long fingers spanned her waist. She'd never been considered tiny or petite. She found comfort in being bigger, taller, a little stronger. Victims might have to curl into a ball and mentally disappear to survive. She'd lived that way too long. Killing her father, trying to save her mother. It all smashed together until, in her head, the answer had come to her. She'd lead with a gun. Have weapons training. Never get caught and risk being the victim again.

The system served her well for years. She'd been on the run, maybe not physically but emotionally, her whole damn life. But with Gabe, she felt free. She could be a smartass, throw his words back at him. Sometimes she even went too far and said crappy things he didn't deserve. Despite her flaws and her attitude, he never lost his control. Never struck out. He actually seemed appalled at the thought of doing so.

He gave her a different kind of strength. A feminine one. She knew she held a certain power over him, that she could meet his needs. He didn't deny his attraction to her or try to hide it. Didn't hold back.

And with him she didn't have to pretend either. She could let go. For the first time in a long time, trust.

The warmth from his hand seeped into her skin. Still he didn't move. Every nerve ending inside her jumped to life, begged for more, but he just watched. Held his ties in one hand and touched her with the other.

"You are so fucking beautiful."

Not what she expected him to say but somehow exactly what she needed to hear. "With you."

"It's bound up in how you look, which is so smoking hot my dick gets hard just watching you walk. That voice, so sexy." He shook his head as a small smile played on his lips. "The things you do with that mouth and that brain."

The words battered her defenses. The awe in his voice, the reverent way he touched her, she knew he meant it all. "I never found big men with beards appealing until you."

He ran a hand over his chin. "I let it go a little for this assignment."

"Did you think I wouldn't like it?"

"When I kissed the inside of your thigh that first time, I knew you did."

The memory floated through her head and her stomach dropped. The roller coaster, spinning-out-of-control feeling assailed her. "Any chance you're going to kiss me now?"

The smile lit up his face now. "Much more than that."

Desperation clawed at her. "Do it now."

"You're not in charge, Nat."

The nickname spun through her. He used it and her insides turned to liquid. She had no idea why. "I feel pretty powerful."

"Oh, you are." He lifted his hand and skimmed his palm over one of the red ties. "I plan to harness that."

"But I won't be able to use my hands." He flirted, so she flirted back. She'd do almost anything to keep him close.

"You can still use your mouth." He bent down and brushed his lips over hers then lifted again.

Quick and short but enough to get the excitement revving inside of her. "Gabe, please."

She knew he liked the begging. She'd seen his eyes widen, grow darker, when she pleaded. When her voice dipped low and got all scratchy with need.

He slipped his fingers around her wrist. Touching his thumb to the tip of his forefinger. Encircling her without binding her. Then he lifted her arm, laying it against the fluffy pillows as his finger went to work threading the tie through the thick post at the top of his bed.

Air hiccupped in her lungs as he slid the tie around her wrist. At the first touch of the silkiness she knew she'd misjudged. Not a scrap of material at all. A thin padded cuff with a long length of red curl at each end.

He tightened the bindings. At first her skin pinched but then it eased around her, soft but strong. She tugged and realized unless she planned on tearing she'd have to wait until he released her. A tiny fissure of fear spun through her, but the press of his mouth against her breasts, over the fleshy part before licking her nipple, stamped out the last of her doubts.

With an aching slowness he leaned over her, letting his chest hair tickle her chin as he fastened the other cuff. After he'd attached both, she yanked on her arms. The bindings pulled tight. She curled her fingers over the material and held on.

He eyed her, staring as his gaze moved over her face before dipping for the briefest second to her chest then back up again. "Are you sure you want this?"

With her mind scrambled and her body starting to shift around on the sheet, she said the first word that popped into her head. "Now."

He nodded. "Right now."

She expected him to move down her body, but he didn't. He straddled her chest and leaned forward. His cock stood long and thick, just inches from her mouth. She lifted her head and skimmed her tongue over the tip.

Just as she was about to lie back down, he cradled her head, slipped his fingers around the back of her neck and into her hair. Held her there with one hand. The other moved to the base of his cock. He dragged the tip across her lips. Once, twice.

She didn't play games. Opening her mouth, she took him in deep. Felt the bed dip again as he put more weight on his knees. She kept sucking, taking him deeper. Her mouth worked as his hand supported her. In and out, he pressed against her lips. Slid to the back of her throat. Never too much. Never too hard. Enough to kick up his breathing and make him rock hard.

When she thought he might continue and end in her mouth, he backed away. His lips replaced his cock in a kiss that left her shaky and aching. Hot and wet. Filled with a mix of longing and need. Every emotion bombarded her. Tiny pulses moved through her.

"You are amazing." He whispered the compliment against her mouth.

She tried to talk, wanted to say something, but he moved back to her breasts. One after the other, side to side, licking and sucking. Caressing and cupping. He didn't leave a single inch of her skin untouched.

Her back lifted off the bed and those bindings pulled tight. She heard a creak and knew the bedpost strained under her hold. The sensual torture continued until her breaths came out in gasps. She'd gulp for air then his kiss would pull her under. Just when she thought she couldn't take the cycle one more second, he slid down her body. Moved to her stomach. Caressed the small bump as he covered it in lingering kisses.

She'd never felt so sexy. From the thump of his heartbeat when his chest touched her to the shake in his hands, she felt his need. She did this to him. She took a strong, vibrant man and turned him inside out. Had him crawling all over her for more.

Then his mouth continued its journey. His tongue snaked down. His fingers slipped between her legs and his shoulders settled into the V he created. Her body vibrated, almost hummed, at his touch. And when he pressed his tongue inside her the winding sensation gripping her stomach tightened even more.

Her skin felt too tight. Too sensitive. He'd turned her body into his playground, running his hands and mouth all over her. Bringing her right to the brink then backing off to taste another part of her. If he wanted her clinging to the edge of reason, desperate for him to move over her, he'd succeeded. She wanted the friction.

"Gabe . . ." He licked that spot that made her vision blur and she wanted more. "There."

Her voice dripped with heat. She heard the tone and refused to apologize for it. The room faded away until all she saw was his shoulders and that dark hair. Just as the orgasm started to ripple through her he sat up. Her inner muscles clenched and she tried to reach for him, to bring him back, but the bindings tugged on her wrists.

Sweat collected at the base of her throat as the need to find her release gripped her. "God, Gabe. No."

Then she saw a flash of something and a wrapper fell to the side. A second later he slid in deep and sure, pressing her thighs back close to her chest and opening her even wider. She could feel his hands on her legs and his cock inside her. He said her name and plunged inside her again.

She tried to hold on to every moment, every thought. To savor each blinding touch, but her body betrayed her. Her hips started to buck and her head shifted on the pillow. He had her entire body in motion as he filled her. Trying to fight off the orgasm as long as possible, she dug her fingernails into the cuffs.

Her body trembled as she came. The grabbing sensation inside of her gave way as a sudden warmth washed through her. She couldn't control her breathing or her body. Her lungs strained to the point of bursting. Her heartbeat hammered in her ears. She felt it all as his body leaned forward and a low moan escaped his lips.

She knew he was coming but she couldn't help him. Didn't have the strength to do anything. Spent, her hands fell back against the pillows with her palms open. Her legs curled around him but she could barely feel his skin. Her body had turned to mush beneath him.

She lay there, gasping. When she turned her head to the side, the room came back into focus. The picture of Gabe and Brandon on the end of the dresser. Gabe smiling and so proud. The big wall mirror where she could have stolen peeks of him during their lovemaking before she lost the ability to think. It all registered, slow at first but then with greater clarity.

Gabe's hot breath blew across her collarbone. His weight pressed her deeper into the mattress but she didn't care. It anchored her. Filled her with an odd sense of security.

"Holy shit." He mumbled the words against her skin.

She couldn't help but laugh. Her body still tingled from the joint caress of his mouth and tongue. He'd been gentle at times and so determined at others. His hands had readied her until every cell begged for release. And when that release came . . . damn.

"You are a man of your word." She could barely get the words out because her breathing refused to return to normal.

He lifted his head then. Balanced his elbow against the bed and pushed up a bit. "And you are pure fire."

From him it sounded sweet. She was about to tell him that when he reached up and massaged her tight arm muscles. Feeling came back in bursts, like being poked with tiny needles. She gasped from the shock as he untied her arms and lowered them to drape over him.

His brow wrinkled. "You sore?"

She rubbed a hand over her opposite wrist then smoothed out the lines on his forehead. "Are you asking about my arms?"

His eyes roamed a little then. "I was, but now I want to know about all of you. You okay?"

He couldn't think he hurt her. That never happened and she would never pretend he did. "I'm great."

She meant that. He gave her so much. Treated her both as precious and as an equal. He had her head spinning and her thoughts jumbled. She wasn't sure what to say or how to handle the rest of her life but she knew, with absolutely certainty, she did not want to leave him yet.

"Are you planning to take me to another safe house?"

"We're staying here."

He didn't say "together," but she heard the word anyway. Couldn't believe she filled it in. That the panic stayed away. For some reason she needed him to know. "I was hoping you'd say that."

His finger traced the line of her jaw. "You're safe here."

The words he didn't say kept playing in her mind. He knew about her father. Understood that she'd never been really safe.

"I trust you." She delivered the truth with more than a little shock.

His eyes closed for a second. When he opened them again they were clear and matched his grin. "Thank you."

The perfect response. Not a surprise he knew what to say. He always seemed to. He hit life head-on and fought for what he wanted. The only bump to his peace was this Rick issue, and it loomed large. She wanted nothing more than to hand him an answer so he could move forward. His needs meant more than her own. Her life carried on in a confusing mess, not knowing what came next. But he deserved to know.

She brushed her fingertips across the line of his shoulders. "Would it be possible to arrange a meeting with Eli?"

"For what?"

"Lawyer stuff. He can pass messages to Bast for me."

"About taking off?"

"No." The thought of that sent bile rushing up the back of her throat. "You said I can stay, and I'm going to."

"Good." Gabe hesitated for a second then nodded. "Eli can come here. He understands safety protocols."

"Not here." For some reason the idea of breaching that line had anxiety swelling inside her. Gabe deserved his sanctuary. She didn't want to take that away. They could use that cabin or somewhere else. "Don't change your life for me."

"Maybe I think you're worth the effort."

No one had ever found her to be worth the effort. "I'm not looking to make your life difficult."

"You're staying here. With me." Gabe placed a kiss on the tip of her nose. "Andy can get in touch with Eli."

She knew the history. Talking to Eli involved Andy, which

meant her deception moved out in circles, swallowing up the very people she wanted to protect. "Is that a good idea?"

"This is about what you need." When she started to protest, Gabe put a finger over her lips. "You come first."

Every word he said tied them tighter together. She'd spent her life pushing and clawing. With Gabe, she cuddled in close. The realization scared her and excited her. Had her brain ticking with denials and plans for a future she never thought she'd have.

She turned it all off and let herself feel.

"Speaking of that . . ." She lifted her hips and rubbed against him. A spark of heat flashed across his face. "Naughty girl."

She slipped her arms around his back and tugged him in even closer. "I was thinking we'd try it without the ties this time."

If possible, his smile grew even wider. "You're in charge."

She felt that vow to her bones.

TWENTY-TWO

Andy saw the outline of two heads through the conference room's shaded glass. Two men at the table, not one. The realization deflated him. It shouldn't. He knew the score. Wade had been clear. Hell, people lined up to talk about Eli being with Wade now.

Fucking message received.

He shoved open the door, letting it bang against the far wall as he walked in. "We meet again." His gaze lingered on Eli's dark hair then zipped to Wade. "I called Eli in."

Wade lifted his hands off the chair's armrests. "Which means you get both of us."

The headaches that rolled over Andy so often after he got back from deployment and after Eli had died down. One ticked up now, threatening to swamp him with a debilitating migraine. "I'm not trying to—"

"Okay." Eli thumped a palm against the wood table. "Let's stick to work."

"Sure." That was the right answer. Andy understood the need to keep the conversation on track. He kept veering off because he didn't want it to be true that Eli finally committed to someone and it wasn't him. He blocked the rush of disappointment and listened to Eli's suggestion. Work only. "Natalie would like to see you."

Eli frowned. "Good God, why?"

"Not the reaction I was expecting." Since she asked for Eli, Andy assumed this would be a welcome bit of news.

"Look, I respect her." Eli leaned forward with his elbows on the table. "What she did to make it possible for me to leave the CIA in one piece is not something I'll forget."

Andy knew buildup when he heard it. "But . . ."

"I owe her. That doesn't mean she likes me. The idea of her calling me for anything is more than a little stunning."

"How could anyone not like you?" Andy joked.

A slight shift had Wade's chair squeaking and all eyes going to him. "And that is why I'm here."

Andy hadn't intended to flirt or touch on an issue that would set Wade off. They sat in the middle of the Tosh offices, and Gabe would be pissed if he came in to find blood on the walls. "Just kidding around."

Eli cleared his throat. "Are we still talking about work? If not, let's get there."

Time to man up, and that meant backing off. Andy's instincts told him to keep fighting but his eyes told him the truth. Wade and Eli wore how comfortable they were with each other in how close they sat together, the stolen looks. The calming change in the way Eli handled everything, problems big and small. There was an intimacy there. More than sex. Something Andy wanted to grab on to but would never try to steal. He had to earn it, cultivate it.

"We're good." They were. He wasn't, but at least now he could turn the corner. Stop picking up guys and limiting every interaction to sex in hope of Eli coming back.

"About Natalie," Eli said, his dark eyes intent and his expression serious. "Is she okay?"

"She's with Gabe." Andy thought that told them everything they needed to know.

"Didn't we already know that?" Wade asked. "They left the safe house, and Gabe has her somewhere else. Rick filled in Bast."

Andy knew about Bast's commanding presence. Knew all about Rick's stubbornness. "I bet that was an interesting conversation."

"Imagine lots of yelling when Bast found out someone in the CIA was having Natalie followed, despite the existence of an agreement that promises that sort of shit wouldn't happen." Eli being Eli, he laid out the issues clean and clear. No tact or waffling.

For some reason Andy felt the need to defend his difficult older brother. "Rick said he's trying to work this out with his client."

Eli nodded. "And Bast is applying pressure."

"You mean threatening the release of whatever information they fear Natalie holds." Andy didn't blame Bast or Natalie. She had leverage and should use it. A file of information didn't do anyone any good if the person holding it died before they could release it.

"Something like that." From Eli's tone it was clear he meant *exactly* like that.

"Is this why Natalie wants a meeting?" Wade glanced over at Eli. "Maybe we should talk with Bast."

Before he could answer, Andy jumped in. "She asked for Eli specifically."

"You're sure she's okay?"

The genuine concern intrigued Andy. The Eli Andy remembered didn't do a great job with putting other people's feelings first . . . or even third. Which probably explained how Andy ended up on the wrong side of the door the second after he floated the idea of them not seeing other people. But this version, the new and improved one, didn't gloss over other people's pain. That realization brought a fresh wave of disappointment washing through Andy.

"Did something happen between her and Gabe?" Wade asked, his voice echoing Eli's confusion and concern.

"Nothing bad, to my knowledge." But some things were private, so Andy stopped there.

Wade laughed. "Interesting answer."

Andy pretended not to notice how good the guy looked and sounded. He turned to Eli before he figured out what Eli saw in Wade. "Gabe wants me to take you to Natalie."

"So, she's close." Eli tapped his fingers against the table.

There were limits, and Andy decided now would be a good time to impose them. "I'm not going to answer that."

"He's going to be able to see where you're going," Wade said.

Eli laughed. "No, I'm not."

Life operated in a much easier way when people understood the score. "Exactly."

"Wade comes with me." Eli sat back in his chair. "That's the deal."

Not that Andy had much choice. Natalie was his client, and she asked for something Gabe thought they could give. That meant dealing with Wade along with Eli. "I'm starting to think you two are a matched set."

Wade nodded. "That would be a wise conclusion."

Rather than sit through another he's-my-boyfriend-and-not-yours lecture from Wade, Andy stood up. "Can you be ready this afternoon?"

One of Eli's eyebrows lifted. "Do we need to pack a bag?"

That seemed safe enough to answer, so Andy did. "No."

Eli smiled. "Then we're ready when you are."

. . .

Gabe grabbed two water bottles off the counter. The fact Brandon left any surprised him. So did the sight of Natalie sitting on the end of the couch with her legs curled up beneath her. She wore those sexy jeans that made him want to drag her upstairs to bed and pull them off. Topped the outfit off with one of Brandon's bulky college sweatshirts. Looked like the southern girl had some trouble adjusting to winter.

She turned pages and kept her head down. Gabe saw a flash of a photo here and there. The scene struck him as so normal when they'd both lived lives that were anything but.

He walked into the great room and handed one of the bottles to her. "What are you looking at?"

"Thanks." She tucked the bottle next to her thigh and kept scanning. "Your photo albums. I found them on the shelf by the fireplace."

He looked at the binders on the coffee table. They stretched back in time to the early days. Brandon learning to walk. Brandon in elementary school. One from around the time of his birth. She had to be bored if she fell back on this entertainment. He paged through them every now and then to remember, but these memories would mean nothing to her.

"I have a television." He picked up the remote and aimed it at the screen he bought solely so he could experience college football practically life-sized.

"I don't really have any family photos." She flipped a page then her fingers and eyes moved down and onto the next. "I'm fascinated by how and why you memorialize all of these moments."

The comment hit him with the force of a punch. Spoken like

a woman who didn't have much she wanted to remember. He hadn't really thought . . . insensitive fucker that he was. "Did you have any good ones?"

"Sure." She didn't look at him. Didn't stop looking at the photos. "That's what lures you in, makes you think things could change. You have dinner outside at the picnic table or go to a family event. For those few hours you have fun and run around. It's not until you get home that the yelling starts and you realize you had fun the wrong way."

Every word sliced through him, making him wish he could make it better. He spent so much time being angry at Rick for fucking up everything and for the decisions being forced on him that he'd forgotten how lucky he was. He had a support system. He ached for her not having one.

"I wish . . ." Jesus, he had no idea how to finish that so he didn't even try.

Her head popped up then. "What?"

The intense stare had Gabe stumbling over his words, but he finally got this thought out. "I could bring him back to life then kill him for you. Do something to make this better."

He meant every word. If there were a way to take on her pain and relieve her of some of it, he would have done it.

She closed the album and leaned an elbow on it. "Seeing you with Brandon makes me smile."

Gabe didn't force the issue. If she needed to change the topic, he would. "He's a good kid."

"*Your* kid."

An alarm bell rang in his head. Something about the way she said it and how stiff she held her body. He sensed he hovered one step away from danger. "Damn straight."

"Maybe you should—"

"Don't say it." He couldn't hear it. Not from her. Not from one of the people he'd come to count on to make good decisions.

"I'm just trying—"

"I raised him." Gabe stood up because sitting made him twitchy. "I fought for him and begged Linda to keep the pregnancy. Actually begged. Paid her money, made her promises. I would literally have done anything to convince her."

The memories rushed over him. They'd been so young, and Linda wanted out. She'd rethought not going to college and no longer liked the idea of being stuck with a guy in the military. Really didn't want a crying baby.

She'd been moved around her whole life thanks to her father's inability to hold on to a job. Maybe that spooked her, or the Rick issue did. Whatever the combination, it took every ounce of strength Gabe had to win the birth battle.

She'd made the choice based on his promises. He'd never broken them. Never would. Never tried to reach her or make her be involved. Raised a good son, just as he vowed he would. "Linda didn't want to be pregnant and certainly didn't want me. I didn't know then about Rick, but she'd gone from having these intense feelings to not wanting to be near me."

Natalie put the album on the table with the others. "You loved her."

"With all the conviction of an overwrought seventeen-year-old who welcomed any way out of his house." With Brandon's birth, Gabe lost his father. The old man refused to be a part of what he termed a *ridiculous* decision.

Over diapers and through deployments and time apart, struggling through the teen years and the times Brandon tried to buck authority. Through it all, Gabe would not have changed one damn thing. Looking at Brandon's face right after he was born sealed the deal. Nothing else mattered the way his son did.

"Now how do you feel about her?"

Gabe didn't have any trouble following the line of Natalie's thinking and rushed to ease her concerns. "My feelings for her faded a long time ago. Trust me, there is nothing left."

"But you have Brandon."

Gabe nodded. "Yes."

"No matter what."

He gave her credit. She'd circled back around. Sounded so reasonable. He knew he should listen, but the idea of allowing in any doubt, even for a second, had him throwing up a wall and backing away. "The DNA test isn't happening."

She eased back into the cushions. "It could prove Rick is wrong."

"I don't care what a test says." He was desperate to make her understand that simple fact. Blood didn't make a father. Being there, actually acting like a father, made him one.

Without Brandon, Gabe had no idea where he'd be. Dead in a desert in someone else's war, most likely. Having a son gave him purpose and direction. Too young, sure, but he didn't really get a choice about whether or not to be responsible.

"But if it would give you an answer, make your life easier?"

He could almost see her mind turn as she analyzed. "I don't need tests or answers. He is my son."

"But—"

"End of story."

TWENTY-THREE

Natalie rarely suffered from an attack of nerves. She decided what had to be done and did it. She didn't waver or weigh emotional concerns. Everything depended on the intended outcome. Once she determined that it was just a matter of figuring out how to get there.

Applying that logic to Gabe and this situation with Brandon proved tougher. Gabe was so strong and practical, but his commonsense approach to problem solving abandoned him when it came to his son. Understandable, she guessed. Not something she could assess from experience, but for him a very real thing. Talking about the DNA test was like touching a live wire.

So, she'd come up with this solution. Even now she stood with the envelope she borrowed from Gabe's desk. Inside she had DNA samples in bags. All an expert would need to provide the answer.

She kept telling herself this was the right course, that Gabe eventually would understand and come to appreciate having the suspense over. She'd only known about Brandon less than two weeks and about the parentage issue for days, and it had her tied up in knots. She could not imagine how Gabe got through the day.

But handing over the evidence proved harder than she expected. About a half hour after they arrived she'd asked for a minute with Eli and Wade and dragged them outside with her. Even now they looked over the land, scanning the hills and far fence.

"This is an impressive place. Even blindfolded I could make out the acreage." Eli's gaze skipped to the pool and what looked like a pool house right next to it.

Wade went the more practical route and pointed at the motion sensors on the fence. "And the security."

"Knowing Gabe, no surprise there."

While their talking gave her more time to mentally walk through her plan, with each pass she became more confused. She just needed to end this.

She turned to Eli as her fingers skimmed back and forth over the sealed top of the envelope. "I need a favor."

Eli frowned at her. "We are not sneaking you out of here."

"I don't want that." The logic jump . . . okay, to be fair she could see how he got there. The old Natalie would have shunned help like what Gabe provided, no matter the form, and kept moving. She instinctively knew that was the wrong call here.

Then there was the part where she didn't want to leave Gabe. The idea of walking away made her throat clog. Filled her with a bubbling anxiety that made it impossible for her to even think.

Eli's frowned kicked up into a smile. "Is this the Natalie I know?"

Now was not the time to debate how much she'd changed and why. She still hadn't worked that out in her own head. Running through it with these two would not bring clarity.

She jumped to the real reason for their visit. Not about her agreement or her safety. About Gabe. "I need you to get a DNA test done. Quiet. No one can know. Not Bast and not any of the MacIntosh men."

"This is starting to sound more like the Natalie I know," Wade mumbled under his breath.

Eli skipped right to the point. "What are you doing?"

She just didn't know what point he was trying to make. "Meaning?"

"Gabe is a good guy," Wade said, moving in closer as the double-team began in earnest.

She thought about stepping back but didn't bother. They'd be on her and rapid-firing questions in a second. She'd trained Eli, and Wade had innate skills of persuasion that impressed even her. "I agree."

"Then why are you setting him up?" Bigger than most guys, tall and broad, Wade loomed over her as he asked the question.

She shot one back. "For what?"

"I have no idea."

They'd gotten off track. Somehow they'd gone from her risky idea to something she didn't even want to know. "This isn't about my case or even about me. This is a personal favor."

"Sounds like you might be in the middle of something it would be better for you to step out of," Eli said, drilling right down to the point that pulled at her.

"I can't."

Wade shook his head. "Won't."

Time to bring out the big guns. Make this a bit more personal. She turned to Eli. "How many times have I asked you for a favor?"

His shoulders fell. "Never."

"That should tell you how important this is." She was calling in a favor she never expected to use. The only thing that made it tenable was that she made this choice for Gabe.

Eli blew out a long, slow breath. "Shit."

"Okay, but be sure," Wade said, as he stepped directly in front of her. "Because whatever this is, you can't undo it."

A breeze blew over her and the trees swayed as she tried to think of the right words to explain. "You ever hide from something so long that it twists up everything else in your life?"

Eli glanced at Wade then back to her. "I spent months doing that and most of my relationship with him trying to un-fuck it."

Wade moved in closer beside Eli. "You succeeded."

Then she saw it. What everyone else who knew them described. The closeness. How in sync they were. The former CIA agent and the crime gang enforcer. Two of the toughest and most lethal guys she knew, next to Gabe. They'd fought, gone after each other until they ripped emotional wounds in each other. But they'd found a way through it. That made her happy for them. "You two look good together."

Wade winked at her. "Thanks."

In her rush to get down to what she needed, she'd messed up . . . again. She looked at Eli. "I didn't mean to throw you and Andy together to get you up here."

She tried to keep the wording neutral in case Eli watched how much he shared with Wade. She had no idea how normal people handled their secrets. She'd spilled her biggest one to Gabe. He'd shared his biggest fear with her. Things that should have made her feel vulnerable while she plotted for a way to use Gabe's weakness, but neither happened.

"You don't need to be careful," Eli said. "Wade knows about our past, mine and Andy's."

Wade frowned at her. "Why do you think I'm here?"

That sounded ridiculous in light of what she could see, right there, so obvious in front of her. "Oh, please. Anyone looking at you or who is with you two for ten seconds can see that Eli belongs with you."

Wade slapped the back of his hand against Eli's chest. "Grant her the favor. Whatever it is."

She held out the file to Eli. "I need to know if these two people are parent and child or child and uncle."

"I think that's two different tests."

"If the paternity test fails, I'll have my answer." Or Gabe would. Her feelings for him, as complex and confused as they were, would not change, no matter the outcome. She'd witnessed his love for Brandon. Let it color and support everything she'd figured out about the man on her own. The real question is what Gabe would do when he found out. How he would feel about her . . . after. But she had to push that aside. This was what she did. She solved problems and this was a huge problem, whether Gabe wanted to deal with it or not. "I have some contacts—"

"This one is on me." Eli tucked it under his arm. "I'll handle it. I probably need two days."

A mix of relief and dread fell over her. "Thank you."

Eli looked thoughtful. "I don't think you've ever said that before."

"There's a lot of things I've never done before." Including getting tied to a man and not wanting to undo the knots again.

Wade smiled at her. "Like sneaking around to get paternity tests."

The answer was so much broader than that. "Like caring what the answer is."

Andy sat on the stool in front of the kitchen island. Gabe stood on the other side. Every now and then, one or the other would take a peek out the matching sets of double glass doors to the backyard. Watch Wade and Eli and Natalie as they huddled in conversation. Something intense had them drawn close and had them ignoring the cool air.

"It's not like you to give away the location of your house to anyone." Andy decided if he couldn't know about the outside conversation he could at least ask a few of the questions sitting on his mind. "I'm just saying first Natalie and now Wade and Eli. Seems like you have a new habit."

Gabe grabbed the pot of coffee and poured each of them a fresh cup. "Is there something you want to ask me?"

"I don't need to." Andy settled for holding the mug instead.

"This conversation is annoying as shit."

"Try being the youngest brother in this family."

"Want to explain that?"

He had to be kidding. The stress between them right now bordered on back-breaking. "It should be self-evident."

Gabe frowned. "How are the headaches?"

Andy almost reached for the base of his neck to massage the area, but he didn't have to. The usual ticking that blurred his vision hadn't started. Not yet, but who knew.

"Under control." That topic could take them to a conversation about Eli, and Andy wasn't in the mood for that. "I've already texted with Brandon."

The kid was so excited about the smile on his old dad's face. The fact his father snagged someone as pretty as Natalie seemed to be something Brandon wanted to brag about. The reaction filled Andy with relief because he knew if Brandon didn't like Natalie Gabe would likely walk away from her. And Andy sensed that Gabe needed to stay by her side.

Gabe must have known that Brandon couldn't talk about anything other than his dad's new relationship at the moment because he rolled his eyes. "That's just great."

"He likes her. Likes you two together. Said you didn't hide the fact you guys were having sex or that she meant something to you." Andy took that opportunity to take a sip. He knew he could count on Gabe to make it really strong.

"I should have sent him farther away to school."

Andy knew the truth—that Gabe hated Brandon being even an hour away. "Which brings me to the next topic—"

"Don't bother." Gabe's mug hit the counter with a smack and he held up his hand to stop the flow of words. "I know Rick is trying to get Brandon to meet up. I guess Rick thinks he can just drop the DNA issue in the middle of dessert, the dumbass."

The idea of Rick taking the choice out of Gabe's hands made Andy sick. Gabe might need to come around on the DNA test since Rick wasn't giving one inch, but not this way. Not with threats or by using Brandon. "He just doesn't stop trying to do this in the most underhanded manner."

"Nope."

Andy almost hated to ask. "What are you going to do?"

"Damned if I know." Gabe put his palms against the counter and pushed back, straightening his arms. He looked down at his feet. "All of the options suck."

"Brandon is a tough kid. You can explain it to him." The words sounded right and the idea so easy, but Andy had to admit if he were in Gabe's shoes he would want this all to go away, too.

"He's already had to hear about how his mom didn't want him." Gabe pushed off from the counter and stood up straight again. "Not that I said it that way, of course."

"You sure this is about him and not about you?" There really wasn't a delicate way to ask so Andy didn't try. His relationship with Gabe remained strong. It could survive some tough love.

Gabe exhaled. "You think I'm being selfish."

"I think you're worried you are going to lose the most important person in the world. Understandable, but it will never happen." Brandon idolized his dad. And Gabe had managed to be a pretty great one. Without a strong fatherly influence of his own or the wisdom that came with age, he'd muddled through and raised a great kid.

"The idea of him not being mine . . . fuck." Gabe started pacing. Went back and forth two times on the kitchen floor before stopping. "Natalie thinks—"

"Wait." This time Andy dropped his mug. It slipped from his fingers and bounced. He caught it before it fell off the counter. "She knows?"

Gabe watched the moves without saying a word. "Yes. It felt right to tell her. I can't really explain it."

Neither could Andy. He didn't know what to do with that information or how to assess it. The news of Gabe sharing such intimate details, with a client no less, qualified as a pretty big shock. Gabe didn't open up much. If he did with Natalie, then whatever they had went well past sex and dating. It was more than just fun for Gabe.

"Huh." Andy didn't know what else to say so he went with that.
"What?"

Brandon's excitement. Gabe's insistence that he work Natalie's job. Bringing her back to this house and keeping her here. All the pieces started to come together in Andy's head. "Maybe there's someone else who's pretty important to you these days."

"Well, I usually like you."

Andy didn't let Gabe laugh this off. Not after so many years of playing it cool with women and holding them at a distance. "Could be you more than *like* when it comes to her."

Gabe's mood sobered. "I want her safe."

They weren't saying the same thing, but Andy was pretty sure Gabe knew that. Felt like a pretty calculated move. "Okay."

"She drives me insane."

That sounded about right. "After years living with you I can say with some certainty that's probably a mutual thing."

"Is it so weird that I don't want anything to change? From right now. Right here forward. I love where my relationship is with Brandon. I want Natalie here."

Andy took that for the huge admission it was. Gabe might throw around talk about keeping Natalie safe, but he really wanted to keep her by his side. No doubt about it. Good thing Andy liked her because, unless Gabe or Natalie screwed up, she might be around for a while.

"No, but I think you should be telling her that." Andy started to wonder what other secrets Gabe had trapped inside that head of his. "And then you need to talk to Brandon."

"I still hate those options."

"Being a grown-up sucks." Andy knew from the kick-in-the-teeth drive over here with Wade and Eli in the car. Neither talked much, but when they did they finished each other's sentences and talked almost in code, about things only they understood because they lived through them together.

The hour had amounted to pure torture. Andy made the drive in record time.

Gabe nodded. "Sure as hell does."

TWENTY-FOUR

Gabe slid his hand up the center of Natalie's bare back to her shoulders and used his palm to press her upper body even deeper into the mattress. Her hair fell over her arms and across the sheets. With every plunge he enjoyed a front row seat to her ass. On her elbows and knees, she opened for him, and he couldn't take much more.

His gaze shifted to the mirror that ran along the wall, parallel to the bed. In this position he could watch her body buck as he entered her then retreated. See those full breasts bounce as he ached to touch them. The lean muscles of her arms clenched in time with his thrusts. Those fingers grabbed fistfuls of his sheets.

The way she moved, so sensual and graceful. Drawn out, as if every shift was picked for his pleasure. Pure magic.

Every second pushed him closer to the edge. Not that he had far to go. He'd prolonged the tasting, touring his mouth over her until they both shook. When he finally entered her a few minutes ago he nearly sighed with relief. Now he bit back a groan as his body begged to come.

The last two days had been like this. Alone in the house, lost in a haze. They ate then they had sex. They'd watch a movie then have sex. Walk the grounds for some air then rush back inside to rip their clothes off. Talk, sex, eat. He'd check in and scan the grounds, but mostly he'd focused on her. He'd never experienced the combination of wild and comfort before.

But in this moment, as his breath clogged his throat and his rapid heartbeat threatened to knock him over, all he wanted was to feel her clamp around him one more time. One of his hands slipped down and over her hip, then lower, until he could touch her. Feel her wetness as she clung to him. Touch off the spiraling inside her.

One brush of his finger and her head flew back. He wanted to lean in and kiss her neck, but his body had other ideas. The burning inside him had taken over. He needed release and couldn't hold back the rush one second longer.

Her tightening touched off steady thumping deep inside him. He curled around her, desperate to be closer, to push in deeper. His chest lay against her back. The heat from their bodies mixed but they kept moving.

She made a noise that sounded like a "guh" as her head finally dropped forward, and her elbows shook and her upper body collapsed into the mattress. Her hair hung around her except for the strands he'd clutched in his hand. He could feel the tiny pulses inside her as the pounding continued to hold him in its grip.

When he finally came, the release felt as if it had been ripped from him, taking every ounce of his strength along with it. The energy buzzing around the room faded and his muscles gave out. He had to balance his palms against the bed to keep from flattening her. Still, he rested against her, anchoring her underneath him. Skin against skin as the harsh breaths rocked his lungs.

With both of them spent, he eased out of her. Fell to his side and watched her. She stretched out her legs until she lay on her stomach. Her hands slid up the bed to land close to her head before slipping under the pillow. But she kept her face turned away from him.

The sex had rubbed him raw. He couldn't even call it sex anymore. The term felt too cold and distant. The intimacy that wrapped around them reached deeper than two bodies slapping together. He'd crossed over into lovemaking, which made something twist in his gut. After a lifetime of protecting his sanity by keeping relationships with women light and away from Brandon, he'd broken both personal rules. With her. Because of her.

Conflicting emotions bombarded him. He still wanted her safe, but not as part of any job. This need to tuck her close and talk things over with her was so new he didn't even know how to handle it. He kept mentally chalking up the change in him to a strong attraction to her, but that didn't make much sense. He'd found other women beautiful before her and wanted to sleep with them. This didn't feel like those. This came with thoughts about a future and a dread over the idea of her leaving the house with that bag and never looking back.

The need to coddle her, protect her, spoil her, learn from her—every sensation hit him as he lay there. The last time he'd known love for a woman was as a teenager. Back then it came in this overwhelming burst. So dramatic and intense, but it burned out fast. A crying baby had a way of putting love to the test, and theirs failed. It actually failed before that when she said she wanted out of it all—the relationship with him and motherhood.

With Natalie he experienced the slow burn, the gentle creeping up on him. Jesus, if he loved her he truly was fucked because Natalie would not rush in with him. She'd be difficult and insist he had the flu or something and would get over it. He ran the risk of her shutting down, or worse, shutting him out. No matter what she would not give an inch. She'd make him prove it.

And he wouldn't expect her to act any other way. That's who she was and part of what drove his attraction to her—her strength and independence.

He reached out and ran a hand over her hair. "You okay?"

That quick, she turned around and she smiled at him. A stray strand of hair fell over her mouth and he pushed it away. Brushed his hand over her cheek and loved the smoothness under his fingers.

"You promised I'd be a panting mess by the time we were done." Her lips were wet as she licked her tongue across the bottom one.

If he said half of the naughty things that went through his head she might just slap him. Though, maybe not. Natalie embraced her sexuality. Of the many things he found so hot about her, that was near the top.

"That wasn't very chivalrous of me," he said, not feeling one ounce of guilt over any of it.

"I'm not complaining." A bit of her southern accent snuck in as she talked.

Good thing she'd worn him out or he'd be all over her again, and right now he just wanted to look at her. To memorize every inch of her stunning face.

He didn't fight the question playing in his mind. The same one he'd been biting back since Brandon went back to school. "Any chance I can convince you to stop keeping your stuff in the extra bedroom and just move it in here with me?"

She pushed up on her elbow and stared down at him. "That sounds like you're okay with me taking over your house."

Damn, but yeah. "Sharing it."

She speared her fingers through her hair, separating the strands as she focused on some spot on the wall over his shoulder. Finally, her gaze cleared and she focused on him again. "I've been on the run a long time."

He never thought she'd admit that. Until that moment he hadn't been sure she even understood her tendency to duck out emotionally. Looked like she did. "You made choices that allowed you to stay unattached, almost demanded that you live your life in a solitary way."

"And now everything is jumbled. For the first time ever when I look out at the expanse of my future I don't see anything." Her head fell back as she stared up at the ceiling. "It's this utter blackness. I can't get it to focus. Can't really think through my options."

"Because you're worried you're being hunted?"

"No." She looked at him again. "Because I don't feel as if I have any choices. I know how to do one thing, and under the agreement I have to walk away from the CIA and all I've known. What's left?"

"You're selling yourself short." She could fight and manage and lead. That was more than most people.

"Ever since my father . . ." Her voice faltered and she cleared it. "When you lose your mom the way I did you make some decisions about your life. You won't be a victim. You won't let your future get twisted up. You'll always have a plan. A way out." She ticked each one off on her fingers.

"Makes sense." He hadn't experienced anything like she had but he understood the intelligence of wearing a protective shell and being prepared for the worst.

"Somewhere along the line I lost sight of all of that."

He'd never met a more competent woman or one so determined to let the blame pile up until it buried her. "Maybe you should give yourself a break? You made the decision to protect your people."

She shrugged. "And look where that got me."

"You would do it again." He didn't have to ask because he knew the answer. They were alike in that way. Loyalty, sometimes begrudging loyalty, trumped a lot of bullshit.

She exhaled. "I would."

"Then stop worrying about the next twelve months or five years." He wanted her to focus on the here and now. On being safe and getting her feet under her again. On them. Not that he could spit those words out in any logical way, or that he wanted to. He'd barely come to terms with the overpowering energy behind his feelings for her. This was not the time for show-and-tell. But he could offer sanctuary. "You are safe here with me. Stay here while you figure it out. There's no rush. Even once we get this stalking thing straightened out, you can relax and think it through."

"You know under that beard and all that gruffness, you're a charmer." She ran a finger over it as she talked.

He pretended to be horrified by the thought. "Absolutely untrue."

"And when you want to talk you can." Her thumb pressed against his lip until his mouth dropped open just a bit. "I'm thinking the whole short responses, not talking thing you did when we first met was an act to show me how big and tough you are."

The woman got him. Gabe couldn't deny that . . . but he pretended to anyway. "Wrong."

"Want to know what's right?" She shifted then, slid her leg over his and moved from beside him to half on top of him.

He fully approved of the change and pulled her over him to let her know. Then his mind started racing. "Sex in the shower?"

"Now, you're talking." She said the words between nibbling kisses on his neck.

Yeah, they were definitely on the same page.

. . .

Eli called before he showed up at the office. The warning didn't make seeing him any easier. He walked in, all tall and so fucking beautiful. Andy almost lost it.

He struggled to keep his ass in his desk chair and his voice even when he saw only one person being ushered inside. "Where's your bodyguard?"

Eli flashed a smile as he closed the door, trapping them both inside. "Wade was needed at the club."

"Sounds ominous." Andy tried to remember how to breathe.

Alone with Eli. Andy had been wanting this moment for so long. Then he learned about Wade and confronting the ex suddenly seemed like an epically bad idea.

"Powerful people sometimes think they can do whatever they want. Wade's job frequently is to advise said asshole members that they can't." Eli sat in the chair across from Andy.

"Sounds like a thankless position." Necessary but messy, though Andy had a feeling Wade specialized in that type of situation.

"He doesn't scare easily."

"Except when it comes to you." The words slipped out as if Andy's subconscious wanted to pick a fight.

Eli stared for a beat or two longer than necessary before answering. "He's fine."

For some reason the clipped answer brought all the old feelings rushing back. Andy remembered spilling his guts once only to have Eli sneer and run as fast as he could for the door.

Andy knew he should back away now. Wade had made it clear Eli was not available. Not that Andy needed the warning. He saw it in every line of Eli's body and heard it in every word that came out of Wade's mouth. They were absolutely together. Bonded, right for each other . . . the whole fucking thing.

Still, Andy felt the need to push. "Your man has a jealousy issue."

"He knows I won't cheat on him." Eli didn't hesitate that time. The words rang out clear and firm.

"Then what's with the constant supervision?"

"He trusts me." Eli's eyebrow lifted. "He doesn't trust you, and since I told him he can't kill you, he's decided to remove temptation."

"He thinks I'll make a pass?" That had been the plan the first day Eli walked into Tosh's offices about Natalie. He'd been with his boss and all business, and Andy's brain cells had started firing. The possibility of a reconciliation floated through as soon as he realized how much Eli had changed. He'd settled down. No longer seemed half feral in the way he moved through life.

"I told him you're not that stupid." Eli's eyes narrowed slightly. "That you know the score."

Andy appreciated the faith in him. Too bad it was so fucking misplaced. If he thought it might work, that it had a fraction of a fraction of chance, Andy would have made a play. Rather than point that out, he went with the question that refused to leave his head. "Why him?"

Eli shifted in his chair. Crossed one leg over the other then dropped it to the floor again. "Don't do this, Andy. I came for business."

"Don't you think we have awesome unsettled business of our own to deal with?" Andy tried to stop the flow of words, but they kept rolling out. It was as if he'd stored the questions along with the feelings and both rushed forward at the same time. Once the subject was on the table, Andy wanted it dealt with. Finally. Once and for all. "Well?"

"I fucked up."

The words sliced into Andy with a painful nostalgia. He would have done anything to hear them before his life had spun out of control back then. He'd wandered down a destructive path after Eli left. Wasn't careful. Gabe had saved his life more than once. Andy finally made the needed corrections, but only after getting some distance and some help.

Still, Eli's admission fed Andy's need to know more. "I'm not arguing, but any chance you could be more specific?"

"I wasn't in a place to have a real relationship when we were together. I told you that, tried to be clear, but still . . ."

And there was the reality slap. Eli never lied. He hadn't made any promises or looked for more. The whole history Andy planned for them originated in his head, from his needs.

The sudden clarity that Eli never really cared for more than sex became the one step too far. Somewhere inside Andy had always known, but hearing the words in Eli's voice would give them power. Andy couldn't handle that. He shut it all down as he flipped open some unrelated file on his desk. "Never mind. Ancient history."

"Is it?"

"No offense, but I've had sex since we were together." Right after Eli bugged out, Andy started having sex with a lot of men. Some he didn't know. They formed a faceless, nameless line in his head. Not his finest or safest hour, but he'd been lucky enough not to damage his health.

Eli laughed. "I sure as hell hope so."

"I got over you." He hadn't, but Andy felt his mind and body inching closer. Eli had changed. But with time passing and Wade in the picture too many doors closed for Andy to hope for anything more.

"Look." Eli sat forward in his chair. "What I'm saying is that

I'm sorry you had to waste one second getting over me. I was a shit back then and the way I handled what you told me—"

"That I loved you."

Eli nodded. "I blew it. I wasn't capable of hearing the words or dealing with them because I knew I was pretty unlovable."

"But now . . ." Andy sensed Eli had overcome that affliction. Sensed it and felt it reverberate like a sucker punch through every bone in his body.

"Wade is the one, Andy."

When Eli repeated it the second time, Andy got it. Hated every minute and felt it to his soul, but he got it. "Right."

"And you are the one who deserved better than me. I truly hope you find him." The words rang with genuine feeling. From the sadness in Eli's eyes to his concerned expression it was clear he meant every syllable.

"I will." Andy didn't say the whole of the sentence—that he would eventually.

Eli stared for a second before pushing ahead. "I need to see Natalie."

The change in topics helped ease the rising tension in the room. Andy grabbed on to the lifeline and let it pull him out of the emotional darkness. Work he could handle. "Is everything okay?"

"Yeah." Eli broke eye contact but just for a second. "She needed me to check on something and I did."

The scent of lying hit Andy. He wanted to dig and ferret out what Eli wasn't saying, but he threw out a softer question instead. "Want me to pass a message on?"

"Sorry, I need a face-to-face."

Something. Andy's mind skipped through the possibilities. Could be she was ready to leave. Andy could understand the need to keep moving forward, but that would suck for Gabe, and he had more than enough to deal with right now. "I'll let my brother know."

Eli stood up. "Call me with the details of my next visit."

"I can have someone else get in touch with the arrangements if that's easier on Wade." Andy could make that concession because he should. He needed to put behind him the days of looking for reasons to talk to Eli or see him.

"Do that if it's easier on you. Wade's a big boy. He'll handle it."

"I'm okay with going through you." And for the first time in months Andy meant it. Maybe he'd finally given up, but he couldn't fight the regret nagging him about what could have been. The man Eli had become was exactly who Andy always hoped he'd be, but the timing passed without them ever getting a true chance. "We need to focus on Gabe and Natalie now."

Eli nodded. "Let's get the job done."

Andy waited for the steady beating to start and the headache to overwhelm him. This time it didn't happen. He felt nothing but a twinge of sadness. Maybe this is what closure felt like. He sure as hell hoped so.

TWENTY-FIVE

Eli had said the tests would take about two days. He showed up in three. Natalie had set this all in motion. She took responsibility for that. Still, standing on Gabe's flagstone back patio and looking at the large envelope in Eli's hand made it all real.

She'd been so practical when she grabbed the evidence and passed it on to Eli and Wade. She solved problems. She found answers. That's how she operated. She kept secret those things that needed to be hidden for security reasons and uncovered those items that needed to be discovered because the knowing would bring relief.

But that was work, and this was personal. The idea of hurting Gabe made her waver in her convictions. She'd gone back and forth and debated. Doubted whether she should get involved. Tried to let Gabe come to the decision on his own.

He'd opened his home and made it clear she could use his place as a base while she worked her way through the mound of problems facing her. Now the practical side of her took a backseat to the side she didn't even know she had. The part she kept buried and ignored. The part that was falling in love with Gabe Mac-Intosh.

Eli glanced at the file then back at her. "Be sure about this, because once you know, once you pass this on, you can't undo it."

The choices played in her mind. She waffled, bouncing from one to the other, knowing the results could emotionally destroy Gabe and sensing whatever ripped him apart would now shatter her, too.

Still, she couldn't shove the truth away. The common sense side of her insisted Gabe needed to know. That in the end Rick wouldn't give his brother a choice. She half wished Eli would have failed to handle the test, but that wasn't his style.

She didn't reach for it. Didn't even look at it. "You don't know what it is."

"It's a DNA test, which means it's about to change someone's life and I don't think it's yours."

Eli got everything else right but the last part. "It might."

"Meaning?"

This was not her secret to tell. She'd already broken too many unspoken rules without smashing Gabe's insistence on privacy to pieces. "Not important."

Eli shifted until his back leaned against the glass and he blocked her view of Andy and Gabe milling around in the kitchen. "Natalie, look. I know we haven't always agreed on every operation and every maneuver."

"Did we ever agree on anything?" She remembered yelling and heated debates. Eli had been a good agent but not always a careful one when it came to his own safety. He'd do anything to get the job done, which meant she'd spent more than a few nights worried the man had a death wish. He'd changed, but those memories lingered.

"You sacrificed a lot—everything—for me to be able to live the life I have now. There isn't anything I wouldn't do to repay that."

The words struck her as the most honest thing she'd ever heard Eli say. He made the vow not just in what he said but with his eyes and tone. "Is this the same Eli who once told me I talked like I had a desk shoved up my ass?"

"That sounds like something I would say." Eli nodded. "The answer is yes and no. I'm smarter now. Maybe a bit more tactful. I know what it means to be in a position to lose something. I no longer zip through life expecting to die or assuming I know the right answer."

Wade. She got the message and what Eli was trying to tell her, but the whole sharing-her-worries thing was not her strong suit. "I'm happy for you. Honestly."

He leaned in a little closer as his voice dropped lower. "And I'm telling you we're more alike than you want to think, so if the information in this envelope is going to wreck something you're trying to build then let me take it back with me and shred it."

"You know what it's about." She didn't have to ask. She knew every inch of his file. His training and skills. Add to that the new layer of personal understanding and Eli put pieces together faster than ever.

"I have a clue who it's about. At least the adult part, and the photos all over the house of Gabe with a kid hint at the rest."

She put a hand on his arm. "You can't tell anyone about the test or Brandon."

"I don't know anything about any of it."

The anxiety welling in her stomach died back down as she dropped her hand. Eli could keep a secret, his and others. "Thanks."

"Gabe's a good guy. Ending up with him wouldn't suck for you."

She figured that was Eli-speak for saying he knew they were sleeping together and approved. For some reason, having her personal life paraded around still stung. "He's protecting me."

Eli scoffed. "Give me some credit."

With the relationship still new and in limbo—with her not even knowing if what she had with Gabe qualified as a relationship—she switched to the other topic that stayed on her mind all the time now. "How did you do it? Adjust to life after?"

"It's a bumpy ride and it still backs up on me some days, but you pick a new start and then go. Do not look back or second-guess. Don't answer the phone when the people you used to work for, the same ones who threatened to wipe you off the planet, come sniffing around for a favor."

Typical Eli. No stray details but he said enough for her to know exactly what he'd been ignoring the last few months. "You make it sound easy to move forward."

"It's not. Not even a little." He tapped the file against the side of his thigh. "But Bast is speeding the process up for you. He's been his usual ruthless self in negotiating on your behalf so that you can then make informed decisions about what comes next and feel safe doing it."

"You mean Bast is threatening people who handle covert op teams for a living." The idea of Bast using muscle didn't bother her. She had to hope he covered his safety and the safety of those he cared about as he zigzagged through this dangerous turf.

But the CIA types, her former people? She had no more loyalty to the men in suits. They'd reached a fair deal months ago, one that sucked for her but granted closure, and if someone in the CIA was trying to tiptoe around it she hoped Bast slammed him for it.

"I think we're saying the same thing." Eli smiled for a second then it was gone again. "The point is it looks like the leverage you're holding is going to work. People are backing off. He still wants you to be vigilant, but he thinks this transition period where you wonder if you will be allowed to move on is almost over."

"I want to be happy about that." But that led her right back to the question she kept avoiding. The file and the answer and Gabe. She decided to stall. "So, you and Andy?"

Eli shook his head. "A long time ago."

But she knew all about it. She'd tracked Eli's private life back then, slim as it was. That had been part of her job, and she knew he'd left Andy reeling. "Did you clean up your mess?"

"I think I finally did."

She felt a stab of regret for Andy. Now that her heart was involved with Gabe the complications doubled. Investment and caring only led to confusion as far as she could see. "Then I guess I'm not the only one who will be moving on."

Eli handed her the file. "That probably depends on what you decide to do with this."

She took it because Andy and Gabe headed their way. The door opened and they both appeared on the patio. Andy more muted than usual and Gabe looking satisfied and in control. The man sure understood the concept of being the king of his castle and carried it through his broad shoulders.

"Everything okay?" he asked.

When she just stood there not really sure what to say and overwhelmed as usual by Gabe being so close, Eli jumped in. "I gave Natalie a status report. Looks like we almost have a deal that will keep her safe."

Gabe frowned. "Again. That's what Bast hoped the last time."

"There's that," Eli admitted. "But when Bast started actually reading from one of the leverage files during the last meeting that seemed to get everyone's attention. It became much harder for the group at the table to deny the existence of the intel."

"I like his style." She'd been grumpy about people stepping in and hiring Gabe, and Bast taking over her case. Those days everything had whipped around her. The loss of control left her dazed and fighting mad. But Bast had followed through on every promise, even the one where he said she'd grow to trust Gabe.

"Soon, your normal life can start." Eli's gaze dropped to the file in her hand then back to her face.

She tried to skate right over that. "Right."

"Andy?" Eli put his hand on the door handle. "Time for the blindfold and—"

Gabe waved him off. "It's fine. You don't need the cover to get in and out. You can see where you are."

The comment shocked her. "Really?"

"I trust Eli." Gabe didn't add any flowery words or descriptions. He put it out there and that said he meant it.

"I appreciate that." Eli shook Gabe's hand then turned to her again. "You get a message to me if you need me."

She knew he talked half in code. If she pulled the trigger on the information in the file and her world tilted, Eli would rush in and help. The idea of a safety net in the form of another person never appealed to her. She preferred to handle things on her own. But this was different. This drove to the heart of a very personal matter, and she appreciated everything from his discretion to his support.

She nodded. "I will."

As she slipped back inside she watched Eli walk next to Andy to the front door with a healthy bit of space between them. At first they didn't talk then Andy said something that had them both laughing. She didn't want to know what.

She passed the file from one hand to the other. Leaned against the back of the couch and ran through Eli's warnings. Backing down from being sure about a course of action was not really in her skill set. She knew how to assess new facts, but the problem remained. The contents in the file and how she went about securing it could drive Gabe away, and she was desperate to keep him close.

She heard Gabe shut and lock the door behind her. A second later his body pressed against hers, his front to her back, and his mouth went to her hair.

She thought about how much they'd both changed in such a short time. He opened his house to her and now widened his trust circle to include Eli. Big steps for a man who proclaimed to be stuck in his ways and fine with that. "You like Eli. Admit it."

"He apologized to Andy."

It made sense Gabe would care about that part. Want to see his brother put back together again. She loved his family loyalty. "How is he?"

"Better."

She didn't press because Andy's private life was just that. But Gabe most definitely counted as her business. "Well, you were very impressive."

"You know what's impressive . . ." Gabe's palm traveled down her stomach to settle on the fly of her jeans.

The man did enjoy sex. He mixed it with talking and sharing. A sort of intimacy she'd never really experienced. So much deeper than the act. "I doubt Andy is even in his car yet."

"He knows better than to barge into my house. Usually an alarm would trip, but this time he'd face my wrath, which is much worse." Gabe slipped the file from her clenched fist and balanced it on the back of the couch. Then his fingers slipped through hers.

At the crinkling sound of the paper her gaze went to the still-sealed envelope, abandoned there but sitting so close. "Good, because we should really talk about something."

His mouth traveled to her ear and his tongue licked around the outer rim. "Getting you naked."

"Before that." Because if he kept touching her, all that would matter would be touching him back.

"Kissing your neck."

"Gabe . . . I . . ." She let her head fall back against his shoulder as his tongue tickled her sensitive skin. "Man, that feels good."

With a flick of two fingers he opened the top button of her jeans. "It's only the start."

"I need—"

His fingers slipped behind the zipper and skimmed down the outside of her underwear. "Me."

Now, it had to be now. She couldn't sit on the information. That would make everything worse. She had to drag it out or forget it. There wasn't a middle ground, and her good sense kept blinking out as need took over.

"Okay, look." She forced her hands to let go of his and turned around. Still in the cocoon of his arms, she looked up and stared into those dark eyes. "I need my brain functioning, and when you touch me that can't happen."

His mouth flattened into a thin line and tension pulled at his eyes. "If this is about leaving, don't say it."

She actually had to shake her head. She'd been racing down one road and he was . . . where the hell was he? "What?"

"Eli comes in here and says you're about to get the green light on your future, and now you want to have a big talk." With his hands on her hips, Gabe pulled her in closer. "I don't want to hear about you moving on."

They'd gone off track. Leaving was the dead last thing on her mind. Her drive to stay with him kept pulling at her to do the right thing and fess up. To give him an answer he might not want but one he needed so he could prepare. "I didn't say that."

His fingers tightened on her. "But it's coming, right?"

"You've been nice about—"

"Jesus, Natalie. I am not nice."

She didn't know how to respond to a guy who got ticked off at being told he was a good guy. "Okay."

"The talk I gave you about staying here for your safety is bull-shit." He swore under his breath. Shook his head. Looked as if he had a battle going on inside him and was trying to fight through it. "Well, not completely, but that's not really where my head was when I made the offer."

She touched him then. Ran her hand along his jaw because he seemed like he needed comfort. "I don't understand what you're saying."

"I want you to stay for me, Nat. I want you safe, sure, but this is way more selfish than that. I want you to be here with me."

Her mind went blank. Every argument and thought shuddered to a halt in her head. "Gabe."

"Yeah, it's too fast and maybe a little stupid. I don't give a damn." He wrapped his arms around her. For a second he leaned his forehead against hers but then he lifted it again and stared down at her with an expression that looked suspiciously like worry. "You being here, sleeping beside you. God, Natalie, it means everything to me."

"You want—"

He exhaled, long and loud and full of pent-up something. "I want you to stay so that we can figure out what's happening between us. I want that future you're considering to include me."

The words sputtered inside of her. Here she was thinking about covert actions in his personal life, and he was offering her a chance that amounted to more than a few rounds of good sex. She shouldn't want the opportunity or crave it so much, but she did. From the start her feelings for him had only intensified.

Still, she had to be smart. That protective wall she erected so long ago couldn't just crash down with a gentle push. It needed to be bulldozed, and it scared her that he might have that kind of strength and staying power. "This started out as sex."

"Sex and protection."

Even that much had been a violation of her personal rule and, honestly, of his. "Nothing more."

He frowned. Looked as if he were preparing for a body blow. "Can you truly say that's all it is now?"

She thought about how he smelled and how he smiled. How good it felt to lie in bed and run her hands over him. Not just for sex. The getting to know him part.

She should lie and stand firm. Not let the toughness slip . . . but looking into those eyes, so full of genuine feeling, and knowing the leaning of her own heart she couldn't cut the ties and walk away. "No, it's a lot more."

His hands cupped her cheeks now, as if he willed her to believe every word. "Then understand that while I do want you safe and I've never forgotten my job is to protect you, the man—not the protector or the president of a security company—the actual man, is hoping you want to stay for him."

If she hadn't been falling for him before that moment, that comment would have sent her flying over the edge. His honesty sealed her fate.

She treated him to a quick kiss and pulled back before he could take it deeper. "For a guy who doesn't say many words, when you do you sure pick the right ones."

His frown disappeared. "Is that a yes?"

She wrapped her arms around his neck and let the unexpected sensation of lightness wash through her. "Yes."

"We're definitely getting naked now." His hands moved to her back and started wandering.

The friction of her body rubbing against his had her thinking about his bed and how much she loved it when he balanced his elbows on either side of her and hovered above her. "No question."

"What's that?" He nodded toward the envelope.

Her gaze slipped to it and guilt nagged at her. She'd open it later. She'd peek inside and find the answer because that's who she was. She didn't let clues get by her. And armed with the information she might be able to ease his pain or push him toward a test she knew would make his world better. But all that came later. "Something I thought I needed."

His hands slid down her back making a beeline for her ass. "And now?"

She jumped up and wrapped her legs around his upper thighs. "I need you."

TWENTY-SIX

Rick had the power to turn a day to shit.

Gabe got the call that his big brother hit the road from D.C. and was on the way. Andy jumped in the car to act as a potential referee, if needed. At least that's what his text said. A few minutes ago the house alarm chirped and Gabe buzzed the far gate to let them in. Now he had to wait it out. See what was so urgent Rick insisted on a face-to-face meeting here, where Gabe never conducted business with Rick.

As if Gabe didn't know.

He'd spent last night all over Natalie, barely letting her rest so he could forget the nightmare closing in. He'd settled one part of his life. Actually found a woman he cared about to the point where he wanted to change his life to make room for her. He'd been in her, over her, under her. There wasn't an inch of her body he didn't know better than his own.

She'd traced every scar on his chest and back and asked for the story behind each injury. With how he felt about her, the level of trust he'd developed so damn fast, he didn't hold back. He gave the details he could without violating confidences. They'd only been out of bed and dressed for a half hour, which matched up perfectly with the time of Andy's warning text.

He heard her footsteps on the stairs and glanced up. She wore jeans and a long-sleeve V-neck tee. This morning she had her hair up and off her face. So beautiful without makeup. Real to the bone.

But something else lingered there. Gone was the sure woman who knew what she wanted last night. Her steps seemed tentative, as if she expected something terrible brewed.

He hated pulling her into the middle of his family battle but it seemed shitty to cut her out or pretend he wouldn't spill later anyway. That's what he did with her. For the first time, he opened up. He shared intimate details and his greatest fear. He knew she wanted to help when she suggested he might want to think about the DNA test, but he'd shut that line of thinking down because he couldn't find his way through the haze of denial that had fallen around him.

Fucking Rick.

When he saw her hesitate on the last step, not coming into the great room with him, he wondered if her apprehension covered more than Rick. After all, they'd turned a huge corner last night. He went from offering her a sanctuary to offering her more.

He wasn't being nice when he said she should stay. Shit, what had that been about? No, he was being selfish. For once, reaching out and asking for something for himself—her. Them together, working this out and looking toward a future.

But with her past and her anti-commitment walls stacked even thicker than his, he understood how he could have shaken her up. In the light of day he might not seem as great a catch. "You okay?"

She chewed on her bottom lip. "Should I stay upstairs while you talk with Rick?"

So, that was it. While she might want to avoid the discomfort, truth was he needed her in the room. It might take her and Andy to keep Rick alive.

"No. I want you here." Gabe held out a hand to her and felt a wave of relief surge through him when she grabbed on.

She stepped to his side and sighed when he wrapped an arm around her. "Is this about Brandon?" she asked.

"I don't know." But he had a sneaky suspicion Rick's patience had worn out.

"This might be battleground day." If the anxiety pounding his insides was any indication, yes.

"We should talk about—"

The sound of Andy typing in the code rang out in steady chirps. Then the door opened, and his brothers walked in with a burst of cool air. Gabe thought that might be an omen.

"Ms. Udall." Rick nodded his hello.

"You can call me Natalie."

"Okay then." Andy rocked back on his heels before walking around Rick and taking a seat on the armrest of the couch. "Now that we have the pleasant part out of the way."

"Your attorney has made his displeasure known. My clients are pulling back." Rick held out a thick white envelope to Natalie.

She just stared at it. "Shouldn't my attorney be the one handing me any necessary documents?"

"In here is a copy of my termination letter and the stated reason why the matter was settled." She took it and Rick dropped his arm. "Bast should be calling soon, or however you communicate, but I thought you'd like to see the copies of the affidavits and other documents Bast sent to the people who hired me. I can't believe your old bosses will sign them, but you, and by extension Bast, do have the leverage."

Gabe wasn't convinced. He'd played games with these types before. They said one thing and did another, just like they had with Natalie's original agreement. They dug for loopholes and called things by new names. Did anything to get out from under the restrictions they'd already agreed to, and when that didn't work they violated the terms with impunity.

For Natalie's sake, Gabe needed to know if this just ushered in a new round. "Are your people ending this in fact or pretending to?"

Rick spared him a brief glance. "Bast doesn't exactly play fair."

"You can't when someone is holding a gun to your head," Andy said.

Natalie tapped the envelope against her open palm. "So, this means the bounty on my head has been lifted."

"There never was one." Rick looked at them all. Met their eyes. "My job was to check on you."

"Come on." No way did Gabe buy that. From the way Andy shook his head, it didn't look like he did either.

"Follow and watch. That was the entirety of my orders."

Except that he had the green light to extricate Natalie or take her down if he saw anything to suggest she was breaking the agreement. That's how these things worked, no matter what Rick tried to sell. The way he lied about it without blinking worried Gabe. They all possessed the skill but didn't turn it loose on family. Rick didn't operate with that caveat. He treated everyone with the same level of detachment.

Gabe knew he should let it drop. They'd talk with Bast and sort it all out. Until then, the best way to handle Rick was quick, in and out. But the tension whipping around inside him called for a bigger response. He'd let so much slide. Heard every new piece of information from Rick and tamped as much of the outward hostility down inside as possible. All for Brandon's sake.

But he wasn't here now, so Gabe let the leash on his anger slip. "You get a good show following us?"

Natalie froze, and Andy made a strangled sound.

"It was either me or someone who would pull the trigger without warning if the mission directive changed." Rick kept on justifying and explaining. Telling his side in a packaged way that sounded like truth but came off as one more piece of blowhard bullshit.

"You're saying you would have disobeyed the direction from your client?" Andy shook his head. "No way."

Rick continued to stand there with his arms stiff at his sides and his posture perfect. More robotic than human. "I would have warned Gabe."

No fucking way. Gabe knew from experience the absolute last thing Rick would do was give a warning before screwing him over.

"Convenient." Gabe didn't even try to mumble. He nearly shouted the word.

"I'm talking about one thing." Rick's voice turned deadly cold. "You're trying to make this about another."

Tension choked the room. They kept glancing at one another, as if waiting for the explosion to come. Gabe decided to diffuse. It amounted to more denial, but he didn't give a shit. "Fine, Natalie is probably safe. We'll wait for word from Bast, who is my client, before she goes anywhere."

"Is she leaving?" Rick asked.

The words sliced through Gabe even when someone else said them. He'd just stopped worrying every second about her cutting out on him. Now Rick raised the issue again.

"She?" The fury rumbled in Natalie's voice.

Gabe didn't like Rick's dismissive tone either, but now wasn't the time for this battle. "Not your concern, but if that's all then—"

"You know it's not."

Andy got up and put a hand on Rick's arm. "Let Gabe finish this job."

Not moving, not ever breaking eye contact with Gabe, Rick leveled his final shot. "I'm going to the campus tomorrow and taking Brandon to dinner."

The words knocked the wind right out of Gabe. Had a mix of fear and fury vibrating through him. He wanted to double over, come out punching—something. But he refused to give Rick the satisfaction of knowing this threat landed.

This wasn't about his ego. This was about Brandon and putting him in a position sure to rip him apart. "You promised you wouldn't go directly to him."

Rick shook his head. "You are waiting too long to make a decision about the DNA test or even broach the possibility of a paternity issue with Brandon."

"The test results won't change if Brandon gets older." Gabe hated to even reference them. Give them any credence, but that fact should resonate on some level. Or it would if Rick's plans were really about Brandon and not about Rick's ego.

Natalie started to say something but Rick talked right over her. "Under that scenario I lose more time with him."

Rage swamped Gabe. Started at his feet and swept over him until the heat thundered in his veins. "And you don't give a shit what I lose."

"Look at this from my side."

Every comment ignited more fury until Gabe could barely see. The room shrank until it was just the two of them locked in this fight. He took a warning step. Got right up in Rick's face, ready to unload with more than words if necessary. "You mean the side where you slept with my girlfriend, lied about it, watched me struggle to raise Brandon—"

"I helped." Rick's yell bounced off the soaring ceilings.

A silence followed the shout. A tense quiet fell over the room. The walls seemed to be closing in and dark clouds gathered despite the sunny day.

Gabe didn't care if they broke every stick of furniture. This was too important and the pounding inside of him screamed for him to take a shot, just one. To take out all his frustration and fear on the brother who didn't care what happened to any of them.

"And now want to rush in, clear your conscience and claim my son as yours." Gabe shook as he spit out the words. His jaw tightened until cracking and he had to ball his hands into fists to keep from reaching out and ending this with Rick once and for all.

Instead of taking the bait and launching the first punch, Rick stepped back. He shook his head as he stared at the floor. "You don't know how long I debated telling you all of this."

Gabe didn't buy it for one second. "Stop acting like the victim."

"Maybe . . ." Rick glanced at Natalie. "We should—"

"What?" Gabe was too far gone to listen to reasoning or anything else. Fire burned inside of him. He'd been putting it out and stomping on it from the day he learned about the affair. Now it raged.

"Ms. . . ." Rick threw out an arm in Natalie's direction. "She doesn't need to hear all of our private information."

"She knows about Brandon and your claims. She is with me." Gabe took another step, but this one put him in front of her. "Do you understand that?"

"You're sleeping together." Rick hesitated between each word, as if he analyzed them as he said them.

"More than that." Andy stood up, too. Now the four of them

hovered around in a tight group, with Natalie just outside of Rick's reach, but not by far.

Rick looked confused. "I didn't know it was serious."

"Why, did you want to make a pass at her, too?" Andy groaned, but Gabe did not regret the smartass comment. Rick deserved the shot. Deserved a hell of a lot more.

"Okay, stop." Natalie shoved them all out of the way and moved to the center of the circle.

Rick shook his head. "This isn't your business."

Not one to back down, Natalie put a hand out, not touching him but close. Her other one rested on Gabe's chest. "Your mistakes are impacting everyone's business."

Rick glanced at her hand. Looked ready to swat it away but didn't. "I am not arguing with you about my life."

"What the fuck." Andy kept swearing under his breath for another few seconds before continuing on. "This isn't just about you, Rick."

"Well, it's sure as hell not about her."

Something exploded in Gabe's brain. She was off-limits and Rick . . . "That's it."

"No." Natalie shoved against him as he closed in. She threw in a glare before looking back and forth between all the men. "Honest to God, I will pull my gun." She focused in on Rick. "And you, dumbass, should not test me."

Andy pushed them all back, giving her some breathing room. He also kept a hand on each brother. "Let's listen to the smart lady."

Gabe wrestled with his control. He'd lost it. Really lost it. Actually wanted to hurt Rick. Inflict some damage so he'd know what it felt like to live in this tumble of confusion and frustration and panic. That realization had him inhaling and trying to get his heartbeat to settle back to normal levels.

"First, everyone stop talking about Brandon's mother like she's a cookie the two of you passed back and forth." Natalie looked around at all of them but stopped on Rick. "Gabe loved Linda, and you were so far out of line that you should be grateful he lets you in his life and anywhere near Brandon after what you did."

Andy nodded. "Amen."

She turned on Gabe. "And you . . . Linda was young and made a mistake and it's over. Not to minimize or diminish, because you are right to be furious and not trust Rick, but you said you don't love her. Let that part fall into history and focus on what—who—does matter."

"This is about Brandon," Andy added.

"Who could be my son."

Andy grabbed Rick's arm and twisted his shirt in his hand. "You've got to stop with this shit."

"Gabe is sitting there, patting himself on the back for raising the kid but that might not have been his right." Rick practically screamed the insult.

He couldn't do it. Gabe couldn't find a place or enough time to dig out of the hole. So, he would fight his way out. "I am going to fucking kill you."

"He's mine," Rick said, not leaving any doubt how he thought a DNA test would come out.

She rolled her eyes at him. "Brandon is not furniture. He is not a possession."

Gabe listened to the words and remembered Natalie's comment about Linda not being a cookie. It resonated. Even humbled him a little, because he had turned Linda into the villain in his mind. Forgot her age and everything going on in her life at that time with her difficult parents and painted her as evil. Something clicked. Not enough for Gabe to turn off the rage, but it decreased to a level where he could think again.

He was about to call for cooldown when Rick pointed at Natalie. "Stay out of this."

She shook her head. "He's not your son."

"Right, I get Gabe's argument about biology." Rick waved a hand in the air. "Save it."

She visibly swallowed. "No, I mean he's really not your son."

Silence crashed through the room for a second time. They all stared at her. Rick wore a look of confusion, but Gabe didn't care about him. He focused on her. She didn't throw out comments just to say them. She backed up claims. She did her homework.

Gabe's mind went blank as he searched for the right words. The hollowness inside him made it tough to hear or think about anything. He touched her arm and brought her around to face him. "What are you talking about?"

"I have the test results." Some of the strength had left her voice. She stood in the middle of the room, more or less between them all, and kept glancing from one to the other.

"What the fuck?" Andy stepped back. Way back until he leaned against the fireplace.

"I had them done so Gabe would know."

Gabe could barely hear her. The words faded. His emotions battled. Relief at the idea of her being right. Absolute crushing pain at the thought of her working behind his back. Doing exactly what he told her he didn't want.

"I'm supposed to trust you?" But part of Rick clearly did. The doubt about the paternity hovered right there in his voice.

"Gabe didn't know." She walked over to the bookshelf next to the fireplace and removed an envelope from the top of a line of books and held it out to Rick. "And you can look for yourself. Reputable lab. Gabe is the birth father."

She'd carried that around yesterday. Gabe fought to remember through the daze that threatened to swallow him.

Rick turned the envelope over in his hands but didn't open it. "This can't be."

"Natalie?" Gabe heard the rough edge to his voice and ignored it.

Sadness filled her eyes as she held a hand out to him. "I know you're upset."

"No." He jerked away from her touch, because that word didn't even come close to covering this betrayal. He had to fight his knees to stay steady and choke back the bile rushing up the back of his throat. "What the fuck did you do?"

"Ran the test."

He didn't know how that was possible. He searched his mind for any reasonable excuse or a way to understand why she lied and worked behind his back. How she . . . The lightbulb clicked on. Those visits from Eli. Here he thought he welcomed the guy into his house to help her legal case when she was just playing games with his personal life.

A strange darkness fell over him. "Why would you do this?"

Before she could answer Rick's flat voice floated through the room. "I was so sure."

Gabe leaned over and ripped the envelope out of Rick's hand. Then he pointed toward the door. "You, get out of my house."

"Gabe, maybe we should talk this through," Andy said in an uncharacteristically hesitant voice.

No, this anger Gabe could handle. The kind aimed at Rick. His offenses stood out there for everyone to see. Natalie's . . . Gabe couldn't wrap his head around her choices. He brought her into his life and told her how he felt. How lost he was about the idea of losing Brandon.

Damn it, he fell for her. Hard and fast and with enough intensity to knock him stupid. Maybe that explained it. The great sex
and growing feelings for her blocked out what he should have seen
happening right there in his house. He lowered his emotional wall
and she jumped over. Jumped all over him.

"Take him outside." He gestured for Andy to usher Rick out
of his sight then turned on Natalie. "Now tell me why I shouldn't
kick you out on your lying ass."

TWENTY-SEVEN

Anger radiated off Gabe and smacked right into Natalie. She could see it in his drawn features and hear it in the harsh whip of his voice.

Something inside her scrambled. The truth had tumbled out of her. Watching Rick stand there, so sure and so smug while failing to take responsibility for any of the damage he'd done. The pain hidden just behind Gabe's fury. She thought she'd settle the matter and then they could move on. Instead she just redirected all of Gabe's rage at her.

She took a step back. "Listen . . ."

"Don't do that. Don't act like I'm going to hit you." Tension pulled at the corners of his mouth and around his eyes. All the light and charm had seeped right out of him. "You know that's not the case."

But his words ripped into her with the force of a slap. It was as if he took every secret she'd ever shared and discounted it all before rolling it into a ball and throwing it back in her face.

"You were not handling the issue." She regretted referring to Brandon like an item to be checked off on a list, but she couldn't call it back. Not when she had so many other things she regretted right now.

"Are you fucking kidding me?" Color washed through Gabe's face, red and angry. "We've known each other for weeks and you think you know what's best for me better than I do?"

Each sentence struck her like a lash, leaving scars. But she stayed on her feet and fought through. "I thought I meant something to you."

"So did I." He didn't move from his position looming in front of her, hands on his hips as he practically screamed the words.

She tried to swallow. Tried to find her breath but she couldn't draw in enough air or force her body to work. "My job—"

"I don't work for you."

He wasn't giving an inch. All signs of the caring man who held her at night and gently brushed his hands over her skin vanished. "I am the type of person who resolves problems." When he started to talk she ran right over his words with a few of her own. "Don't even think about throwing the fact I was fired in my face. You will regret it."

He stared up at the ceiling for a few seconds, possibly trying to stem his rage, but when he looked down again all the signs of him being furious held in place. "I told you I didn't want the test."

She plowed through that fact as she pushed forward. She'd known that would be a problem. That's why she hesitated and held back the envelope. Why she debated looking inside, but she had. As soon as he fell asleep last night, she snuck downstairs and found the paperwork right where they'd left it on the couch. She scanned the contents then tucked it away.

Now it haunted her. Good news or not didn't seem to matter to Gabe, and that's the part she didn't get. "We both know you couldn't hide from it forever."

"We talked about this." Her knuckles turned white as he tightened his hold on his hips. "I was clear."

His words floated through her brain. *End of story.* She couldn't exactly claim confusion about his meaning. "Very."

"But you decided. You took away my choice."

"I thought . . ."

She eased away from him toward the couch. Standing behind it suddenly felt safer than standing in front of him unguarded. One glance at the open front door and she realized they were alone. Andy wouldn't come rushing to her aid. Not on this.

Gabe leaned in. "You thought what?"

"I don't know." God, she didn't. It all made sense to her at one point. This is what she'd done for her team. Rushed in and fixed the problem before they stepped into any more danger. The steps made sense to her. Now to put them into words. "I wanted to help, and I figured if I knew the answer I could prepare you."

His eyes actually bulged. "That was your plan?"

Sugarcoating her thoughts now didn't make much sense, so she grabbed on to the top of the couch cushion with all of her might and let the facts spill out. They would condemn her or not in Gabe's eyes. She didn't have any control over that. "If the news turned out to be bad, I planned to tell Andy and get his help. If it was good, like it was, I'd hope to ease you into the idea of a test, knowing how relieved you'd be."

"You were going to let me wait, make me tell Brandon about the possible outcomes even though you would have known everything was fine?" She didn't have time to answer. Didn't even have an answer to that. Gabe stepped right in front of her. He nearly shook as his jaw clenched. "I'm not a fucking child."

"Obviously."

"I don't need to be handled or for the woman I'm sleeping with to sneak around my house for evidence." A nerve in his cheek visibly ticked. "That's what happened, right? You took something of mine and his."

"We both know how DNA tests work." Hearing the details wouldn't help, and she couldn't take much more.

Her emotional shields kept rising and she tried to hold them down. She deserved some of his wrath. She just never expected his rage to catch her up and toss her around the way it did. If this was how deep the blows went when you fell in love, she'd stay single and uncommitted forever.

His exhale sounded like a harsh cough. "Do you really not understand what you've done?"

"Solved your problem. Brandon is yours."

"He was always mine." Gabe's voice rose until it echoed through the house. "That's the goddamn point. Who donated the sperm was not my concern."

He kept saying that. She thought he probably even believed the words on some level, but she didn't. When it came to Brandon, Gabe couldn't hide his vulnerability. "Yes, it was. That's why you balked at finding out the truth."

"I was trying to spare Brandon."

"At least be honest and admit that you hid from the truth for your sake as well as for Brandon's." Under all the guilt and the blame he kept heaping on her something else poked through. A hint of temper and it slid in before she could bite it back.

"You don't get to be angry or disappointed in me right now."

"Fine. But I'm the one who stepped up and tried to resolve this. Your solution today was to beat up your brother." Gabe's expression went blank but not before she knew she'd hit on the truth. Those threatening steps. The words. Gabe had been on the verge of breaking into a full knockdown fight. "You think I didn't notice? I know you."

He shook his head. "You don't. If you did you never would have made this choice."

The punch came. Not actual and not aimed at Rick. A verbal shot that hit her right in the stomach and had her fighting not to double over. "So, that's it? I didn't live by your rules, so I blew it."

"Don't make me the bad guy here."

Then it hit her. That's what this was about. Finding a bad guy. "You expected me to disappoint you. Maybe that's why it was so easy to ask me to stay. Because you knew I'd screw up, then you could kick me out and go back to licking your wounds."

Gabe shook his head. "You are pushing it."

"Are you going to hit me, too?"

"For the last time, I would never hurt you." He thumped a fist against his chest. "I am not your father."

"And I'm not Rick." The words ripped out of her in a hiss of anger.

"Hey." Then Andy was there, stepping in the middle of everything with a pale face and hands that seemed to shake as he moved. "What's going on in here?"

"Where's Rick now?" Gabe asked his brother the question but kept his gaze locked on her.

"I dropped him at the cabin. Your guy is going to meet one of his employees who will give him a ride back. I'll take his car."

Something about what he said or the way he said it set her on edge. "Did you stay to make sure I don't steal Gabe's silverware?"

Andy's eyes widened. "I see this is going well."

She felt something crack inside of her. A tearing sensation echoed through her followed by an intense pain. Every muscle ached.

She had to get out of there. "You know what? It is."

Gabe's eyes narrowed. "What does that mean?"

"Better we find out this isn't going to work now." Her voice cracked so she stopped and started again. "If you want a woman who follows your orders and stays in line, I'm not her."

"I never said that."

She couldn't hear him. Thoughts and arguments filled her head. She bounced back and forth from desperate to furious to drained. With her reserves depleted and her body inching toward falling over, she tried to get to the bottom line. "Okay, maybe I screwed up."

Gabe's mouth dropped open. "Maybe?"

"But I did it because I care about you. Because I wanted to fix the mess that seemed to have you stuck and frozen and in so much pain." There it was. The absolute truth. She'd messed up and handled this all wrong, but she got to that place because of her intense feelings for him. Because she was falling in love with him.

"I was handling it." But most of the anger had left Gabe's voice. Now he sounded more resigned . . . something neutral and emotionless.

"No, you weren't." The last of her energy drained away. She could feel her body list to one side and tightened her grip on the couch to keep from bobbing. "But you have your answer now, and I'm happy for you."

"My concern is about us at the moment, not Brandon."

They'd jumped way past that point. Right into that famous avenue of no return. "Don't you get it? There is no us."

Before she could say anything else, she turned and headed up the stairs. She needed to gather what few things she had and slink away. She'd never crawled in front of a man. Never broke down. She teetered on the verge, and with everything else she'd lost tonight she refused to lose her dignity, too.

"Where are you going?" Gabe asked.

She froze on the second step. He still didn't seem to get how shredded she was. Good, then she'd press on like she always did. Head high and shoulders back.

"Wherever you're not."

Gabe heard the door upstairs click shut. He'd gone numb and his brain threatened to shut down on him. All he could do was stand there and stare at the empty staircase.

Andy's voice broke into the silence. "That didn't go well."

"Do not even think about sticking up for her." Having to deal with one more thing . . . Gabe couldn't do it.

During his life he'd been shot at, stabbed. Been left to raise a baby mostly alone and lived through his brother's betrayal, but Natalie tore him apart. Her retreating back and those final words shattered every bit of happiness inside him.

"Of course not." But Andy's voice suggested it wasn't as easy to pick sides as Gabe thought.

"She stole property—"

Andy shrugged. "Probably a hairbrush."

"—and lied to me." Conducted a DNA test on *his family* without telling him. The invasion struck so deep he couldn't figure out how to dodge around it.

"She got you an answer."

The only relief in an otherwise shitty half hour, but if Gabe thought about the findings for two seconds he'd be on his knees. He could celebrate later. Now he needed to make her understand that the ends did not justify the means. "That's not the point."

Andy's eyebrow lifted. "Isn't it?"

Doubt broke through the other emotions bombarding Gabe. All he wanted to do was call Brandon and hear his voice. No, that should have been all, but now he thought about Natalie, too. He wanted her to . . . do something that would make it easier to get past her choice without feeling as if he'd been duped once again by someone he loved. And he still did love her. If that didn't make him the biggest sap, Gabe didn't know what would.

Desperate to keep treading water and not just lose it altogether, Gabe looked at Andy. "Please tell me you see the trust violation."

"I think you've been turned around and ripped inside out by Linda and Rick and your time overseas and with worry over me and Brandon. You've been in charge for so long, without a break, and been the one who calls the shots that you missed the part where you were hiding from an issue that had to be put to rest."

Gabe didn't know what those factors had to do with anything, but he sure hated the sound of the list. "You make me sound like a fucking prize."

"She equals you. She is never going to be easy."

Andy still talked as if they were a couple. That had been blown apart. Even looking at the scattered pieces, Gabe couldn't figure out what they were other than splintered and fighting. Two things he didn't want. "She won't even admit she should have told me. She said 'maybe' she messed up. I mean, come on."

"And you won't admit she saved you." Andy made a tsk-tsking sound. "Seems like the perfect pair to me."

Gabe stopped and took a mental step back. Andy wasn't yelling or crucifying Natalie for her actions. He almost joked, as if everything happening now amounted to not much at all. "What's your point?"

"Did you really ask her to live with you?"

So, Andy had been hiding outside, listening, for longer than Gabe thought. He'd heard and there was no use in denying the basic gist of his offer to her. "Not in those words."

"Now who's being difficult?"

"People get close and then they lie to me." The admission cost Gabe something.

Andy sobered. "Some did and you deserved better."

"Including her." A noise above him had Gabe turning around. Natalie thumped her way down the stairs, with her boots smacking against each step as she carried a duffel bag over her shoulder. "What are you doing?"

"Leaving." She kept right on walking. Breezed past him and headed for the front door.

"We're not done," he shouted at her retreating back.

"Oh, we're done." She turned around and tapped her hand against the side of the duffel. "You bought all of this for me, so charge it to Bast. I'll pay for everything when I pay my legal bill."

A chill moved through him. The idea of her leaving cut deeper than the idea of her running the DNA test. He didn't even know what to be angry about anymore. It all merged together until his head pounded and he wished they could climb back into bed and start this shitty day over again.

Then there was his real job. Keeping her safe. "Where exactly do you plan to go?"

She held the bag's strap in a death grip. "It's fine for me out there, remember?"

"That is not what Rick said." God, if after all this his words caused her to run out and get hurt or worse . . . there was no way he could live with that. Gabe knew that much.

"I'm a big girl."

"You're running. Just like you always do."

She didn't look away from his stare. "It's a skill that works for me."

Andy cleared his throat. "I can take you to D.C. or wherever you want to go."

The offer had Gabe's head spinning. "What the hell?"

"She wants to leave," Andy said.

She shook her head but didn't move any closer to the front door. "I'm fine."

"At least let me take you to the cabin." Keys jingled as Andy pulled the chain out of his front pocket. "Then you can scatter from there."

"Deal." This time she did reach for the doorknob and pulled.

The numbness returned. A deep, black nothingness that made Gabe hope for the return of his anger. "So that's it?"

She froze but didn't turn around to face him. "You made this decision."

Then she opened the door and stepped outside, leaving it open behind her.

Gabe watched her walk down the front steps and look out over his open front yard. He turned on Andy. "What are you thinking with that offer?"

"That you have until I get to the cabin to figure out letting her go is the wrong move." Andy's voice dropped to a whisper. "I'll drive slow, but get there fast because losing her will be the biggest fucking mistake you've ever made."

The words had Gabe jerking with surprise. "I am not running after her."

"You sure as hell better be. And you need to make a big gesture."

Andy kept talking like the problem had been resolved. Any way Gabe put the pieces together in his head he could not make the puzzle come out that way. "She's the one who fucked me over."

"Again, you didn't pick an easy woman." Andy slapped the back of his hand against Gabe's chest. "Man up and fight for her."

Andy headed out, following Natalie's path. But Gabe just stood there, trying to figure out the last few roller coaster minutes. Good news. Horrible news. Keeping Brandon safe. Losing her forever.

Misery and relief swamped him. He'd never dealt with confusion like this. Never felt as if so much rode on the next decision he made. Not that he had much of a choice. Despite everything, including the gaping hole inside him, he loved her. Forget falling, he'd fallen already.

His gaze went to the peg in the kitchen and his car keys hanging there. Getting in that vehicle meant fighting for her and forgiving and letting the hurt go. Staying right where he was, wallowing, fit more with how he felt, that she needed to stop running and deal with him, anger and all.

He headed for the stairs. By the third step the weight of the potential loss hit him. His knees buckled and he grabbed the railing. Alone sucked. Being without her would prove unbearable. He didn't have to live through those bleak days to know he was right.

After another few seconds he headed back to the kitchen and grabbed the keys. Now he had to just hope the right words would come . . . and that he wasn't too late.

TWENTY-EIGHT

Natalie stared out the car window and watched the trees whiz by. She traced her finger over the window until she couldn't handle the silence one more second.

She glanced over at Andy. "Just say it."

"You have balls."

She watched the gate shut behind them as they drove off the main property and headed for the road. She couldn't hear it but imagined the clanking of a jail cell, only this time it kept her out rather than protected her inside. "Gabe is furious."

"Yeah." Andy made the final turn and headed for the cabin.

"He refused to listen."

"Did you give him a chance?" Andy never took his eyes off the road.

Natalie studied him, looking for any signs that his anger matched Gabe's. But nothing. Once or twice Andy even whistled. He'd cut it off as soon as it started, but he wasn't yelling.

That took her mind to the other brother. The one who heaped

all trouble on the family only to find out he'd been wrong all along. She almost felt sorry for him . . . almost. "Rick was not going to let this go."

Andy nodded. "I agree."

"So, I sped up the process." She felt the need to keep talking, to justify, because if she let her mind wander back to Gabe, the pain would settle in. Arguing gave her a focus. The quiet would eat her alive.

"That's where your reasoning goes haywire." Andy pulled into the space next to the cabin.

"You should have run the test."

Andy scoffed. "Now it's my fault?"

An old pickup sat just off the main drive in the gravel. With it being daylight, there were no lights on and it was too cold for windows and doors to be open. The structure showed no signs of life and Natalie hoped that meant Rick had moved on. He needed to grieve but he should do it in private.

"You're his brother." She didn't have siblings but she knew that family loyalty meant something.

"And you're his girlfriend."

The word spun through her and landed with a hard thud. "Hardly."

Andy turned off the engine and faced her then. "You're sleeping with him."

"That was sex." She suddenly felt trapped. She reached for the handle and opened the door. A welcome rush of cool air blew over her.

"That's not what he said."

No, he'd made promises or said things that sounded like promises. He offered her a place to stay and a future to plan for. Then he snatched it all away, and she couldn't figure out how to feel anything. "Well, he forgot whatever he said there in the last few minutes."

"He can yell."

"I'm not a fan." She got up because sitting there made her twitchy. She needed to move. First came the planning, but then she'd have to hit the road. Snow would settle in soon and she wanted to be long gone before getting stuck in that.

Andy got out and stared at her over the roof of the car. "You never yell?"

"You can be annoying."

"Not the first time I've heard that." Andy slammed the car door. "Gabe points it out now and then."

"I suppose you think that shows we have something in common."

"No, the fact that you're a lot alike suggests you have something in common." Andy laughed at his joke.

Natalie couldn't even muster up a smile. It was as if she'd been cut off from amusement and now she just spied a long stretch of dreary loneliness in front of her. She'd never dwelled before on the idea of going through life alone. She assumed she'd have her work and that would be her focus. Then Gabe walked into her life making promises and she understood why people planned.

When Gabe snatched his offer and her hope away, he snatched those promises, too. "I just . . ."

"Care about him."

She met Andy at the front of the car, right near the overhang of the cabin porch. "I thought I did."

"Come on. I don't believe for a second your emotions shift around that easily."

She never thought so either, but so much had changed that she wondered if she even knew her own thoughts anymore. "It was so hard to watch him . . . the Rick thing . . ."

Andy nodded. "I know."

"Now at least he can have some peace." God, she wanted that

to be enough, but it wasn't. She ached for more. She wanted to be in one of those family photos on his fireplace. She could see her life beside him.

"That's very martyr-like of you." When she glared, Andy laughed. "What, you know I'm right. You're giving up and limping away."

She dropped the duffel by her feet and prepared to push the pain and disappointment away so she could settle on a strategy. "You can leave now."

"You're stuck with me."

"What do you want me to do? I mean, you clearly have an agenda here."

"You could try fighting for him." Andy glanced at his watch then at the main road. "You gave him ten seconds to process what you did, which you know was not great. You did the testing for him, but you knew taking that on over his objection would be a problem or you wouldn't have snuck the test out." Andy smiled. "Through Eli, I'm guessing."

She thought about Wade's warnings and the way Eli counseled her to take another course of action. Maybe they'd all been right.

"Gabe was so angry back at the house." She could still hear the rage vibrating in his voice as he yelled.

"Some of that was leftover from dealing with Rick. Some of it should have been expected because you were talking about Brandon and Gabe is damn protective of his son."

It all sounded so logical when Andy spelled it out. But her way made sense to her, too. "It's just easier to—"

"Run and hide."

She talked over him. "Not get involved in the first place."

"Too late." Andy nodded at the incoming car. "Your boyfriend is here, and right on time."

. . .

Gabe slammed the car door. Almost ripped the thing off its hinges. Not out of anger. Relief poured through him at seeing her there and it fueled him.

He walked around the front of the car and joined Andy and Natalie. Tried to ignore how good it felt to see her again even though they'd only been apart a few minutes. This whole lovesick fool thing he had going on would take some time to get used to.

He stopped right in front of her with his hands on his hips. "You forget something?"

"You missing a toothbrush and looking to blame me?"

She just didn't stop. Never backed down. That character trait he loved so much kicked him in the ass now. "I guess that's what you used for the test."

"Your electric toothbrush was a problem. I had to improvise."

"I'll figure out what's missing from my stuff later." He could not think about the specifics now. He'd get wrapped up and slip into anger and he needed to handle this a better way, preferably without pushing her further away.

She shrugged. "Send me a bill."

He went back and forth between wanting to shake her and needing to kiss her. He had a feeling life with Natalie would always be like that. "A man protects you and you walk out without saying thank you."

"That's what this is about?" She threw her hands up in the air in an exaggerated gesture. "Fine, thanks for keeping me alive even though I could have done it on my own. Are we good now?"

She reached for her bag, and he skipped over the nice parts and the easy parts and went right for the part that would grab her attention. "What about the sex?"

Andy whistled while Natalie stood back up, nice and slow. "Excuse me?"

"I'll wait over here." Andy pointed to a random spot five feet away. "I'll be listening to everything but pretending not to. Carry on."

Gabe didn't wait for Andy to get lost. Not with Natalie right there, looking ready to kill. "The sex."

"What about it?" A strip of red stained each of her cheeks. "Was that part of the services or extra duty?"

Anger. Good, he could handle that. "It was pretty damn great."

"This is the way you want to play this scene?"

He didn't actually want a scene. He wanted to say what was in his head and heart and shut down any talk of her leaving him. They could work their way through the rest. Andy was right. Being with her guaranteed life would never be easy, but Gabe loved that about her. She didn't just agree and live her life to make him happy. She was this amazing, smart, sexy beautiful woman.

Now he had to convince her. "But that wasn't my favorite part of being with you."

"What, was there a position we failed to try?"

Gabe ignored Andy's laugh and her sarcasm. "One or two."

"Go to hell." She reached for the bag again. This time touched the handle.

He launched into the part it hurt to say. The admission that made him feel weak when he'd spent so much of his life being strong. "You did what I couldn't. You stepped in when I let my emotions and my needs cloud my judgment."

Her gaze softened and some of the heated fury left her face. "You were right. Brandon was yours and was always going to be yours, no matter who donated the sperm."

"But he deserved to know."

"I saw you together. Your dad skills are not in question."

That meant something. Everything, actually. Being Brandon's dad had been his life for so long and would always be a huge part of it, but now Gabe wanted more. With her. Not just sex on the go as he'd done most of his adult life. A real relationship, filled with risks and rewards.

"My boyfriend skills suck though, right?"

She sighed. "I wouldn't know."

He got that she wasn't ready to believe that she mattered. He vowed to keep talking until she did. "You also gave me perspective. I'd blamed Linda for so long that I forgot how much her life sucked with her son of a bitch of a dad, and how much she wanted out. We were dumb kids and got so much wrong, including the part about not using a condom."

That was the biggest epiphany. The toughest lesson Natalie taught him. All the rage he'd focused on Linda over the years as he silently judged her for her choices, it was time to let that go. They had been kids when they met, human and flawed, in trouble and facing only bad choices. Linda may have failed in some ways but she followed through on the only promise that really mattered, to give birth to Brandon and let Gabe raise him.

She'd never come back and tried to pull Brandon away or put him in the middle. In the end, maybe that made her a good mother after all. She did what was best for their son, and Gabe would appreciate that from now on.

"None of that excuses her sleeping with Rick, of course," Natalie said.

Gabe almost laughed. Yeah, he wasn't quite ready to forgive and forget that one. "No, but she was young and almost as messed up as I was."

"You're pretty put together now."

If she only knew how close to imploding he was. "Nope."

Natalie frowned. "What?"

He drew in closer and exhaled in relief when she didn't back away from him. "Seeing you standing there with that damn bag, ready to leave, is ripping me apart."

She looked down at the duffel then up at him again. "You kicked me out."

"I actually didn't." She started to talk, but he rushed to explain. They had enough to fight about without adding a he said/she said to the mix. "You ran before I could hurt you, and I get that. It's second nature for you. A reflex that kicks in when you get scared."

"It sounds like you're psychoanalyzing me."

Guilty. "Maybe a little."

"You could take some responsibility. Your words hit pretty hard back there."

"I'm sorry." He'd taught Brandon to admit guilt when he deserved it. Gabe tried to follow that lesson now. He didn't remember any of what he'd said to her. He'd been so spun up, so lost, that he came out kicking and fighting. She'd borne the brunt, and he vowed that would never happen again. "I have a temper, one I can rein in."

She glanced at Andy, and he nodded. Then she turned back to Gabe. "Okay, that's good."

Wariness still played in her voice and she didn't do anything to bridge the gap between them, physical or emotional. He knew that signaled the need for him to step up even more. "See, the other thing you gave me was a chance at a future. Instead of being a pathetic single guy kicking around a big house, missing his son and venting his frustrations, you showed me that life can go on."

For a second she looked ready to really listen, but then she started shaking her head. "This can't work."

The words punched at him, but he let the blows glance off. "Why?"

"We're so different."

This argument he could overcome. "We're not." He took both of her hands in his. "We both need to be in control. We both have a tendency to emotionally shut down."

She made a face. "We sound like quite a pair."

He shot back with a smile. "We really are."

"We had great sex."

He knew a last gasp when he heard it. Rather than get angry or take the bait, he pushed what he wanted one more time. "I'm not denying that. We're on fire in bed. Out of bed we were starting to build something."

She squeezed his hands. "Until I disappointed you."

"Nat, baby." With a gentle tug he pulled her in closer. His hands went to the small of her back. Anything to touch her, to feel the comfort of her skin and smell her shampoo. "We are going to disappoint each other, grate on each other, fight each other."

"You're not selling this very well." But she looked as if she were biting back a smile.

He took that as a good sign. "But I am not going to leave you."

She blinked a few times as her head pulled back. "What?"

"When it comes to family, you haven't experienced much in the way of calm and staying power. I can give you both." He brushed his hands up and down her back, trying to soothe whatever fears she had left, and he sensed this was one she kept buried deep. "I was a dad at eighteen and managed to get Brandon through school without any of the big problems."

"Like?"

"Jail, drug rehab or fatherhood." The trifecta of terrifying for parents.

"That's quite a list."

"But if one of those would have happened, I wouldn't have given up on him. I don't hit. I don't cut and run. I don't give up on people I care about." He willed her to understand, to see how big of a promise he was making to her. "Not when I fall as hard as I did with you."

"Fall?" Her shoulders relaxed then and her body eased against his.

He didn't require even a second to think this part through. His need for her never strayed far from his mind. "Hard and fast. Even back at the very beginning when you pushed me away and called me names."

She hesitated for a second as she gnawed on her bottom lip. Finally she said the words. "A defense mechanism."

The last of the tension spiraling inside him vanished. "Not a very successful one since it just made me want you more."

"That's kind of sad."

"I'm not denying that either."

"I know the right answer is that I should have stayed out of your private life and let you figure it all out in your own time. But, honestly, that's not my personality." She skimmed her hands up and down his forearms. "Not that it excuses me sneaking around your house, picking up DNA."

The words still filled him with a twinge of frustration, but he needed her to know nothing about their relationship—and that's what it was—would be once and done. Some issues would take time and nurturing. Sometimes she'd need to be patient and let him come around. "Making a go of us means talking stuff through."

"I tried."

"We should probably give each other more than one shot before we throw up our hands and give up."

She placed two fingers against his lips and rested her forehead against his. "You're right."

"Then don't leave me." The harsh whisper tore out of him.

She lifted her head and her gaze traveled over his face. "Gabe."

"Any chance you're falling for me, too?" He had to know hope at least lingered there. He didn't need much to keep the spark going, but he could not do this alone.

Her hands traveled the whole way up to his shoulders. "Yes."

He didn't dare jump in. Not when he could have heard her wrong or might have misunderstood. "Say it."

"I am falling for you." Her fingers played at the base of his neck. Slipped into his hair. "Already have."

Every word freed him. They washed over him like a cleansing shower, drowning out the doubts and pain. But he sensed she held something back. "And?"

"It scares the crap out of me."

He didn't fight off the lightness flowing through him now, because that made two of them. "Trust comes hard to both of us, but I do trust you."

She winced. "Even after the DNA test."

This time Gabe didn't hesitate. He understood why she did it, that she was the type of person who would do it because she solved problems. Over time the shock of all of it would fade. "Even after that."

"I never meant to hurt you." She caressed his cheek.

He caught her hand and placed a soothing kiss in the center of her palm. "I know."

"And I didn't want to leave."

He knew admitting that meant a lot coming from her. She wouldn't throw the words around. Neither would he. "Then come back to me."

She shook her head as a smile broke over her mouth. "Yes."

"Yes?" She held her tight against him, not wanting one inch of air to separate their bodies. "No more running."

She practically jumped into his arms. "You're stuck with me."

"Most romantic thing I've ever heard." Andy shook his head. "Now get back in Gabe's car before I shoot you both."

"Your brother is a killjoy," she said between kisses.

"Don't worry. I'm not inviting him back to the house with us."

TWENTY-NINE

Natalie couldn't keep her body still for one more second. She lifted up and then sank back down on the impressive length of his cock. Her legs shook on the mattress on either side of his thighs from the force of holding back her orgasm. Her fingernails dug into his shoulders as her body rocked back and forth.

She wanted to milk every ounce of feeling and stretch out the last few minutes. After a week of rolling around in the sheets, exploring every acre of his property and every inch of his house, so few secrets remained between them. Neither held back any information about how they liked to be touched and what they liked during lovemaking. He knew this was her favorite position and rolled over so she could be on top pretty often.

His mouth continued its gentle assault on her breasts. He licked and caressed. The joint pressure from him being inside her and around her, touching and tasting her, sent the last of her control crashing. She couldn't wait another second. She came with her head tilted back and her hair slipping over her shoulders.

His body shook under hers and she squeezed those tiny internal muscles together one more time. His groan broke through the sensual haze winding around her. She tried to say something but gave into the exhaustion pulling at her muscles after the shaking stopped. Her shoulders fell forward, and he caught her against his chest.

Her body pulsed in the aftermath as his orgasm overtook him. His hands shook and his breath rushed out of him. When the vibrations finally stopped, he settled back into the stack of pillows behind him and took her with him.

In the darkness of the cool room, she took stock. Every minute of the last few days had buzzed along with her love for him getting bigger and brighter. They'd talked with Brandon and she'd checked in with Bast and Eli. It looked as if the bulk of the danger had passed, but Gabe still watched over her as if she were a precious commodity someone might try to steal.

He made her feel powerful and beautiful even as he protected and nagged and otherwise acted like the Gabe she'd known from the beginning. The usual pangs of worry no longer assailed her. She didn't spend every day panicked about her job because she knew that would all somehow work out. She didn't have to beat back the urge to run or be alone. He let her be who she was and never punished her for it, and she thrived.

Her hand snaked up his body to wrap around his neck. She couldn't find the strength or will to sit up, so she settled against his shoulder and let her mouth linger over his throat.

"I love you." The words eased out of her as if they'd been sitting on her tongue just waiting to tumble out.

Her eyes popped open and she felt her spine go stiff. Maybe he'd fallen asleep or not heard or . . .

"That's a big word," he said in a rich, deep voice.

The words vibrated through her because he spoke right by her ear. She thought about hiding in the crook of his neck but decided there was no reason. She could say it, take the risk. If he wasn't ready, she would wait. For the first time in her life, she'd step out on the emotional limb and hope he'd eventually join her.

"Hey." He put a finger under her chin and lifted her head. "Any chance you'd be willing to say that again. I'm thinking a lot louder and while I'm looking at you."

The courage turned out to be inside her all along. She didn't need to dig to find it. Of course the big smile on his face and in his voice didn't hurt.

"I love you." This time she said it in a full voice, dipping down to her soul and letting the words ring out.

He closed his eyes. "Oh, thank God," he said in a whisper.

She slid a hand over the back of his head and leaned in to kiss his forehead. "I never expected it, certainly didn't plan on it, but you crashed into my life and turned it upside down."

He winked at her. "In a good way."

"In the very best way."

"That's good since I am so stupid in love with you I can barely see straight." His fingertips danced over her cheek then down to her lips. "I didn't even know love could be like this, so overwhelming and bright and healing."

Every word touched her. He wasn't the type to break out in poetry or make big grand gestures, but he'd proven from the start that he would make concessions for her. He'd bend the rules and change his life around.

His love humbled her. She didn't know what she'd done to deserve it but she refused to push it away. "Gabe."

"I don't care how many days have passed or how much more we need to discover about each other. That future together, the one we hinted at and almost blew, I want it." He repeated the words he said to her every night. "Stay with me."

This time instead of saying she would, she went with the answer that played over and over in her head. "Always."

He kissed her then. Not one of those sweet ones and not one that spiked her temperature. This one rumbled in the middle and held a promise. One she could feel and taste. This man had staying power. He would not break her. Would not walk away.

She lifted her head and stared at him. Even a few days ago she wouldn't have broached this subject. She would have enjoyed what they had and not rocked their calm world. But she felt empowered. "We need to talk about something."

His smile fell. "Uh-oh."

"Rick."

During a recent visit, Andy told her the divide between the brothers stretched even wider now. Rick didn't call or contact any of them. Brandon, who didn't know what had happened behind the scenes, didn't understand the complete communication blackout. Andy was starting to worry. It was time for Gabe to step up and be the head of the family. Be the loyal, decent man she loved so much.

Gabe groaned as his head fell back into the pillows.

She kissed his chin. "It's time."

He opened one eye and peeked up at her. "Can't we hide here and have more sex?"

She knew then he wouldn't disappoint her. He'd step up this time like he did every other. He'd grumble and try to negotiate. She'd grumble back, though a part of her really loved that playful side of him.

She trailed a finger down his chest, down between their bodies. "I'll make a deal with you."

He nearly jackknifed into a sitting position. His head whipped up that fast. "I'm listening."

"If you're a very good boy and reach out to Rick . . ." She drew the comment out and could feel the excitement rise inside him while he waited.

"Yes?"

"I will be a very bad girl for you." Right as she got the words out the room spun around. When it came into focus again she lay on her back with two hundred pounds of bearded hot male leaning over her. "That was subtle."

"There is nothing subtle about my love for you."

Her insides turned all soft and gooey when he talked like that. The sensation was new to her and she loved it almost as much as she loved him. "Something else we have in common."

"And, Nat?"

"Yes, baby." She used the endearment and said it in that smoky tone because she knew it drove him wild.

He lowered his head and whispered the word against her lips. "You have a deal."

Gabe sat in the conference room at Tosh two days later and decided he would do just about anything for Natalie. The fact that she sat next to him, looking all cool and professional in a slim-fitting black pantsuit. So proper, except that she flashed him a peek of the lacy pink bra under her shirt as they got out of the car. The one that barely covered her nipples. Then there was the admission that she "forgot" to put on panties.

The woman was going to be the death of him and he could not wait to see what she planned next. But he had to survive the next few minutes first.

Gabe stared across the table at Rick. He'd been in the chair for all of three seconds and was already moving around. Gone was his characteristic smoothness, that outside veneer of control.

From the slight beard and the ruffled hair Gabe wondered how long it had been since his brother showered.

Rather than draw out the moment, Gabe went right to the point. "Come to the house this weekend for dinner."

Rick's head shot up. "What?"

"Brandon is coming home for a visit. Some sort of break. Who knows. The point is he misses you." Gabe promised Natalie he wouldn't hold back anything and the warmth of her palm against his thigh reminded him of that fact. "Hell, Rick. I miss you. The old you. The one before our worlds collapsed."

"Before I ruined everything, you mean."

"I didn't say that." Over the last few days Gabe had tried to imagine being in Rick's shoes and couldn't. His older brother had made so many mistakes and tried to hold on to the wrong things, but he loved Brandon and Gabe couldn't fault him for that.

Rick glanced over at Natalie. "Is this coming from you?"

"Gabe misses you. I don't really know you. Not the Rick who Andy and Gabe talk about. Not the uncle Brandon describes as the best fisherman in the family."

Rick visibly swallowed. "My life has been a shitshow lately."

Mostly of his own making, but Gabe didn't point that out. Might have, but Natalie squeezed his thigh and he guessed she was making a point and not a pass with Rick sitting right there. "Let's find a way through it. Get back on track."

"You forgive me?"

Gabe hesitated because there was still a part of him that couldn't believe his own brother betrayed him in such a painful way. But years had passed since the cheating and they had to move on from the rest of it. "Give me a chance to, okay? Earn it."

Rick nodded.

He would never be the one to issue a big apology. That's who Rick was, and as Gabe sat there, with a son in college and a woman by his side who satisfied his head, heart and body, he could afford to feel some sympathy for Rick. He had nothing to fall back on but his work.

Maybe the DNA test had been his way of gaining a foothold in the outside world or dealing with his injuries. Gabe didn't know what went on in Rick's head but he knew he wanted to get Natalie home and thank her for this moment. She pushed him to be the better man. She opened this door. Whether Rick walked through or not was up to him, but Gabe wouldn't walk away from his brother.

"So, six?"

"Sure." Rick wiped a hand over his growing beard and glanced at Natalie again. "You're sticking around?"

"I'm living with your brother," she said in a firm voice, as if daring Rick to say something about that.

"Always said Gabe was the smartest one of all of us."

With that, Gabe relaxed. Sat back in his chair. "I have my moments."

Rick eyed Natalie once more. "Any chance you're looking for a job?"

She snorted. "We would kill each other."

"I could use your skills."

"No." Gabe didn't mean to shout the denial, but when they both stared at him, he guessed he did. "She's taking some time off."

Rick shrugged. "I'm talking about later."

"She has to think about my offer first." When she looked at him, Gabe figured he might as well make the offer now. "I want you to throw in here with me. Help me run operations from here."

"When were you going to ask me?"

"Soon." One night in bed when she was all soft and a bit more open.

She exhaled and nodded. "Good."

A new rush of relief hit Gabe. "Good?"

"I plan on working my way into every part of your life." Her hand moved a little higher.

"I support that plan."

"On that note, I think I'll go." Rick stood up. "But I am happy for both of you."

Gabe stood and reached his arm across the table. A handshake might be a shaky start, but at least it was one. "And we'll see you on Saturday."

Rick took the outstretched hand then nodded to Natalie. "Right."

Gabe watched the door shut after Rick left. It seemed like he walked a bit taller going out than he did going in. Gabe hoped that was true.

"See, that wasn't so bad." Natalie snaked her arm through his.

"Don't think I won't be collecting my reward tonight." He really wanted to start right now but there were rules in the office. And he regretted writing every single one of them right now.

He leaned back against the conference room table, and she slid into the space between his outstretched legs. "I bet I'm naked during this reward."

Gabe thought his heart might have stopped. When her fingers trailed down his chest to land on the top of his pants, he was pretty sure his lungs cut out. "We can't have sex in here."

"Absolutely not." She reached for his belt. "That would be naughty."

He loved this side of her, so in touch with who she was and what she wanted. "But I do like you naughty."

"It's all so confusing." A jingling sound filled the room as she opened his buckle.

"Maybe I should explain. You know, step by step." His hand slipped inside her jacket and he wanted more.

"Any chance there's a lock on that door?"

When she leaned in and pressed her lips against the side of his throat, his common sense blinked out. "I sure as hell hope so."

Before he could get up or drop his pants or do one of the hundred things she tempted him to do, she brushed a hand over his jaw. "We are perfect for each other."

"From the start." And only grew from there.

She smiled at him. "I love you."

Hearing that made all the stresses of the world disappear. "I love you, too."

She kissed him, slow and oh-so-sexy. Her mouth still touched his when she started speaking. "So, when I work here do I get to boss you around?"

His body hummed with his need for her. "For you? Anything."

"Then lock the door."

ABOUT THE AUTHOR

Bestselling and award-winning author **HelenKay Dimon** spent twelve years in the most unromantic career ever—divorce lawyer. After dedicating all that time and effort to helping people terminate relationships, she is thrilled to write romance novels full time. Her books have been featured at *E! Online* and in the *Chicago Tribune*, and she has had two of her books named "Red-Hot Reads" in *Cosmopolitan* magazine. When not writing, she teaches fiction and romance writing at MiraCosta College and UCSD and generally wastes a lot of time watching bad Syfy channel movies.

HelenKay loves to talk with her readers and can be reached through her website, helenkaydimon.com, or her Facebook page, facebook.com/HelenKayDimon.